Recipient of the

1989 Eugene M. Kayden National Translation Award

Esther Tusquets

The Same Sea As Every Summer

El mismo mar de todos los veranos
Translated and with an afterword by Margaret E. W. Jones
University of Nebraska Press, Lincoln and London

Originally published by
Editorial Lumen as
El mismo mar de todos los veranos,
© Esther Tusquets, 1978
The paper in this book meets the
minimum requirements of American
National Standard for Information Sciences –
Permanence of Paper for Printed Library
Materials, ANSI Z39.48-1984.
Library of Congress
Cataloging in Publication Data
Tusquets, Esther.
[Mismo mar de todos los veranos.
English]
The same sea as every summer /
by Esther Tusquets ;
translated and with an afterword
by Margaret E. W. Jones.
p.   cm. – (European women
writers series)
Translation of: El mismo mar
de todos los veranos.
ISBN 0-8032-4422-3 (alk. paper). –
ISBN 0-8032-9416-6 (pbk. : alk. paper)
I. Title. II. Series.
PQ6670.U8M513   1990
863'.64–DC20   89-38371 CIP

Publication of this volume is assisted
by an award from
the Eugene Kayden Foundation.

Contents

. . . And Wendy grew up   J. M. Barrie

I walk through the heavy, creaking glass-and-iron door and submerge into an atmosphere that is contradictorily purer – less light, less noise, less sun – as if I had taken refuge from the dusty, dirty morning, those suffocating, obscene mornings of the first days of summer in my city that has no spring, into the stony coolness of a very old church, where there is a faint smell of dampness and cold, the cold of a winter not yet driven away in here by the summer heat, and in whose air myriad rays of light from the high stained-glass windows intersect. I like semidarkness and silence and remain standing on the threshold, my back to the door, which closes by itself behind me with a click, while my eyes become accustomed to the darkness little by little and begin to make out objects in the shadows. Shadows which, in any case, I have always known by heart, because here, as in old cathedrals, very few things have changed, and so I smile at the statue before I see it, and when I finally make it out, I don't know whether I am really seeing it or sensing its presence because I know it so well. He is sitting, relaxed and confident, one hand held out in a friendly gesture, low, palm up, a reassuring gesture like the one we use with an unfamiliar dog who is unsure of our intentions, a gesture of approach that is the next thing to a friendly pat. And yet, at close range, a little higher, the noble Hellenic face is absorbed in who knows what daydream, so remote that it is difficult to reconcile the eyes gazing into infinity and the ecstatic smile with the cordial gesture of the extended hand, although, of course, we have known each other for a very long time, so I disregard it, and smile at him without resentment even though he doesn't look at me, and in an automatic, mechanical reflex infinitely repeated throughout so many years, I look curiously between his legs. An old game or an old rite. For curious, anxious girls, remotely – only remotely – excited, or for mature women who return years later, who take refuge here as in the naves of old cathedrals, as one always returns to dark underground places, or perhaps not always, perhaps only when something hurts us terribly in the outside world or something ends or everything seems too stupid. So I continue the old game or the old rite, and I look curiously – really curiously – between his legs, and confirm with a sigh of relief – even today with a sigh of relief – that everything is in order and that his penis appears exposed between his long legs, between his smooth bronze legs. And now my mother, an uninhibited, playful, willful, and stubborn mother, much more beautiful and much more distant than any statue, a mother who never needed to take refuge in old cathedrals fleeing from the light, the implacable, offending light, and who passes through here only briefly, as one should pass through vestibules, because after all we are talking about a vestibule and not a church or a cathedral, just the vestibule of an old house in the middle of the city, a mother forty years younger than that English-style mother who sends me postcards bursting with "greetings" and "love from" in her inordinately large, steady handwriting, from cities whose names I scarcely recognize, but in which I picture her only too well, taking over with her sure, athletic step, her lithe body still young, still beautiful – beauty, I haven't forgotten, is rooted and begins in the bone structure – in clothes that might seem extravagant on another woman but which on her have just the right amount of elegance, looking with her ironic, hard, lapis-lazuli eyes – although sometimes, seldom, they could also be kind – at public officials and natives, and I believe that the natives are always more nativelike, the officials twice as official under that blue gaze of an elderly English lady who wanders condescendingly among her possessions, unaware that the world has changed, even that it can change, because where her hardness doesn't reach, her charm infallibly does, and, let's face it, what my mother takes with her wherever she goes isn't exactly family pride but a goddess's haughtiness. And now, as I was saying, from forty years ago, my mother emerges from the shadows, walks up to the bronze youth – he may be Mercury, because I am almost sure, though I can't make them out clearly, that there are little wings attached to the back of his ankles – resolutely yanks from between his legs a fig leaf also made of bronze but unmistakably added to the original sculpture, looks at it mockingly, makes it jiggle between her long fingers – beauty begins in the bone structure – of her perfumed hands, then wrinkles her nose, frowns, and with a quick intake of breath, her suppressed laughter bursts out, shaking her shoulders and, like a breeze, stirring the lace, the ruffles of her silk blouse, of her velvet suit, the feathers of a magnificent boa that caresses her bare shoulders – the broad shoulders of a Greek goddess, because beauty begins in the bone structure – and my mother glances around conspiratorially at the happy mortals she deigns to consider her friends and, while they stand on hind legs, make the colored ball dance on the tips of their noses, wag their tails in crazy, frantic movements, the bronze leaf disappears rapidly into a crack in the moldings of the pedestal, into the flowerpot with its faded, dying fuchsia, into the deep creases of the frayed velvet sofa on which visitors were theoretically supposed to wait and where I never saw anyone wait, into the deep, bottomless well of the elevator shaft, on top of the very door frame that leads to the concierge's room, or into the very mail slot of the three maiden ladies (and I don't know why my mother does all of this with rapid, hurried gestures, because this scene, the innumerable variations on the same scene, always takes place when everyone is asleep and I am the only one on the lookout in the house), and a few hours or some minutes later, as the new day begins, because this mother with the steely look and mocking smile – and the word *mother* is merely the name with which I connect her to me in a very phantasmagoric, tentative way, since motherhood doesn't define her at all, doesn't exhaust or perhaps doesn't fit among the possibilities of her magnificent essence – likes to commit her insolent villainy, I repeat, protected by conspiratorial midnight shadows or by the timid light of early dawn, and it is when the new day begins, when the three ladies, the three old-maid sisters who live on the mezzanine – for there had to be three of them, as in children's stories – at the top of a staircase with a marble bannister, much more sumptuous than the stairs that the rest of us tenants use, a luxurious carpeted staircase that leads exclusively to their apartment, the three sisters who spend their life grumbling about the misuse of the elevator, the dirt that invaded the landings, the light bulbs on the huge crystal chandelier in the vestibule which we tenants supposedly exchanged for others that were burned out – and not even the postwar years were sufficient cause for such stinginess in a bourgeois apartment house – and about the servants' boyfriends who even came inside with them or nuzzled them against the outside doorway, the parties given by the girls on the sixth floor, where the phonograph throbbed too loudly – and how could those half-deaf women hear it from the mezzanine – but above all ceaselessly grumbling in unappeased irritation at the boundless insolence of the laughing blond goddess from the second floor, so sinfully foreign in her own city – or rather, in theirs – who swept through the vestibule in her furs and her laughter and left behind her an unmistakable perfume which lingered for whole minutes, as Lucifer's sulfurous smell prolongs his appearance in Christmas plays, the same perfume that I sought in her handkerchiefs, in her glove box, in the lace of her petticoats, and it is when the new day begins that the three maiden ladies, three dried up, incredibly chaste dragons, an aggregate of shrill little squeals, indignant snorts, creaking bones and corsets – because the three ladies kept their breasts, which in former days must have been voluminous, pitilessly compressed in steel corsets, which in the end caused them to melt away and disappear, leaving them thin and smooth – the three maiden ladies, with their bulldog leading the way – a bulldog in the person of the female concierge, because real dogs frightened them as much as my mother or the bronze penis that the Greek god brandished between his legs – and I think that both of them, the statue in the vestibule and the woman on the second floor, were a single entity in the eyes of the three ladies, equally beautiful, equally menacing and inso-lent, equally indestructible and unbanishable from their lives, since they didn't dare or were unable to evict us from that sec-ond-floor apartment we had occupied since the war ended – in-solent or not, we were indisputably on the winning side, above all suspicion, despite Mama's playfully unorthodox ways – and they couldn't find a convincing excuse, for themselves or for the tenants, for removing a valuable sculpture that had been in the vestibule forever (they must have heard something to the effect that a nude in art isn't a sin) – a bulldog with broad haunches and a deep, hoarse voice who preceded them in their investigations on the stairs and in the vestibule, while the stri-dent gibberish of sharp squeals and deep barking – in neither case human sounds – reached the half-opened door where I, forty years back, was spying, and they scurried up and down the vestibule and the conciergerie like hysterical fleas, peered into the street, searched in the shadows of the elevator shaft, poked their malevolent fingers into the crevices in the statue, the folds in the sofa, disturbed the thick accumulation of dust under the carpet, looked into the shades on the sconces, and searched in the caramel-colored crystal prisms of the chande-lier that hung from the ceiling, because right there, dangling

among the prisms, tied with a little pink bow, there appeared
one fine day the famous, the high-minded, the most virtuous
fig leaf. And although I didn't see her put it there, the child
imagines her mother, suppressing laughter that is only a bit too
sharp at the moment when it bursts out in her amused excitement, lifted by two handsome men with blue eyes – there were
always handsome men, young men, elegant boys with blue
eyes around Mama, whom the goddess deigned to call friends –
not by my father, my father isn't under the chandelier; the
happy mortal whom the goddess deigns to call "my husband"
smiles a little off to one side by the street door, and I don't
know – the child doesn't know – whether his smile is disap-
proving or secretly amused, or whether her father has already
set out on the interminable road toward indifference and boredom; he smiles from the door, takes short puffs on his pipe and
observes the group crowded together under the crystal chandelier, while my mother sways gently in time with her laughter, cradled and rocked by her own laughter, and holds up, like
some trophy of liberation – what liberation can there be in the
forties but this one, and that for a very few, for the assembly of
the victor-gods – the little bronze leaf. She teeters for a few seconds, tries to balance it on top of the slippery glass branches, to
hook it on the wires holding the prisms, and at last – now her
laughter definitely loses its harmony and breaks out uncontrollably, that laugh of Mama's that was always a little excessive, and the girl must have heard it that night, as on so many
other nights, if she were looking out of the half-open window
of the second-floor apartment, and it might even have awakened the three flea-ladies, the three dragon-ladies, if their deaf-
ness were not so extreme – her fine, white, long hand slips
quickly, like a playful, purring little animal (where? the three
frightened virgins and the bulldog wonder), into the heavy,
thick hair that smells of invisible honeysuckle (where? the girl
wonders), between those incredibly white breasts that inex-
plicably always make her a little sleepy and remind her of the
sea, or perhaps the hand rummages around – the fleas are too

appalled even to cross themselves and the bulldog growls in fright at the spectacle – perhaps with a fleeting, half-glimpsed movement, it rummages under the wide chiffon skirts, under the soft velvet skirts, under the sumptuous gold lamé skirts, and now her mother, literally dying with laughter and about to lose her balance on the arms that hold her up and that sway under her tottering weight, her mother raises the fig leaf in one hand and in the other a short silky ribbon, of a scandalously intimate pink color, and a second later both are hanging there – the modest fig leaf and the brazen little ribbon – provocation on provocation, provocations not added but cubed, dangling among the prisms on the solemn crystal chandelier. And there they stay all morning like a triumphal standard, while the amused child, who is now definitely on guard at the window and who discovered the leaf and the little ribbon much earlier from her lookout post, sees the three skinny fleas with their strident shrieks and the dark horsefly with its deep, hoarse voice hop crazily around the vestibule and then suddenly fall silent, paralyzed, heads upturned and all four mouths gaping, their ability to understand, their ability to react with outrage overwhelmed by the unexpected magnitude of the offense, destroyed, swept away, nullified forever by that different kind of mother, so much a part of this city and nevertheless like a foreigner, a mocking, belligerent mother, with her easy laugh and white hands. Until one day the fig leaf, perhaps concealed in a perfect hiding place where it will spend years and years, perhaps eliminated by an ever-victorious mother who has grown tired of the game but doesn't want to give up, or maybe even secretly whisked away by the three maiden ladies fed up with hopping up and down, waving their arms, and always ending up as losers, or even by the bulldog with the hoarse bark, who doesn't wish to continue wasting her mornings in monotonous sniffing in corners behind her virginal, hysterical mistresses, while the woman who is always guilty but never convicted, the unmistakable object of all suspicions but never caught – her indelible perfume doesn't constitute conclusive proof, that

7

unique, inimitable scent of the mixture of her cologne with her skin being absolutely unmistakable only to me – sleeps soundly on soft pillows similarly perfumed, her blond hair sumptuously spread over the downy feather pillows, one hand sticking out, resting on the linen sheets; so one day the fig leaf disappears for good. And the sculpture is still here, with his pleasant, condescending gesture, the dog-petting gesture, the noble Hellenic face absorbed in the noblest – or the silliest – of daydreams and his penis definitely, insolently, triumphally between his legs, he is still here, forty years later, and I smile at him as I go by, and he answers me with an acquiescent gesture of friendly complicity, almost of affection, although I am not, this is obvious even to a bronze Mercury, the woman with the amused and defiant laugh, with the mocking frown, with the beautiful, purring hands, the beautiful, marmoreal, distant lady, ever victorious, with whom he long ago made a pact between statues or between gods, in any case not between human beings.

T he apartment has been vacant many years and my mother, or perhaps Julio, or both in unison, as they did so often with so many things, must have wanted to sell it for a long time – what sense is there in keeping this huge, empty apartment, implacably invaded day after day by dust and dampness, in the middle of the city which relatives and friends have been deserting one after another until they have left it reduced to a district of banks, offices, and travel agencies -- they probably stopped trying only because they were too indolent to face one of my obscure fits of stubbornness that they neither understand nor excuse, but which, perhaps precisely because they are incomprehensible and inexcusable, dimly disturb them, and anyway what difference did it make if they kept this apartment, with expenses almost unchanged for thirty years and a concierge – not the old bulldog, but a blond Andalusian girl, one of those Andalusians with blue eyes and firm white flesh, two or three children constantly chirping around her – who can come up a few afternoons to open the windows for a while, shake out the carpets and run a dust rag over the furniture. Or perhaps the three of us foresaw that the time would come when this complex, well-tuned machinery, whose upkeep cost them so much effort, was finally going to come crashing down on our heads – or perhaps only on mine – and that Julio would leave once again for parts unknown, the grotesque captain of some ghostly yacht, together with a celluloid blond, only this time – it might well have happened ten years ago, or it could have waited another ten to happen, or perhaps it might never have come about – everything was going to seem too silly to me, excessively banal, a vulgar story, tirelessly repeated, which had to be cut short before reaching the intolerable nausea of its conclusion, and then the neat, polished papier-mâché universe in which I had been trained to live was finally going to collapse on me, and it is possible that the three of us sensed that I would then have to seek refuge in my first burrow. And here I am, suitcase in hand, looking rather like a prematurely aged orphan girl, while the smell of closed space and dampness assails me, and from the threshold I see the endless hallway, so long and dark, the dust particles dancing crazily in the rivers of pale gold that filter through the leaded windows – the windows from which I used to spy on my mother's triumphal arrivals at night and, during the long winter afternoons, the comings and goings of the tenants – a hall onto which the doors of the bathroom, the kitchen, Papa's study, the guest room open, the dark hall onto which all my childhood fears opened and which I now follow to the living room, where one after the other I open the three balcony windows that face the avenue. It is like looking down from an unknown and craggy island, a cliff at the water's edge, onto a slightly rough sea of tender green colors. I hear the wet slapping of the waves, incessantly repeated; I would like to doze to that sound – I always loved to fall asleep in some place where I could hear the sea – and if I pay attention and make an effort to penetrate behind this dance of greenery, if I half close my eyes to soften the excessive light, I see some

9

remnant of the submerged city appear: gray asphalt pebbles on the sea bottom or the swift, fleeting movement of a fish car in the waves. I know that later, as we move into the summer, the sea will turn darker day by day, dustier in some places, more golden in others, the pure emerald green color already long gone, until, pulled off by the wind, it finally vanishes – soft piles of rotting reddish leaves on the sidewalks, around the trees – and allows the presently submerged city to emerge in its autumnal splendor. And then you will see from here, from any of the three balcony windows on this second floor, that the tree trunks are black, with the blackness of an inevitable death sentence. But we are only at the beginning of May, and autumn is still very far away. I think that this year I was unaware – that this year I didn't want to be aware, as I was, only once, a thousand lives ago – of the arrival of spring, that I have half-heartedly watched the bare branches in vain, only to be distracted at the exact moment, that most brief and fleeting instant, when the leaves come out, clean little points, tender buds, against the blue sky, or, viewed from here, the first amorous surge of the waves under my windows. In my city there have been years – very, very few – that had some early warm days with a pale sun and light, weightless air. On days like that, it was possible – at least it was once, a thousand lives ago – to see the innocent green emerge, the frightened virgin buds, adolescent nipples, stiffen and grow under the still cold air. But this year, as in almost every year in my city, summer has invaded too soon, suddenly, and when I finally realize that winter has ended, the trees are already bursting out in luxuriant green. Undulant matron's breasts under my windows. But in any case it is the sea, and I like for my house – my old house, my only house, my parents' old house – to be surrounded by waves like this once a year, and for my city – so different, so vulgar, so impoverished – to recover for a few days its magical illusion of a submerged city, while I revive the remote dream, remote and childish – or aren't all dreams perhaps childish and remote? – of living at the seashore, of falling asleep lulled by the sea, on an island, on the summit of a cliff, at the top of a lighthouse.

This softens the impossible obscenity of the month of May, of the parks and gardens in May in my city without candor or spring, with that turbid, closed smell that strangely invades the open spaces, a smell of slight putrefaction, May flowers slowly decomposing before the blue-and-white Madonna, a rosary between her fingers, in the chapel. That was also a long time ago. I am at a time in my life when everything is already long, too long, ago. In those days May was the month of the Virgin and of flowers; perhaps it was also the unacknowledged month of impossible love affairs, and while lilies and white roses – the only roses that I detest – were dying an ugly death on snowy altar cloths embroidered with gold thread, we dreamed of bridal chambers filled with tuberoses – and I never imagined that much later there would be a morning when I would open a door, laughing, my arms filled with tuberoses, and that never, never again could I tolerate the perfume of these flowers without a touch of nausea – of bridal chambers filled with tuberoses, where the warm sensuality of their smell goaded us to pretend to swoon, and still-faceless young men – princes from the Orient? handsome boys with blue eyes? – whipped us unmercifully with mimosa boughs, until our buttocks, our backs, our breasts, were covered with a fine golden dust. Out of the greasy corolla – the color of dead flesh – of the lilies, appeared yellow penises enveloped in fuzz, and even more obscene, more filthy, more putrid, were the tiny white flowers – I have only seen them on the Virgin's white altars during the month of May – surrounding the roses and the lilies like a rain of semen. In the afternoons – the water in the vases emitted a nauseating smell, also fleshy and dead – we would remove those vases – green, blue, with little gold stars – from altar cloths starched, embroidered, and ironed ad infinitum by rough, virginal hands, and we carried them to the sacristy to change the water and replace the flowers: every morning, by turns, we bring one of those horrible sprays of white flowers.

The sacristy is almost dark at this time and very cold. Summer hasn't arrived here: only the obscenity of the lilies, the withered opulence of wax roses, the filthy little semenlike flowers, the stench of so many decomposed corollas in clouds of incense – and once again the bridal chamber, there is no longer any doubt now, with an Oriental prince with jet black eyes, greedy lips, black hair, right out of an expurgated, and for that very reason doubly exciting, version of the *Thousand and One Nights* – and anthems for several voices – all out of tune – in Latin. But we slip away, laughing shadows, clumsy, silly apprentice-bacchantes, through the shadowy chapel, we run our curious, not entirely innocent, fingers over the long, rough yellow penises, full of fuzz, we hide alone or by twos in the confessionals, we get drunk on the fine pollen of the flowers, so golden and malevolent. And one afternoon in May, in the side chapel, the same one used for spiritual exercises, with those dreadful, dissonant voices, at one moment a low, purring, almost romantic whisper that caresses all the lilies-of-the-valley while barely touching them, that touches our hair and cheeks like a breeze, like the wing of a bird, then a tremulous howl, sustained in unbearable high notes, which sets fire to all the *Primaveras* and possible Venuses who might rise from the sea and which nevertheless, beyond fear, or clinging to fear, forming a single entity with this desperate fear of the unknown, gradually discovers a strange pleasure, as if Savonarola himself had us there, bound and naked, bound and naked at his mercy, while he clawed our backbones with a very long and Luciferian fingernail, from our buttocks to the napes of our necks; in the chapel of fright and ecstasy, culmination and abyss of permissible, unwholesome confusions, we discover – one May afternoon – a dead nun in a white coffin. The thundering voice from the pulpit that violates us and the cloying smell of May flowers brought her here, surrounded her with thick candles, lit and smoking in the penumbra, with innumerable white roses, and someone has slipped an enormous rosary into her wrinkled, stiff, yellow hands. And although we peek furtively into the chapel and speak in excited whispers, the temptation to look and the fear of what we are seeing holds us on the threshold; although it seems like the first knowledge, the first voluptuousness, also exciting and tremulous, of what death must be like, we don't plumb the depths of horror and barely experience any feelings of anguish, because we know with a strange certainty that she never was alive, alive like us – so distant – or perhaps she isn't really dead now, and this is only an indispensable, clever touch, reality and life trying to outdo each other, transcending one another in the accurate picture that fleshes out an ensemble of aromas and images. Mays in the chapel, Mays with Latin anthems for many voices, with clouds of incense, Mays, the month of Mary and of ageless mummy nuns who always die in the spring. Stifling and lascivious Mays, with a tightness in our chests and a special taste on our lips – perhaps only the desire to be whipped with mimosa boughs in a bridal chamber, in a death chamber filled with tuberoses – and watching from these balcony windows the same sea as every summer being born green and new, in short, playful charges.

The blond goddess with the white hands, the elderly lady of Anglo-Saxon bearing who sends me greetings and postcards from cities with names I've never heard of – and who has of course not interrupted her trip, how could I have thought that she would, how could I have imagined a reaction from her, if not maternal, at least human, that would make her return here from the other side of the world, so I wouldn't feel so alone in my old burrow, although she did indeed send a very wise letter, for once a letter and not a postcard, slightly alarmed, full of admonitions to be prudent, and she even telephoned me a couple of times to explain to me how nervous my absurd decision has made her and how much I have aggravated her tachycardia and insomnia with my actions, so that the poor woman can hardly get to sleep in the luxurious suites in South American hotels from which she leaves every morning to photograph old stones and picturesque natives; surely I have ruined the pleasure of her trip, as I have so many other pleasures in the past, with my odd behavior, always inconvenient, one more in the long list of an absurd daughter's oddities and offenses, and I also suppose that she must quickly have gotten in contact with Guiomar, both of them very serious, one on each end of the telephone line for the international call that joined the miserable village in India with the brand-new American university, both lamenting in a duet a foolish daughter and a crazy mother, and I wonder where the devil I fit into this genealogy of Wise Virgins, a twisted link in an irreproachable chain, while they come to a perfect understanding behind my back, the goddess and the doctor, exchanging opinions about the difficult little girl, as if about some little dog they had found run over in the street, with a broken leg, and they don't know what to do with it, because it bites, furthermore, and it worries them so, although not enough to stop photographing ruins or interrupt the thesis on the brain functions of a certain type of mouse, and return here for a few days – the blond goddess with the white hands, I repeat, never liked this dark, shabby old house, too large, full of twists and turns and irritating resistance. She always tried to impose her ideas of order, luminosity, and beauty on us – on this apartment and on me. Time after time new doors were opened up, windows sealed up, rooms were joined and divided, the old paper or paint on the walls was covered with paper or new coats of paint, the colored tiles – so beautiful – that traced their geometric or floral borders on the floor, were buried under beige, pink, bluish green carpeting, the gilded moldings on the coffered ceiling were coated with layer after layer of plaster. And there was a constant uproar of furniture arriving, laboriously carried up the stairs – the men puffing under its weight, from landing to landing – or hoisted with pulleys and inserted through the three balcony windows, furniture which, barely having arrived, began a frantic gallop through the apartment, from wall to wall, from room to room, soon to be cast aside, sent into permanent exile, swinging once again in empty space over the curious heads of the passersby, or bumped on the turns of the staircase, to the irritated snorts of the concierge. The lady liked what was new, the latest thing, what was shiny, so very un-European in this, so characteristic of our city that at times I wondered if there didn't exist a secret accord, an evil conspiracy, between her and the mayor, between her and the councilmen, between her and the worthy merchants of this city, to keep on replacing, destroying, renovating the most beautiful and cherished things. The lady also liked little girls who were blond, unquestionably Anglo-Saxon, very Aryan, heirs of at least another twenty generations of still other blond little girls of their same lineage, girls dressed up in their little knitted caps, their precious little tartan dresses, in illustrated magazines from abroad. And while the apartment was filled with cabinetmakers, painters, decorators, plasterers, and antique dealers, the dark, long-legged runt, too thin, too dark, with an indefinable quality that invariably ruined the harmony of her movements and appearance, something always too little or too much, was dragged to dressmakers who specialized in children's clothing, French hairdressers, deluxe shoe stores, to tennis and dance classes, to horrible children's parties, all the little girls with very fluffy skirts and little white socks, watching the performance of a couple of very sad clowns and some folkdancers wearing mended velveteen pants – the men – and loose-fitting knickers tied above their knees, so their legs couldn't be seen in the fluttering of their skirts – the women. All for naught. Because the mother with the easy nonconformity and insolent laugh attacked us for years with her terrible, furious remodeling, with her Olympian rationalism, with her foursquare, perfect aestheticism; she attacked head-on, and her eyes – so frightfully blue, so ruthlessly light – when they pierced me, left me disarmed and naked, and her white hands seemed capable of giving new form, of simply giving one form to the universe, and she was, oh magic mirror, the most beautiful and the most intelligent of all the women in the kingdom –

my father and all his friends were there to testify to it – so beautiful and so intelligent, oh my queen and lady, that thou art no longer even human – nor hast thou the humanity to imagine, to accept the fact that thy daughter needs thee now, lost in her first burrow on the other side of the world, although I don't know what use you would be here at my side, since the natural channels of understanding and tenderness have been broken for years, perhaps they always were, and it is definitely better, much better, that neither Guiomar nor you change your plans for me – but my mother could never, never deal with us, because both of us, the house and I, mute, passive, dark, stubborn, offered her a doubly ferocious resistance, filled with sickly shadows, with unhealthy hidden dampnesses, with incredibly tender, secret underground places, with forbidden Dionysian pleasures. In that frantic moving of pieces of furniture from their place, exiling them, opening up new windows or walling them up, repainting the walls time and again, the house still remained old and sad, a burrow warm and open to daydreams. Through the almost infinite layers of plaster, tenacious garlands of gold, the residues of old colors, the secret bower where witches congregated, emerged on the ceiling. At some point, the paper that had covered the walls before always showed through again, and if it didn't reappear, the brand-new wallpaper or the spotless coat of recent paint was then spoiled immediately by the dampness or mold, the tasteful monochrome would crack, the elegant, symmetrical line of the design would break, and the terrible, crazy, friendly shapes would emerge: a headlong cavalcade of steeds and dragons, enchanted princesses with long golden tresses – Rapunzel, Rapunzel, let down your hair – frightful hanged men who dangled from twisted branches, a piece of tongue showing between swollen lips, and their enormous feet swaying grimly above the marsh where the little mermaid who wanted to be a woman lived in friendly and apprehensive relationship with the daughter of the king of the marsh. And although everything decrepit, whatever possesses any hint of grotesqueness or sickness, whatever rocks gently above the emptiness of pretentiousness had no place in the shining, steely-edged universe of a Hellenic goddess or a sorceress queen, and although the playroom frequently overflowed with expensive and marvelous toys, always with instructions in some foreign language, and a Made in Japan, Made in England, especially Made in Germany printed in some corner, never like the toys I saw in other children's houses, there appeared again and again, imperturbably, mysteriously untouched, the celluloid doll with one missing arm and no clothes, only a half-raveled knitted cloak, without doubt the poorest, ugliest, and sickest of all dolls, or the plush bear, half-bald and quite scorched since the day someone left him next to the stove, or a book that mysteriously appeared – someone must have brought it, but who could have brought a thing like that? – a book written in an indecipherable language – it wasn't German, or English, or French, or Portuguese, or Italian – and that came to me and to our house with half of its pages already torn out and lost, but whose remaining pages contained the most beautiful sketches I had ever seen, about which I could – given the indecipherable nature of the text – freely invent all kinds of stories. I think that we – the old house and the dark girl – sealed a pact in the darkness. We invented strange Orphic myths, secret subterranean rites, to escape in this way the goddess of light, Athena tonans; tenaciously we introduced disorder, anguish, what was ambiguous and mutilated, into a universe that was believed to be, or at least was willed to be, perfect. And in this burrow, in this enchanted, evil, and touching grotto, Wonderland and Never-Never Land flourished.

Until the trunks of the trees turned black little by little and the city changed and the birds – years ago, when I was little, there were great numbers of different birds in the trees along the avenue, birds that lived here all year round and birds that arrived each spring – emigrated toward higher districts, outlying districts of residential neighborhoods, the same districts toward which we and all our friends emigrated. And my mother covered the pictures and the furniture of a house that she hated with white dustcovers – hardly anything was taken: everything had to be new, shiny, unused, in the place where we were going to live – she instructed the concierge to air out the rooms from time to time, and she never talked of renting or selling because sometimes she was simply too indolent for a confrontation with me. Although perhaps she didn't foresee this, perhaps she couldn't imagine that I would return here one fine day, little suitcase in hand, looking faintly like a prematurely aged child, that I would once again occupy my single girl's bed, my adolescent's bed, a beautiful bed with foot and head of gilded metal, with a crocheted counterpane, and I would spend hours – time has lost its meaning – leaning out of the three balcony windows overlooking the avenue, or extracting – very slowly, almost without purpose – the living-room furniture from its white shrouds. Allies, friends, always accomplices, the furniture emerges without protest – meekly – from its parenthesis of shadows and silence. And first I touch them, I caress them through the dustcovers and sheets, I imagine their contours and draw them in my memory so that, only after this previous encounter of touch and caress, can I pull cautiously on one end of the sheet, on the edge of the dustcover, where the dust has traced deep gray furrows on the folds, and leave them naked, naked in the May sun and in the noise that rises from the chattering, noisy – although submerged – city of eleven o'clock in the morning. (The sun pours through the open balconies at this hour and the light golden dust of the early morning hours suspends its dance and seems almost motionless in the streams of light.) Then I collapse into the leather armchair where my father used to read the newspaper and doze at nap time, or on the soft, warm carpet, or on the couch with big cushions upholstered with curious drawings of ancient maps and navigation routes, and I think that perhaps later on, on another day, I will move on to the library. Uncovering the other furniture and removing the dust from the books one by one, and, meanwhile, I will leaf through them

them unhurriedly, mixing fragments at random, the archetypal and puritanical little women of Louisa May Alcott, the grandiloquent gestures – so literary – of the men, but especially of the women, of Somerset Maugham or Stefan Zweig, or these delightful translations into French, in which Ovid, the Song of Songs, or the Satyricon barely escape pretentiousness only to fall into the realm of pornography. Perhaps I may even rediscover the pleasure of my adolescent readings, the reader I was and who died – there are so many I's that have died in me – so long ago now: disordered, chaotic, unorthodox, uncritical, but voracious, omnivorous, and passionate. Because now for the first time in many, so many years, I have all the time in the world. (I also have, for the first time in many, many years, perhaps for the first time in my life, all the loneliness.) After numerous shipwrecks, I have recaptured time. And there isn't, I am sure of this, anything better to do, anything more important, more urgent, than to take unhurried possession of my parents' house – the only house that really was ever mine – to stroll through rooms and halls, to open the three balcony windows overlooking the avenue, to look at the sea of leaves rising, rippling under the windows, to watch the submerged city, to reestablish contact with the complicitous furniture, to reread so many half-forgotten books, or to stretch out anywhere, a glass within reach of my hand – I have started, oddly enough, to drink Cuba libres again – a mixed pile of records playing one after the other on the phonograph, all that remains of my life focused on seeing the little dots of light dancing in the air, on half-hearing the noises that rise from the street as I doze, on telling myself again for the thousandth time the interminable, the inexhaustible old stories.

All time lies before me: no goals, no commitments, no schedules, no one waiting for me anywhere at any time. No one who thinks of me, no one who imagines me wandering despondently through this old house – because only my mother and Guiomar, and perhaps Julio – yes, perhaps Julio, too – know that I am here, and my mother, who naturally hasn't interrupted her trip, undoubtedly thinks of me in a nervous and irritated way, that ever-unpredictable daughter who robs her of her sleep and never quite fits into her plans, and Guiomar undoubtedly wonders between a seminar and a lab session what can be done with this incorrigible mother, one more problem in a labeled series of problems, but neither one really thinks of me; I don't really exist for either of them, just as I have never been able to exist for Julio either, because had I truly existed for him just as I am, for a single instant, the miracle would have taken place, or at least everything would have really been different – I carry my nostalgia from room to room, huddling wounded – wounded? – in the deepest part of the deepest burrow, because I have shut myself in here, as a sick animal takes refuge in its den, in a probably hopeless attempt to build magic bridges between this prematurely aged girl, who dangles pathetically and grotesquely in midair over the most frightful loneliness – not being thought of by anyone – and that sad girl who had no other company but her phantoms; perhaps I have come to rediscover my old phantoms, or to find myself in that child who, although she was sad and solitary, did indeed exist, prior to the falsification and fraud of all roles assigned and assumed. In this timeless time, I have removed the dustcovers from the furniture, in room after room, I have dusted an endless number of books, I have repeatedly leaned out of the three balcony windows – and I have seen the tone, the liquidity, the light of the sea, at different times of the day – I have lounged on the four couches here, I have curled up in the leather armchair, knees to nose, I have drunk Coca-Cola straight, with lemon, with gin and even with brandy – always with an elusive taste of early youth – and I have told myself so many stories, half-invented half-remembered half-dreamed, sentimental stories, sad stories, that repeat a single failure with different melodies. I have examined the closets, I have plunged into the mirrors, I have strolled through the landscapes in the paintings. And I return once more, and always, to the central balcony window, and I lean out over the sea, and on this sea which is now gray – darkness is falling – the lights shine warm and tremulously, it is a sea with a thousand boats, with enormous, motionless, resplendent ocean liners, with buzzing super-fast motorboats overtaking and chasing each other on the waves. Just in front, separated from my cliff by only a short space of sea shadow, bedecked with blinding whites, with aggressive blues, with sparkling reds, multicolored and fantastic, indisputable master of the night and the waves – it hardly exists in the mornings, and only in the early evening hours does this phantom ship begin to take on new life, its light slowly increasing in the same measure as the daylight decreases – a magnificent enchanted castle in a fabulous amusement park, a most luxurious pleasure yacht, a sumptuous Venetian gondola anchored by order of the doge under my windows: directly in front of the windows, then, is the movie house that opened when I was a girl, that was being constructed for months while I waited incredulous and passionate – because to have a movie directly in front of my house was a marvelous possibility when I was seven eight nine – that I watched get bigger, take on color, grow bejeweled with lights and movie posters and then at last to be there myself one afternoon, clinging to my grandmother, a grandmother still young, still beautiful, with white hair, very light blue eyes, blue like mother's but without their metallic hardness and shine, porcelain skin, clinging fast to my grandmother, rapt, with bated breath, while the pink lights coming from a thousand golden shells and softly coloring the turquoise blue upholstery, the cream-colored curtain, the carpeted floors, were slowly dimming. Now, so many years later – the golden shells have been chipped for some time, and the cream-colored curtain was also done away with a long time ago, leaving only the bare screen; the turquoise blue upholstery on the seats was replaced with dark maroon a long time ago – I seem to hear music on deck – although the most foolish and the most handsome of princes doesn't appear anywhere – and I see hurrying couples, laughing groups of young girls, mamas with many children plunging into the deep hold of the ship, into the very jaws of the enchanted castle. And – a little further on – the second vertex of the magic triangle of my childhood almost disappears into the gray of the waters: it is a dark vertex, almost without lights of its own, and it fades away, as the day is fading, into the waves. This second vertex is a dark grotto: six steps and a world of secret nooks. You dive, you submerge, and now deep down, when you turn upward, when you look back up, you see magnificent rivers of emerald light that descend to the depths, the radiant surface of the sea never as beautiful as when seen in reverse from below, from the deep abysses of a sea grotto, which at this time of day make the shadows twice as gloomy, now that the emerald greens are toned down. The grotto is crammed with musty shelves overflowing with treasures. Incredible Caran D'Ache pencil sets with thirty-six colors, each one different, even though there are only seven colors in the rainbow and you can make the other colors with them if you wish; for which reason the exuberance of the thirty-six different pencils acquires a touch of ostentatious extravagance, of almost sinful and exotic excess – even today I can't walk by a shop window displaying a box of Caran d'Ache pencils with its thirty-six colors without stopping – luxurious sets of silver compasses asleep on the blackest or most scarlet of velvets, ready to leave their dreams and create a strange universe of impossible circles; huge, soft art-gum erasers, with smooth rounded edges, on which Snow White and the Seven Dwarfs and Prince Charming move languidly – he is always a bit stupid although this time he may be neither the silliest, nor the most handsome, of princes – complete sets of art postcards, with hippodromes and fat ladies surrounded by little blond children, and women, also blond, with huge straw hats, women Mama would describe as having a lot of class, and vases bursting with multicolored flowers – which have no smell – and small, expensive, stupid-looking dogs wearing little blue bows; and mysterious – bewitched – boxes sleeping under the dust of the furthest – the highest – shelves, whose contents we may never learn, and blotting paper with brightly colored designs, such a rare treasure that not even the most spoiled child has ever used one of these blotters, because they aren't for sale, and for this reason they don't have a price; one must obtain these priceless objects by means of merit or by flattering the two griffin-ladies, of indeterminate sex and age – two griffins who were probably androgynous and immortal – intemporal in any case – who rule over the grotto, who hand you the pencils and the cards on silhouetted chromos covered with a shiny metallic paint that dyes our fingers with silver, two arbitrary or magnanimous griffins who at times capriciously grant one of the blotting papers and who one day may even open the mysterious dusty-bewitched boxes on the highest shelf before your astonished eyes. I think I could well submerge again into the grotto any afternoon – if I am still capable of diving to such secret depths – and buy a little bottle of India ink. Or better yet, an entire box, a fragrant box of the whitest wood, like everything else brought from Germany or perhaps from Japan, in which the little square bottles are lined up evenly, an impossibility become reality, because the box contains not only blue ink, black ink, even red ink – red like blood on the windowsill of a sad queen – a more or less predictable red, but also this absurd collection of orange ink, mulberry ink, maroon ink – though all my maps always turned out so badly despite the multiplicity of colors – that culminates in the implausibility of yellow ink and white ink, a complete absurdity. I may go down any afternoon and buy myself a box of India ink, the most expensive, the largest, the one that has the most labels saying Made in Japan or Made in Germany, the one that has the most colors, and I will also buy sheets of shiny cardboard, cream-colored cardboard, pink cardboard, gold cardboard, and maybe the sexless, ageless griffins will feel especially benevolent and will give me a brightly colored blotter, made for children – there are no longer any children, only Guiomar, who is so different, so far away, so legitimately a grandaughter of the elegant Anglo-Saxon lady, of the traveling goddess, who naturally hasn't interrupted her trip, the goddess who destroys the cults of Demeter as she passes, who has never and will never know anything about secret Dionysian celebrations; and I can't remember if this shop even attracted Guiomar's attention, or if she ever collected chromos or blotters – they might give me a blotter, although it is very possible that they no longer exist either, one more thing among so many that have ceased to exist, because Anglo-Saxon ladies and their grandchildren only write with a ballpoint pen – if filling out postcards with an enormous handwriting that only leaves room for the greeting or covering large graph paper with tiny flylike writing structured into a game of numbers and formulas is writing – but there may still be one hidden, solitary blotter left, a sole survivor of the extinct species, in the deepest recesses of the sea grotto, just as I survive – a prematurely aged girl – in the dark halls of an empty house.

T he bell rings insistently, and for a few seconds I resist opening the door, because I don't think it can be anyone who is looking for me – it would be quite improbable for Mama or Guiomar to have decided to leave off telephoning excited remonstrances, wise restrained advice, and turn up here, which is the least they could do if they really wanted to play some part in this sad story, in this sordid story from which I emerge crippled, dirty, aged, as if from the waters and the dark mud of a marsh that swallows up everything – and for a few seconds I feel the apprehension and the fear that Julio could be here, ringing, on the other side of the door, with his most irresistible smile and a bunch of red roses in his hands, but I end up opening anyway, incapable as I have always been of not answering the insistent ring of a telephone, of not opening to a knock on a door, of not ripping open the envelope of a letter addressed to my name. Equally incapable of missing an appointment. An entire lifetime – in the periods in which there was a concrete reason to justify it, but also in the long periods in which there was no possibility at all – waiting for something marvelous, permanently waiting for something unexpected to happen. I laugh at myself and at this waiting beyond any hope, but I open the door, and it is not Guiomar, not my mother, not Julio; it is a warm voice in the darkness of the landing and the entrance hall – I haven't turned on the light – a slightly hoarse voice, a voice accustomed to say only trivialities but which often has a tense and excited inflection, as if some seventh veil were being removed before an astonished and amazed audience, although she herself is neither astonished nor surprised at anything, and it seems absolutely natural for her to find me here – or could someone have told her? – in this house where no one has lived for years, and through which I wander like a shadow seeking to capture my old phantoms. She quickly asks me about Guiomar, about Julio, and before I can give her an answer or invite her to come in, she has already gone down the dark hall in front of me and has plunged voraciously into a passionate monologue about herself and her circumstances, a monologue I know well because it has followed me at intervals since my adolescence, always takes up again at the exact same point, and seems never to have been interrupted, although it is a bit strange that it could have pursued me here. It is a pretty, serious voice, a bit scratchy and sensual, betrayed by the vices of its class, a false excitement – which reminds me faintly of Mama's – and her mouth seems to be filled with an excess of vowels, which often end on an accented syllable as they push past each other, and those "refined" sentences, almost always ungrammatical, almost never complete or finished, her conversation so loaded with double meanings and unfinished statements. I wonder where this slow, tumultuous, amusing, clumsy, incorrect, and distant speech characteristic of the women of my class could come from. It may be due to some biological change, perhaps a subtle modification effected on the vocal cords of a long line of properly nourished women – just as hands like my mother's are the result of an interminable series of women with idle hands – or perhaps in the past some extremely snobbish, delightfully chic woman, somewhat given to pretentiousness or with a slight speech defect, imposed this fashion on a group and the fashion was then perpetuated throughout the ages; perhaps they send us to the Sacred Heart Academy or the School of Jesus Mary just for this – or also for this – for us to learn this very same tone of voice, this adulterated, terrible Spanish spoken by the refined ladies of my city. Only I didn't learn it – like so many other things – and sometimes I wonder why I never spoke like that, why, even as a little girl, I never had the distinctive characteristics of the tribe, why I always floated in this uncomfortable no-man's-land. And my friend occasionally intuits this, because then her voice hesitates, stops, teeters anxiously on the peak of a sentence, as if she didn't know exactly to whom or where to address herself, and then the sentence is inserted into another, different, often contradictory, one or languishes sickly or expires in the recurrent, saving ellipses. But this awareness – and they all feel it – is only a fleeting and disagreeable intuition, the awareness that, despite so much evidence, I may possibly not be one of them, the agent who has infiltrated from a foreign place and, because he is foreign, therefore is dangerous and an enemy, but the awareness vanishes immediately, and a few seconds later Maite's monologue has regained its enthusiasm, its confident harmony, all suspicion rapidly cleared up, any doubt calmed in the vague and simplifying certainty – only my mother and perhaps Guiomar can no longer attain this certainty – that I am somewhat strange but definitely one of them. It isn't bad, for variety's sake, to have a friendship that is a bit eccentric.

The closer we get to the living room and the lights, and without being quiet for a moment, the voice begins clothing itself in blond curls, fleshy lips, aggressive breasts, pretty legs in black stockings in a herringbone design, legs which she tucks under her when she settles on the couch. Now she looks at me with her bright eyes – the eyes of a perverse girl who begins to catch the drift of some practical joke – and, incredibly, her soft laughter doesn't hamper her talking. This strapping girl whose name I hardly knew, a name heard distractedly when they called roll, a "present" pronounced in a rather more deliberate way than the rest of us did, as if it had a special meaning or as if she were really more present, pronounced in a small, hoarse voice, a voice that hardly suggested the naughty child's face or the body that seemed designed to make blouses and dresses burst open, a body in which any other women might have felt uncomfortable but which with dashing grace Maite carried through the world like a banner; this strapping girl, who came up to me one fine day in the cafeteria at the university – when they still had not done away with the comfortable old couch that offered us a warm communal shelter along the walls – and imperiously held out a copy of the *Letter to His Father* to me and demanded that I read it: because it was exactly her situation. I don't know whether this was her usual way of approaching people who more or less interested her, but that is the way I met Maite and the way I met Kafka. And I enjoyed myself with Maite, because her hoarse voice was then at a savory and fascinating stage in her conversation directed to no one in particular – long before the inevitable deterioration – and we even got to be friends, or perhaps only comrades, to the extent that one can be the friend of a voice engrossed in a monologue, one that looks for listeners rather than interlocutors. Although I never understood what relation there could be between the voracious, greedy girl – a hoarse voice, pretty legs, round, aggressive breasts – self-satisfied, enchanted with being herself, remotely nonconformist about something rather vague, an unbridled snob, who spent her college years tirelessly delivering speeches – her voice and tone never losing their identification with the Sacred Heart Academy – about the mirrors in the houses of assignation, their towels in warm tones, their jets of warm water crisscrossing the bathtub in all directions, lights that can be turned on and off from the bed, and directly above the bed, slightly tilted, another mirror that takes up almost the entire ceiling, a mirror in which are reflected – surrounded by plaster Venuses and Cupids – the two naked bodies, the voice going on and on about the smuggler boyfriend wanted by Interpol who invited her to sumptuous parties on American yachts that had recently arrived from Nice, and who, before descending the boarding plank, stuffed her skirts with marijuana, or about the custard the lady concierge cooked secretly that she and another boyfriend who was a fairy devoured in the hills outside the city, their greedy piggy lips giving and taking kisses, while the short, mustached detective hired by a very worthy and desperate father – mouth watering, penis straining against his ill-fitting pants – got hot and sweaty; I never understood, I used to say, what relationship there could have been between this buxom girl – skirts and blue jeans groaned under the pressure of her hips and the buttons of her blouses popped and flew happily through the air – playful and aggressive, and the sickly loner from Prague, if it were not that both shared a taste for telling stories, for embroiling themselves in a monologue that went on and on and – for him, but not for her – perhaps substituted for life.

A bit mislaid in time, a bit out of place, I now have before me this hoarse, "refined" voice, this monologue which finds me at intervals but which has been following me forever – Maite, the only girl from the bourgeoisie with whom I coincided at the university, perhaps for that very reason the only one I have continued seeing regularly afterward – her lips firm and dark, her little rosy tongue ready to lick, the little tongue of a big silky cat, a lazy cat who licks her whiskers indifferently but deep down is lying in wait, her perfect teeth ready to bite; Maite asks helter-skelter and obviously absentmindedly about my mother, about Guiomar, about Julio, finally; and now I suspect that she has come for this, that perhaps they have sent her for this, I feel almost certain that she knows, that they know (and who could have told her?) that Julio has left once more for parts unknown (it is curious that I can only imagine him on the deck of a yacht, a blond at his side, the glass with the fashionable drink in his hand, wearing a sailor's jacket and cap: the overaged, undistinguished hero of television commercials), though his return is so well known, so certain (a return that my mother and Guiomar promise and guarantee in a duet, as if I could doubt for an instant that he was going to return, or as if it could affect me in the slightest), only this time he won't find me when he returns, because I have escaped to my old burrow, I have left the fold (and apparently this does justify their following me here, their sending this big, pink-tongued cat to spy on me in the ancestral grottos of my early dreams), but Maite hardly seems to listen to my answer, my "I don't know how Julio is; he has gone away" – could she actually have come all the way here for a different reason? – and she pounces on the past with frivolous arpeggios, she proposes – horror of horrors – a dinner with our old classmates and asks me who I see from the old days – it is clear now that she isn't listening to me because evidently she hasn't come up here to talk to me about this, although perhaps it wasn't exactly to find out my quarrels or lack of them with Julio either – and when I tell her no one, that I don't see anybody except her sometimes, I suddenly remember that I saw Marcos in London. Marcos or what is left of Marcos. Besides, the dinner, if it comes to pass, will be a dinner of dead bodies, a phantoms' feast, a banquet of multiple Stone Guests, the ghosts of the most brilliant generation of the post-war era, most of them inexorably defeated by total, unmistakable, gross failure – is self-deceit ever impossible? – most of them defeated by gross failure, some vanquished in a more subtle – just a little more subtle – way, by the grotesque, infinitely lamentable parody of having succeeded triumphantly, perhaps a laughable success that incurs the rancorous hatred of the majority (the cut-and-dried failures) toward those few of us, because success is never enough, because it is never real, because it never came at the right moment – at times a bit too soon, at times definitely, desolately late, always at the wrong time – because above all it never resembles what we longed for in our childhood, and what we longed for in our childhood is exactly what we have been searching for our whole life and the only thing that perhaps could satisfy us, because there is an offensive and insulting difference between reality and desire, because success has always had an exorbitant and crazy price or because it has been given to us for nothing and consequently is worth nothing; it only manages to give us a laughable success that makes defeat much more painful and above all much dirtier, so that we, the presumptive winners, suddenly find ourselves shamefacedly justifying our successes, or absurdly pretending to believe in them, or secretly envying the authentic, first-born, unequivocal failures. And if at least it were a question of a really honorable dinner with thin, remote Stone Guests, with cavernous and monotone voices, with splendid silences, with smells of moss and closed tombs, cold marble and slow movements: a really honest dinner of phantoms at which no one would play games any longer – all games having already been played and lost – in which no one would try to act clever or feign or pretend anything; if we would meet only to be together for a while in silence, to look at each other understandingly – to look at each other compassionately – and shake hands sadly when we left, at an honest wake for so many dead dreams; to meet without housing developments in Ibiza or country estates, without Spanish departments where one is invariably the chairman's right hand, without having finished dissertations – without perennially delayed dissertations – or articles published, or photos of our kids – children for all those years and grandchildren before long – among the napkins soiled with sauces and sangria, on the tablecloth where overflowing ashtrays and shrimp shells accumulate and on which wine is invariably spilled – and someone has dipped his finger in it, raised it to his forehead and anointed our foreheads – without that grotesque collection of dressed-up couples, open shirt collars on English wool sweaters, because we are unconventional and snobbish enough that the men no longer wear ties – fortunately, Julio has never attended one of these dinners, with or without a tie – the women, of course, with their pearl necklaces, with their mink or astrakhan coats, or the nonmink or nonastrakhan coats made of cheap fur, with crocodile purses, and their silly giggles and stupid possessives, where the monstrous lie, which nobody believes, grows, protrudes, and bursts like a boil, the lie of believing themselves alive, important, even – almost – happy. Because now – while Maite prolongs a monologue that I no longer listen to, sure as I am that there will be something, a gleam in her eye, a nervous gesture with her hands, or above all a special tremor in her voice, something that will warn me that the moment has arrived when she will undertake what she came to tell me, if indeed she has come to tell me something and not merely to pry into my loneliness without Julio (what can they know about what my loneliness with Julio has been like for almost thirty years) – now I remember – and I would tell it if I thought that Maite would listen to me – that I saw Marcos in London, and I would explain to Maite – if there were the remotest possibility that she would understand – that scarcely had I entered the house, on the very threshold, as in that ambiguous and alarming moment when the beautiful heroine, that fearful, irresponsible, beautiful heroine, usually scantily wrapped in a silk robe that slides softly over her shoulders and half opens on her warm breasts, usually with a flickering candle in her hand – the beautiful heroine, instead of throwing all the bolts and piling the furniture against the bedroom door – whoever made me leave the hotel and venture like this into the shadowy lair of a friend from the past – or perhaps it wasn't the foolish heroine with the scantily covered breasts, but rather her bold companion who has followed her this far, loving her in silence and knowing that she is lost and in danger in the Transylvanian forests – the heroine or her companion, it's all the same – from the exact moment in which they push open the creaking door that leads from the relative security of the bedroom to the secret wings of the castle – the atmosphere very different from the London apartment, but at bottom the same – they feel that vague apprehension, the first, very brief onset of fear, quickly overcome with a frown and a shrug of the shoulders, the vague, but very sure apprehension that something isn't right. And you forge ahead, and in these first steps, in this fearful first incursion into the castle, you don't find anything that you can definitely qualify as alarming, the huge chests and Gothic candelabras are beautiful, the rusty old armor, even the very instruments of torture, so natural in an ancient castle belonging to a duke with such a distinguished genealogy, the so-called Spanish furniture so natural – how could they have obtained these horrors in a city where every-day things are almost always so beautiful? – the plastic flowers in Murano glass vases, the color television presiding over the room, the Gauguin and Renoir reproductions, so natural in the London apartment of a Spanish professor, or almost natural, or at least not very alarming, although you feel uneasy at any rate, and it seems that the candle flickers, on the point of going out, although it doesn't go out completely, not even when a crazed bat flies quickly across the room, even brushing the blond hair pulled back with a pink ribbon, the throbbing swell of the beautiful heroine's breasts, now more agitated – I should have stayed in the bedroom, I shouldn't have left my hotel – or her friend's black hair; and in Marco's apartment, it is a crazy, emaciated, and hysterical kitten, hissing and spitting, that scratches my legs and rips my stockings and dress, finally hiding under the sideboard, fur still bristling and whiskers stiff. And now the slight apprehension, the remote uneasiness turn to alarm, and the heroine wonders for the first time if it would not have been better to have entrenched herself in her relatively safe bedroom instead of rushing out half-naked to explore an-cient castles with a flickering candle in her hand, and if I didn't want to stay in the hotel, I could have gone shopping or into the first movie house I came across and limited myself to deal-ing with Marcos during conference hours, because what the devil is this lady looking for here and who asked her to stick her nose into other people's business. And the alarm doesn't come merely from the Gothic chests, the old armor – vases overflow-ing with multicolored plastic – and the torture rack where you can still make out traces of blood, it doesn't even come from the quivering brush of a bat's dark wings or from the hysterical scratches of a half-crazy cat, but from the suspicion that perhaps all this might not be entirely fortuitous but is rather scenery carefully arranged by someone for some reason, and this someone, who repels and frightens us but who nevertheless attracts us enough to drag us to the middle of his lair, fascinated by the unexpected and mysterious, or perhaps fascinated deep down by what we have always known we are going to discover there, this someone is arranging these foot soldiers, his emissaries, on our way and sending them to meet us, in a frightening crescendo that can only end in him, that can only end in her. Surely he is already spying on us from the dark shadows at the end of the winding staircase, from behind the half-closed kitchen door, even if he still sends one last emissary, more intimate, more familiar, even more pathetic than the poor cat: a warty hunchback wrapped in rags of unhappiness or a fat little blond girl, snot-nosed and beribboned, a flabby, dull, impossible little girl, and the candle goes out, and we definitely feel sick, and we know with absolute certainty that we can no longer go back, that the secure warmth of our bedroom is gone, the warm refuge of stores or London movie houses, and that when we go out into the street and return to our hotel – if indeed we do return some day – we will no longer be entirely the same. And here she is at last. With a broad, twisted smile, doing the honors of the castle, turning each supposedly friendly gesture into disdain or a threat, offering a strange-tasting Burgundy wine and some moldy biscuits – as if they really came from a rusty cupboard in a Transylvanian attic – while the cat hisses furiously, the little girl makes a pest of herself, and the room fills with blind, crazed bats. The count-who-sucks-the-blood-of-tender-maidens-of-languid-tow-haired-pages: the terrible goddess-mother-devourer-of-geniuses-devourer-of-children-devourer-of-child-prodigies. Triumphal and irrefutable in her mediocrity, absolute center of a sordid world created by her for her own glorification, in a malevolent atmosphere where conversations, the beginnings of conversation, fall like dead birds around us, a malevolent atmosphere where trees can't grow or nonplastic flowers survive; she is thoroughly comfortable with the fat little girl who devours bonbons in a corner, looks at me squint-eyed, and bellows for no reason, thoroughly comfortable with the neurotic cat who jumps at your legs or your neck, always on the lookout for the careless instant when you turn your back on it, comfortable in this marvelously successful scenery where by means of astuteness, complicated calculations, and an ancestral tradition wisely handed down from female to female, one makes an uninhabitable lair out of a supposedly ordinary apartment – and now I have just discovered, on the farthest shelf of the bookcase, lost in the castle of a thousand horrors, the black snout of the little cloth dog that I gave Marcos so very many years ago, and I have to concentrate all my attention on the biscuits and the Burgundy, on the unsalvageable ridiculousness of the situation, so as not to intensify this ridiculousness by bursting out crying – an uninhabitable lair where she fattens and devours her lost and found Hansel, daily fatter and more phantasmal, a Hansel who no longer even has anything to say at the sessions of the convention or in the paper that he himself is presenting, because he stopped loving words a long time ago, he surely stopped loving them at the exact moment that he stopped loving himself, that Hansel with the beautiful eyes and velvet voice, with his loyalty to the party, his sharp, impertinent questions in class, his fondness for good Burgundy and French cognac, his learned disquisitions on Provençal literature, a Hansel so committed and exquisite that he seemed predestined for one of those women with an overly large mouth, a very sad, deep gaze, a lithe step, who discourse in a serious tone on solitude and death in Bergman's films, who seem to talk to death face to face and play a dangerous chess game with indifference, one of those women who have obviously understood something that the rest of us don't see, who – always drifting – have established a complicitous pact with the unknown, somewhere over our empty heads. A Hansel now drained of himself and who has nothing to say, nothing to say to me, in the living room with the TV and the plastic flowers – and the sad snout of my old dog peeking out from the books on the highest bookshelf: he kept it in spite of everything for so many, many years – while we drink half-spoiled wine and munch moldy biscuits and his wife scolds him because he drinks, because he smokes, because he doesn't talk, because he works too hard, and as hard as I look in vain for the little bloody spots on his greasy neck, the unmistakable signs of sharp sucking teeth, and I don't find them, this is a Hansel drained of his life, a poor guy who lost his shadow and his smile at some point, a Hansel who is not alive, who becomes phantomlike and gets fat, who in any case doesn't live his life, or what could have been his life, or a halfway coherent prolongation of the life that I once knew, although he may live and breathe with a plantlike life, in this curious closed, cloistered world, where plants lead a plastic existence, a double metamorphosis that is brilliantly appropriate; and in any case, in the worst or the best of cases, his razor slash won't soil the nylon carpet with his greenish sap, nor will he blow his brains out in front of the red lightbulbs in the fake fireplace made of fake marble, the shot muffled by the noise from the television, and such pale blood, hardly even green, could barely be made out on the carpet; one won't permit even the smallest rebellion, the smallest decency of giving the schizophrenic cat – surely incorrigible by now – to people who can have a cat, or of sending the blond cross-eyed little freak – after all, she is his daughter – to an institution on the opposite ends of the earth. And although he avoids my accusing or desolate looks, and I know that he will carefully dodge my questions, although he certainly does seem a bit uncomfortable, one can't say categorically that he is unhappy – no more unhappy than average, I am sure he would tell me if I could catch him alone in one of the halls at the convention, no more than average, because he decided so long ago that life cannot be, could not have been, different – he gets fat and phantomlike, and vegetates monstrously among plastic flowers. That is all.

I start to explain to her that I saw Marcos in London, but

her monologue already reaches another point in the discourse, and Maite doesn't seem willing to interrupt it even to listen to me. Perhaps she has also acquired something of great goddess mother devourer protector of men geniuses children, but she smells very good, she has lovely legs and pretty breasts, she leaves her children at home and doesn't seem to have changed much: skin-deep nonconformity and an enormous penchant for playing games. And as I curl up resignedly on the other end of the couch, arms around my drawn-up legs, and look at her without paying much attention to what she is saying, her voice, always intense and excited, suddenly takes on that minimal inflection, that slight, almost imperceptible change in tone, that I have learned to detect after years and that tells me she is beginning to speak about what she really has come for: and it is very strange, because it isn't about Julio, or about his cute young blonds or redheads, or about my possible lovers or lack of them, it isn't even to criticize my desertion by my mother or Guiomar. Maite is talking about a Colombian girl, she is giving me a delirious, melodramatic picture of a wild, solitary aristocrat, who rides Thoroughbred steeds bareback and whips the palace servants with her riding crop, an intelligent, sensitive, exquisite girl – that doesn't jibe too well with the detail about the riding crop – who apparently has been attending my course on Ariosto for some days and whom I never noticed. And it is very strange that Maite has come all this way to talk to me precisely about this, but there is a malicious gleam in her blue eyes which tells me without a shadow of a doubt that everything is part of a game, a silly, frivolous game, one of these games that excite her and make her feel good and alive, but in which she never risks, or ever did risk, too much personally, like visiting the houses of assignation in the city, only later to be wed as a virgin to a man who had not taken her to any of them, or carrying contraband goods under her skirt, safely shielded by her apparent ignorance, by the powerful name of a family above all suspicion, or flirting with a friend she knows isn't interested in women in order to excite another poor fellow who really is interested in them, but who wouldn't dare approach her for fear of disapproval. Society games that aren't too dangerous.

I submerge to spend the morning in another of my ancient wells of shadow. I sit at the same little table, pushed up to one of the half-open windows overlooking the inner courtyard, and without having to ask for them, they bring me my books and papers. They haven't seen me for many days – Have I been sick perhaps? No, no, I haven't been sick – although it is possible, I think, as I smile and say, "spring fever," and the attendant says to me, without a smile, that I work too hard, and as usual I get confused and entangled in one of those verbose, long-winded speeches, full of contradictions and nuances, in which ultimately not even I know what I want to justify, whether my would-be industriousness or that profound laziness, that deadly lassitude, about which my invincible puritanism continues to feel guilty, however unsuccessful that puritanism may be in making me commit myself seriously to something, in making me give up this ridiculous pose as a highbrow amateur, of a clever, sensitive, refined lady who whiles away her leisure hours with literature, although in any case the attendant has spoken for the sake of speaking: it is incredible how many things are said and listened to in the course of the day just for the sake of listening and saying, and he no longer hears me; he offers me a light (now he does have a smile), asks me if I want a Coca-Cola, and, still smiling, goes off toward his desk, his smile evaporating in the air as he walks away, because he becomes a strict, stern old cat again, ready to grumble at every request and to dispense volumes of art history one by one to all the insolent kids who study for exams here, the cat who climbs onto the high Cheshire stool – Off with everyone's head! – it is possible, I think, that I don't feel as well as usual, although I am not exactly sick, but I have the exacerbated, delicious sensitivity associated with convalescence, or that keen sensitivity associated with the period of waiting that precedes

37

metamorphoses. And it is very possible that I haven't come here to work today – I scarcely look at files and papers – but because in this library there was – as there is now – the same silence broken by whispers and laughter, the same tenuous light as in the chapel with the dying flowers, the snow-white altar cloths, the little nuns who lie in a side chapel among lilies and roses and who have been dead forever. An aquariumlike slipping in and out of the bookstacks and a confused murmur of prayers. The smoke from our cigarettes, so ritualistic, so transcendental, like clouds of incense. And what is this? A hand covers the bottom of the illustration. The priest-king of Knossos sixteen B.C. And this one? Nefertiti, Tell el Amarna – it can't be too easy. And this one? This one? Amiens, Rheims, Botticelli's *Primavera, The Nightwatch*, the mosque at Damascus. Mechanical associations between pictures and words, without digressions, without reflection, without pleasure: we maneuvered without pleasure among things that perhaps we might have learned to love, among things that I have come to love by laborious and inverted paths many years later. I wonder if they still study that way for the first year art exam and if they are still looking at the same history in so many, many volumes through the smoke of their cigarettes, through the prayerlike murmur of secrets – Vézelay you two went to Castelldefels and then what did he say to you? Nothing – thirteenth century – he said it was impossible – while the light reaches us through the windows overlooking the patio, filtered and colored with green and gold by the branches of the trees, and the floor plans of Gothic cathedrals blend with mysterious evocations, and the other end of the room is full of old mummies who leaf through the newspaper and give us dirty looks – with old mummies who pretend to consult files and papers and look at them with annoying curiosity – and even the attendants, even the fastidious Cheshire cats who have lost their smile in the air, give us dirty looks, because we don't give tips, or because we make too much noise, or because art history has twelve – were there twelve? – volumes and we never remembered what was in each one or which one we wanted to look at. And the long tables overflow with books, notebooks, and papers – could Juan Ramón and Zenobia's translation of Tagore's poems, could the verses of Omar Khayyám be among the books? Certainly not novels by Sartre or Camus – as butts and ashes overflow the ashtrays that are always in short supply. Everything a bit excessive, because surely they don't need to consult so many books and could do without half of their notebooks and papers. Too many whispers, too many butts – scarcely smoked – too many gestures. Even their seriousness, especially their petulant seriousness, is excessive. As usual, they make me slightly annoyed – they have been here all these years, we have been here years and years, before, during, and after my time, too identical to each other, to ourselves, crammed together around the big, long tables, noisy, insolent, and timid – because I too have something of an old mummy about me now, something of a Cheshire cat without a smile, but today I observe them with interest – perhaps in reality today I have submerged into the shadowy well only to find them – because it is May, and it is a stifling, strange month in which many things seem to come back to me connected with memories of exams, of flowers in the chapel, of the incipient sprouting of tender shoots – although this year I didn't see the first leaves appear on the trees either – with the taste of strawberries – you can hardly find strawberries in this city any longer – with long walks toward the sea, or perhaps everything is due to the fact that Julio has undertaken a stupid trip bound for nowhere for the thousandth time, and everything seems too silly to me, immensely empty, even my desertion by my mother and Guiomar, and Maite came yesterday to my parents' home to tell me a curious story – she was telling a thousand stories, but she came, I am sure, to tell me a single story, with which she succeeded, no matter how it may irritate me to recognize that I was manipulated that way, in setting my interest in playing games and my curiosity into motion – and it is certain that, for one reason or another or for all of them, today's May is becoming mysteriously linked with Mays now far away, and it is as if all these years – almost thirty – which were supposedly solid, supposedly fulfilled, supposedly fruitful, these almost thirty years that comprise what should have been the fullness of my life, with all that I have lived, have known, have done during them – have I lived? – were suddenly nothing but a banal and somewhat stupid parenthesis – as if my existence were basically as stupid as my mother's or Julio's – a flashy, vulgar dream lacking interest and sense when taken apart, a parenthesis that now, suddenly, could be erased magically at any moment, a dream from which I could now finally awaken and return to the one and only reality – without dream or parenthesis – of my adolescence and my childhood.

I am behind the desk – definitely on the other side – on the platform, and just by stretching out my hand, I can touch the blackboard at my back. And a little further, between the blackboard and the first of the high windows, a relief map of Spain. Greens and ochers attenuated by the dust of a thousand years. I didn't believe that they still made this type of map, although it is very possible that it is the same one from back then, useless and forever forgotten between the blackboard and the first window, because the strange thing about my return this October – this time on the other side of the desk and on the platform – is not the things that have changed, the uncontrollable outrage of time, of so many years, of almost thirty years – I returned to the university after almost thirty years and everything was, of course, very different! – the surprising thing, the incredibly strange thing, is that here – as in the shadowy well of the library – almost nothing has changed. You wake after centuries with the prescribed words already on the tip of your tongue: "Where am I? What does all this mean?" You are ready to glance around with astonished wonder, but the glance of astonished wonder happens by itself, only in this story what produces it is that you are in the same place and among the same objects as when you went to sleep, because in the Enchanted Forest everything has slept while you slept for the very same one hundred years, everything has slept under the influence of a good fairy so that you won't feel uncomfortable when you awaken. The same benches of dark wood, with inscriptions patiently carved during the drowsiness of the classes – some, many, have probably been added, but surely those from my time are still there, unharmed by possible new coats of paint – the same tender, wavering green behind the panes of the high windows – you don't hear, but you can see the murmur of the trees in the plaza, and just seeing those branches moving up there, it is as if all the warmth of spring were brashly seeping into the still-cold, dark classroom: it was on mornings like these, in the Mays of exam time, when spring murmured outside and inside it was still the worst of winter, mornings in which we were already at the classroom door, about to enter the library or the seminar room, it was on mornings like this one when we would suddenly decide that the very essence of human freedom, the fullness of an existence in which our truest essence was rooted, consisted of something as simple as going out into the street and walking down to the sea (the Ramblas were like a big, green, purring cat, the tip of its tail submerged in the sea), and if we all had not gotten out of bed when the alarm rang, had not dressed and breakfasted quickly (to be there at nine on the dot), had not run the risk of running into the chubby little priest in the hall who supposedly taught us Greek or Latin, because we escaped from class minutes, seconds before the arrival of the teacher (now I am on the other side of the desk, on that grotesque and worm-eaten platform that will fall down any day now, and perhaps I don't recognize the faces of the boys and girls who probably sneaked off toward spring right next to me as I was coming inside and going against the current into winter), if we had not known that there were only three four fifteen days to go before exams and there still remained ten fifteen twenty all the lessons to study, perhaps walking out into the street and down to the sea (first filling our mouths with the taste of a thousand strawberries submerged in whipped cream) would not have assumed that character of a gratuitous, free, almost perfect act, and I believe that in part it was the expression, the words that we liked so much, because cutting class and walking down to the sea sounded good, and at that time, perhaps more than at any other moment in our lives, our performance was influenced by the magic of words and we enjoyed playing our roles as we loudly and disdainfully pushed our way along the shadowy walk, interrupting each other, overdoing poses that we had just learned, often poorly learned at the movies or from books, we acted out an impossible *House of Troy* for the old people who – like the attendant in the library – would look at us reprovingly from their benches, for the women that we almost knocked down on our way and who puffed and snorted like aggressive whales behind their children and their shopping carts, and this was definitely a performance in their honor (young insolent students who cut class and walked down to the sea), then more than ever obliged to present an image, to turn ourselves into a show, to live by words, as if being young did not by chance entail, as it always had and I imagine still does today – because they don't seem so different to me, however much they smoke grass, make love freely – freely? – wear blue jeans and haven't read, don't even know what *The House of Troy* is – lying hours on end in dark rooms behind locked doors, sick from smoking, from literature, from this lethal May air, our bodies limp, restless, and exhausted, struggling clumsily in the sadness and in the anguish that had been pursuing us since adolescence – or perhaps, as in my case, since childhood – and which now, on the verge of disappearing, or at least becoming transformed or toned down, reached its final paroxysm and seemed on the verge of destroying us, poor victims of the greatness and servitude of being only seventeen years old, because among ourselves, in rooms overflowing with smoke and the strumming of guitars, between the cheese sandwiches still associated with our childhood and the Cuba libres of our newfound freedom, we admitted that we were alone and sad and frightened, infinitely bereft of support and direction, but on the street, and especially on the Ramblas, and above all during exam time, if we walked down to the sea, we felt obliged to present this noisy, violent, somewhat irresponsible and insolent image, this image that was brought out in us and then rejected by those unsmiling old people sitting on the benches, the whale women behind their children and baskets. The same benches of dark wood, the same tender, wavering green behind the tall monastic windows, the same platform, worm-eaten and threatened with collapse even then, the same long old desk – as old then as it is now – the same relief map of Spain. All a bit grimy. Worn, grimy, dusty. Cold. Today I feel an urge to go up to the map and run my fingertips carefully along the peaks of the mountain ranges, submerge them in the river basins: if not for this, what is the purpose of this absurd map, lost forever in a university classroom where geography has never even been taught? But since I am on the other side of the desk and on the platform – the fact that I don't really know why or what the devil I am doing here is another story – since I definitely can no longer fill my mouth with a thousand strawberries with whipped cream at the farmers' market, because strawberries are almost nonexistent this year in my insipid city, and where there used to be stands, a sinister supermarket opened a short time ago, since I can't walk down to the sea, because I have lost my companions and spring and even the desire to do so, it will be better for me to stay very, very still at my place, talking to them about something – as soon as they finish filling out the cards with a few questions that I gave them simply because I didn't know how to begin today – without giving them an opportunity to take me, now that I have almost finished the course, for a half-crazy person. In mid-May, with the trees waving their tallest branches behind the high monastic windows, with all the murmuring and the stifling sensations of spring in the wide plaza, with the parks more obscene than ever as the luxuriant new leaves burst forth, with all paths open to the sea – I wonder if the Colombian girl could be walking along one of them now, or if she is under the magnolia in a flowering garden, or sitting with the idiots who stayed behind and are toiling over the cards – it seems absurd to be installed on the other side of the desk, on the platform, absurd to be here this morning. But it seems even stranger that they – I repeat that I don't think they are all that different from us, although they wear sweaters and blue jeans, have their hair curled or long, their cigarettes or joints (that certainly has changed) permanently lit – hand the cards to me one after the other with great seriousness, return to their places and sit down in silence, their eyes fixed on me – not on the tall branches – while I begin to talk to them about Ariosto.

A t last, here she is, before me, holding out a piece of paper. Long, soft, chestnut-colored hair falling down her back, honey-colored eyes, prominent cheekbones, and a gray raincoat belted at the waist: today it is raining behind the tall monastic windows and the tender green of the branches turn gray. During these last days of class, almost without realizing it, I have been involuntarily checking the rows of serious faces on the benches and trying to make one correspond to Maite's delirious description: indomitable Aztec princess – no, there never were Aztecs in Colombia – night-dark eyes, hair blowing in the wind, riding wild horses bareback; thin, pale lips, bluish temples, small breasts, and long legs, climbing the palace staircase three by three – a palace in a tropical jungle? A palace on the seashore? Perhaps a palace on the most aristocratic side of an old Castilian plaza? – and with her riding crop – still damp and warm with the sweat and foam of the horse – beating the barefoot servants with black braids who help her to undress, to take off her boots, to take a bath, and who then bring in the tea service on little inlaid trolleys, on massive silver trays; with absent look, furrowed brow, an ironic and impatient grimace, disdaining princes and ambassadors, first consuls, intellectuals both visiting and resident, at the receptions of her father, the tyrant, while a mother who is very ivory, very European, very languid – "very French," Maite told me – lies dying endlessly among feather cushions and lace coverlets. I have been inventing faces, composing scenes, secretly amused and irritated by the realization that I have been manipulated once again by someone who doesn't understand me at all, but who knows how to press my buttons so skillfully: that malicious Maite, with her greedy lips and wonderful legs, who is walking around here stupidly turning on lights, although she has never understood what electricity is, this shallow education of genuine females, that scandalously clumsy but terribly effective manipulation – my mother and even Guiomar herself have something of this quality – that facility for finding sordid motivations or of causing embarrassing problems. Because Maite knew, with that odious feminine astuteness for setting into motion and profaning unknown mechanisms, that her delirious description, that cloying soap opera that she came to my home to offer me and that should have repelled me if only for its defects in style – for the total absence of any style – that delirious description which she, of course, didn't believe for an instant, which didn't have the slightest effect on her, was going to launch me – even though I didn't believe it either – into making up stories, pursuing images, because my adolescent immaturity is always ready to respond to any offer, to accept everything that has the prospect of a challenge, to take a relatively serious interest in the game, even in the silliest and most predictable of games. And so a long series of images stirred up by Maite preceded the real and demythifying presence of this pale face, framed by straight, dark hair, this definitely insignificant presence, which sends into confused and scattered flight so many faces with the blackest of hair and sea green eyes, so much long tawny hair that coils to the knee, malevolently alive, so many golden locks – Rapunzel, Rapunzel, let down your hair – capable of drawing me to the most hidden of enchanted towers without doors or stairs, so many dark-skinned brows, so many sensual mouths with the clinging aroma of tropical fruit. Because Clara (surely she was the one who wrote on the card without signing it, where her favorite authors and books were to be put: Shakespeare, Homer, Peter Pan) is here at last, the predictable finale to a first act that could not end – now I know – in any other way. Only surprisingly thin, surprisingly young – her appearance even younger than what her real age should be – surprisingly defenseless and insignificant, suddenly blushing a little and with a slight, very slight tremor in the hand that holds the paper out to me, a paper in which many things are set forth, claimed and demanded, which I glance at without seeing – I am going to sign it at any rate – because – while I sign it and I explain to her that Maite spoke to me about her, while I invite her to have coffee – I am thinking that she had to be the one who wrote Shakespeare, Homer, Peter Pan, and as we go down the dark staircase with the peeling walls, I remember that my cafeteria no longer exists, because they got rid of it many, many years ago, after a tumultuous year – I had finished my courses and was working on my doctorate – in which one of the first university leaders, a tall, thin, rather colorless fellow, made speeches standing on one of the benches in the patio of the College of Liberal Arts, the year when the police broke in for the first time and all of us – teachers and students – ran down the halls, took shelter in the lecture halls, the luckier ones having climbed over the park railing, the year when the first lampoons appeared, the first pamphlets, the first graffiti, and when – one glorious day – one of the madcap freshman girls climbed the tower and set the bell of freedom, of a new era, ringing deliriously, while we heard it in astonishment from the lecture and assembly halls, from the park – the throngs in the plaza heard it – and even the police stopped their savage beating for an instant, and although the gesture made no sense, had no effect whatever, and any leader of any one of the emerging cells that were beginning to operate at the university would have totally opposed such a gratuitous, senseless act, because we all knew, and she better than any of us, that she would have to come down from the tower sometime, before, doubtless long before her group – did hers exist? – or mine or ours or whoever, could have taken any share of power, before anything remotely like an era of freedom could have been established, even before the police withdrew, although, I repeat, it was a silly, purposeless move, but how beautiful to hear that clear, unaccustomed sound ringing for a few minutes, for multiple, entire, complete minutes, in the new morning, to the fury of the cops, who, after the first moment of stupor had passed, renewed and intensified their beating; I think it was the same year that the students and some professors locked themselves in the auditorium – also without any possible objective, the only possible outcome being that we came out with our heads down and smirking, hoping that the policemen would not beat us on the head and that we would not be deprived of our identification papers for too long, the students especially hoping that they wouldn't forfeit their enrollment fees or their passport or the academic year (as the only outcome possible for my crazy libertarian student was to come down from the tower and find herself at the mercy of the men who were waiting below for her or who had already started up to get her) – we were, or we believed we were, masters of our destiny in an inviolable and inviolate enclosure, and, although the time was still not ripe for anything, and outside, in the city, an environment hostile to us, a closed-minded lack of understanding was growing in the people congregated in the plaza or listening to the news on the radio, nevertheless, something had begun to change after so many years, as many years as most of those young people had been alive, something warm and fragile, but heady, was being born, and that act of ringing the bell in senseless frenzy (although the police waited patiently at the foot of the tower and outside, in the city, almost nothing was happening), that act of shutting ourselves up with no plan or purpose and seeing a very special kind of intimate solidarity emerge for the first time, was terrible and beautiful and encouraging (although the cops were waiting at the door and further out, in the city, in the kingdom, hardly anything was happening then). And now, going down the dark, peeling stairway, I remember all this, prompted by the somewhat delayed recollection that the bench along the wall no longer exists, the bench that was so inviting for talk sessions, clandestine meetings, and secrets, where Maite came one day to tell me that she was like Kafka, where Marcos pontificated on Oriental philosophy with his beautiful, velvet voice, where I met Jorge some – not many – years later, the cafeteria where passionate meetings and semiclandestine gatherings took place later on, and doubtless for that reason it was closed for an entire year, and then when it reopened the bench was no longer there, the little tables were distributed equidistantly and encircled by hard-backed chairs. And the cafeteria, without the bench, without its nooks, isn't a good place for a first coffee, so I grab Clara by the elbow and push her up the stairs again, then out to the street, to the Pasaje de los Cerezos, and then further up the street, toward the top of the blue, cloud-covered mountain, which at other times is very clear. And, as I rush her up the street, neither of us saying a word, hurried and rapidly as if we were arriving nowhere very late, I wonder if Clara is looking through the treetops, as I do, for a dancing cow flying to the moon or if she hopes to see the curly-headed twins peeking out from behind a tree trunk.

The third vertex of my childhood's magic triangle – toward which I drag Clara this morning of our first meeting – doesn't rise in the air like an ostentatiously bedecked ship, nor is it sunk in the gloom like some underwater grotto: it opens right onto the street, to the surface of the sea, and has just the right quantity of light. It is almost empty at this hour – although in the afternoons it is filled with women and greedy, screaming children – and the gray, rainy morning air filters tenuously through the panes in the door and the windows. We sit down in a corner, here, indeed, on a soft velvet sofa, and wait in silence for one of the bored waitresses to abandon her tenacious inertia behind the bar to come and find out what we want. Clara keeps stubbornly silent and doesn't even glance at the great mirror that covers the wall, where, in the lower part, a

careful, tiny, very elaborate handwritten menu – almost un-
readable from here – makes an objective, critical, absolutely
scientific and aseptic analysis of the contents: number and kind
of scoops, type of syrup, additional cherries, almonds, liqueurs, chocolate or whipped cream, while above these minute
letters appear the colored drawings, so suggestive and so un-
aseptic: magic rivers of chocolate and currants, foamy oceans
of whipped cream, inaccessible peaks of praline, of lemon, or
of coconut and orange, such fragile, shimmering flans, in a delirious apotheosis of the tenderest ochers, the pinks of a sunset
cloud in spring, the ivory of pale princesses afflicted with a
mysterious, incurable disease, blood reds, ebony blacks,
whites whiter than snow, very pretty drawings, much prettier
than real ice cream, and nevertheless this isn't the most important part – not the exhaustive, scientific explanation of the contents, not the delirious apotheosis of forms and colors – because the most important part is the name, placed on the upper
part of the mirror, in huge, multicolored and richly adorned
letters that make a striking contrast with the correct, uninter-
esting handwritten menu on the lower part of the mirror, so no
one could be misled. In the old ice cream shop with its soft velvet sofas – why is Clara so stiff, so straight, so uncomfortable,
on sofas made for sinking, for submerging, for languishing –
with velvet sofas and English engravings where excessively
blond children swing their arms and chase golden hoops
through park greenery, with storybook names, mythical
names, in a world where instead of whipped cream you think
Snow White and red is never just red but blood red and the sea
is not an accidental encounter of a lot of salt water but a blue
immensity where the most enamored of mermaids hides, in
this deceitful and malevolent world, I learned to live the wrong
way, choosing words, never realities. And it is a pity that the
mirror – which, after all, is limited – offers only predictable,
orthodox combinations, and that one can't shock the bored
waitress – who, besides, would remain totally oblivious and
indifferent – by requesting sinful, incompatible, forbidden

49

mixtures, inventing perverse or impossible dishes each time, instead of asking once again for the same ice cream – the one place where my hesitant forays through the mirror have been ending for more than forty years – although this rainy morning, lemon does not tempt me, nor the thick liquid that covers and oozes from the cherries: in this velvet corner, next to a girl I have just met, who has followed me here but who neither speaks nor looks at me now, in front of our blurry reflections in a mirror, amid fancy letters and multicolored drawings, in your honor, most tender mermaid with adolescent breasts and beautiful tail-that-is-almost-legs, I eat an ice cream flavor that I really don't like, because in one way or another I always return to you – that confused, gray mirror-image of a dark woman who always returns to the same places – and to worship you, mermaid, she hit her head on the rocks, ignoring the crowd of Japanese hidden behind their cameras, all identical behind their cameras, ignoring the hoards of sentimental Swiss, of Germans who are so well informed and so supposedly thirsty for what they suppose forms part of a supposed culture, multinational fat and panting ready to be swallowed up again by the tour busses that wait in an interminable line behind the green hedge that borders the sea, ignoring all this and approaching the water, over slippery stones, over rocks that are turning green, right up to the point of breaking her head open with a stupid slip, in a stupid attempt to touch your impossible legs, born of your impossible love for a silly prince who never understood anything – just as the Japanese who photograph everything don't understand anything, nor the Germans who have already read everything before getting here, read it in the guidebook before leaving the hotel this morning, nor the Swiss or Belgian or Tahitian sweethearts who are now kissing each other, right now, before the most impossible of loves, because it turns out, my dear mermaid, beautiful child of the most beautiful story, that this prince of yours wasn't even a dreamer, it wasn't simply that he didn't manage to understand because of some evil misfortune – I assure you that the sea witch had a minimal role in this story – he was simply a little stupid, and there was never any mystery in his distant eyes, only foolishness, a radical – not fortuitous, but irrevocable – lack of understanding about the nature of your magical underwater world, and a very short-lived, shallow, vulgar desire to sit gluttonously at the banquet – this banquet that always seemed alien and repulsive to you, mermaid – at the banquet of life, a very short-lived desire to paw plump little princesses, as shallow as he in their aspirations, princesses with little piggy mouths and good-looking legs, high-minded princesses from good families – earthbound, of course, never underwater – that's all it was, dear mermaid, and that dark woman approaches on a certain day, foolishly stumbling, slipping on the damp moss, among fat albino women, necking sweethearts, photographic equipment, and guidebooks that explain "you" in seven eight nine ten languages, all to place the tip of my fingers, this sensitive, intimate part of my fingertips, for one second on the cold smoothness of your tail-that-is-almost-legs – so near and so far from the sea – the equivalent, my underwater princess, of approaching during the night – and, in a certain way, I approach like those people – the whispering waves as a background, your sweet little face a dream of love, in order to cut off your head with care and with rage – oh, too late, it is always too late – with what pleasure, to cut off your head slowly, as the saw moves forward millimeter by millimeter through your tender neck, with what pain, and then with what desolate love, to throw that insipid girlish face into the deepest, most undiscoverable part of this ocean which she never should, which you never should have left, because it is necessary to cut off your head or put grotesque satin and lace brassieres on you, and God knows you don't need them, daughter of the sea with beautiful adolescent breasts (even though the English lady and her extremely learned granddaughter scream in a duet that this is an incomprehensible act of vandalism, nor would it be any more comprehensible if I told them that I approached in the darkness with the assassins, that together with them I decapitated and mocked you, and I would have raped you if I could – I am sure if they had been able, that they would have raped you – with your useless bronze genitals where the sea spiders spin their dreams), or it is necessary for one fortuitous second to caress (beyond any possible ridicule or shame, trying not to think what the elderly Anglo-Saxon lady and the Harvard lady doctor would say in a scandalized duet, the divine Athena and her most brilliant priestess, or perhaps on the contrary thinking about and discovering a new incentive in what they would say, because it is more shameful to love you than to decapitate you, it is more terrible to caress your tail for a second than to cut off your head or put satin bras on you, at the risk of getting a concussion or wetting my behind or ruining a little Japanese man's photograph, or giving him the picture of the year, who knows), so it is necessary to caress your tender, your salty, wet tail-that-is-almost-legs furtively, for one fortuituous minute, as it is now necessary, dear mermaid, to eat in your honor ice cream that I really don't like, but which bears your name, as I wonder once more whether you and that distinguished fool, your prince, and the magical storybook world where I learned to choose words and fall in love with dreams, haven't all helped make our lives, my life, such a mess, although Clara understands nothing of all this and looks at the drawings and the names without seeing them – Little Black Sambo, Snow White, Little Mermaid, Tropical – and it doesn't even occur to her that she has before her the possibility of choosing and becoming hopelessly lost along the paths of pleasure, since the youngest of the three princes has also reached the crossroads and how do you choose between mocha and strawberry, between names that indicate flavors or something more secret, more intimate, and infinitely more dangerous than the flavors? But Clara understands absolutely nothing today, and I am not going to give her the key, although I think that nothing good can come of this pale, insignificant, thin little girl, who prefers black coffee without sugar to the most fantastic ice creams or to the glorious crown of foam and snow on top of thick brown chocolate, a little girl who absentmindedly dips the sponge cakes I offer her in her bitter coffee without even realizing that she is eating them, in the same way as she lights her cigarettes one after the other and smokes them voraciously – her fingers are yellow with nicotine – obsessively, addictively, and without pleasure.

I wake up late, with a sudden start, after the long, almost always dreamless sleep that follows an excessive dose of barbiturates, with a bitter taste in my mouth, blurry eyes, my whole body enervated and numb – seemingly incapable of getting used to a house without people, to a room which I don't share with anyone, to a large bed that I hardly fill by myself – and this sudden, unsubtle transition from leaden sleep to total awakeness makes me feel almost sick today, absolutely incapable of submerging again into a warm, soft-hued doze, even for a few seconds, incapable of reproducing those childhood holiday mornings, when I would also wake up with an anxious feeling – and I didn't need any Valium or Aneurol to sleep heavily – anxious about being late, dreading the dark coldness of the street, anxious about unfinished homework or unlearned lessons, remembering suddenly that it was Sunday, and stretching in the warmth of the sheets, and going to sleep again reassured, and reawakening in a little while with fleeting, more and more fleeting alarm and quicker and more complete consciousness of a holiday morning until I would reach the point where this minimal level of anxiety, this believing for a second that I had to get up, began to form part of the total pleasure of knowing that I could stay in bed. Now every day is Sunday – I never teach before eleven in the morning, so neither here nor in Julio's house is there the slightest shadow of pleasure in my awakenings. I wake up abruptly to this dusty, stifling, hostile May. And in a little while I am thinking about Clara, about the taciturn Colombian girl who sips bitter coffee, who smokes addictively and without pleasure, who hardly speaks, who, it seems, loves Shakespeare, Homer, and Peter Pan, who carries subversive papers hither and yon for the perfunctory signatures of lady professors who vegetate too far away, for too long, in places too distant from the realities of life, that Colombian girl about whom I know hardly anything, and it is surprising that I can think about her so much, with hardly any concrete facts for my thoughts to grasp, because Maite's delirious explanations have crumbled – useless now – since there is no possible coincidence between them and the girl about whom – of course – I still know almost nothing, but who is, at least in some respects, near and real. So I think about her in hieratic ecstasy, my thoughts about her incoherently blended with the memory of other magnificent awakenings almost forgotten now, when I had just graduated from the university – and I had known Jorge for a very short time then – now unafraid of exams, of being late, of cold darkness, or the unfinished homework of my childhood mornings. Parallel rays of light reflected from the window glowed on the ceiling just above my head, and the same hand that opened the blinds – a hand that was not Sofia's, that soft hand, with such fine, almost transparent skin, that had woken me up morning after morning in my childhood, and about which, during those glorious months after I graduated from the university and met Jorge, when every morning I woke up to life as if to a party recently organized in my honor, I never thought at the time, although I wonder now how I could have managed not to remember it for a single minute, to survive without it, without its protective, soft contact, all during this empty infinity that has lasted millions of years – the same hand that raised the blinds, with the slats fixed precisely so that my eyes, just emerging from sleep, would become gradually accustomed to the light, a hand that in any case was not Sofia's, but the successive hand of so many maids that my mother brought home and dismissed, would offer me cold orange juice in an enormous glass with a gold rim and little gold stars all over. And I would take it with both hands – I wonder if Clara, in her tropical jungle palace, would do something like that, although mestizo hands probably served her mysterious juices with poisonous, exquisite names on silver trays – just to feel the cold of the glass against my warm palms. And, while I sipped it, I would hear the bathtub being filled in the next room, and inevitably my mother would burst in, still in her bathrobe, her glasses and the newspaper in one hand, the other – still white and smooth, still very beautiful – gesturing rapidly in the semidarkness, to explain to me how poorly she had slept, the remodeling she was planning to begin in the apartment, how dreadful it was for a daughter like me – that is, supposedly unsalvageable – to go off on a trip without first stopping at the dressmaker's (perhaps that was the reason why she had slept so poorly that night, in fact, every night, despite the Valium or Veronal pills, and it is curious, I think now, how we end up, by strange paths, resembling mothers with whom the remotest resemblance seemed impossible). I smiled, secretly amused, because it was clear to me that if my mother knew about Jorge – that I had met Jorge, what he was like, and how I loved him – if my mother knew that the man I was waiting for had finally come into my life, and that very soon we were going to say good-bye to everyone, that very soon I was going to break with that grotesque future that they had been planning for me carefully and uselessly, that I was going to leave a world that was not – that I had never been able to consider – my world, and I was also going to break off with my secret underground places, with the forbidden, incestuous love that had bound me to the Minotaur, because Jason or Theseus was there and would take me with them on the Argonauts' ship to an unknown, although dreamed-of, planet, where at his side I would begin a life that wasn't even imaginable but for which I had been destined forever; if my mother had known all that, the remodeling of the apartment or the inappropriateness of my wardrobe – why should my wardrobe matter to me, if I could use nothing of it on Mars? – would have suddenly lost all importance and my mother would have had – as at any rate she did have some months later – something serious and worthwhile to work on and to get annoyed about (since she seemed to enjoy suffering because of something and sleeping horribly almost every night) – except it was too late for me then, and there were no longer hopes or inhabitable planets, because even the earth had ceased to be habitable – but certainly at that time, those days of the magnificent awakenings during my only youth, that was so brief, the years of my desperate struggles were behind me, my tumultuous, Bacchic tantrums to escape her Olympian, omnipresent influence, and the moment seemed to be drawing near when, as winner of the trivial, almost playful, final skirmishes, I could go on the attack and loudly proclaim, "The war is over: I have won," and the goddess's only remaining weapon would be her last, somewhat ignoble card, a bit dirty, but tremendously effective: her growing old (in a metamorphosis that left us disarmed and defenseless because we were so astonished: the hundred-eyed dragon transfigured into a defenseless little cat, a white mouse, a little bird fallen from its nest from flying so much, and not from ignorance of how to fly), and perhaps because I knew that the war was already won, perhaps because in my imagination I anticipated the final card, the last piece that my mother would inevitably move on the chessboard, I hadn't yet spoken to her about Jorge and was waiting until I was on board the ship, until the ship weighed anchor and put out to sea, to tell her from the bridge, now without any ill-will, even rather gently: "Our war is over, and I have won"; because in those days, Mother Juno was still very beautiful in her bathrobes of scarlet, blue, turquoise, pale pink velvet, in her silver or gold slippers, sometimes satin with pompons, her sometimes crimson mules, also embroidered in gold and silver, while the royal hand fluttered frantically without stopping – too frantic for such a little thing – too frantic for a goddess – but with winged grace, and her withering look assumed almost human dimensions. Everything about my mother – her body, her handkerchiefs, her dresses, her gloves, even the very clothes that she had put away years ago on the highest storage shelf – had an unmistakable scent: of thyme and forests and lavender. Sometimes I would sit at her rosewood dressing table, decorated with white tulle and pink velvet bows, in front of her set of brushes, bottles, and combs, and I would uncork the bottle and put her cologne on my hair, on my dress, in the palm of my hand, and the perfume was similar but different, a faithful but inferior evocation of the scent that emanated from her purse when I would look through it, from her neck and breasts when she bent down to kiss me – and for my mother, bending down was always a more intense movement than the real distance that separated us would call for – and from her fairy's hand that rested on my forehead a few moments during nights of fever. And when I think about the mother from my childhood, with her blue eyes that could really and not metaphorically flash rays of fire, or perhaps cold rays of ice, which in both cases left you as if struck by lightning, nailed fast to your chair with terror in your heart, my mother, with her reasonable, carefully chosen words, so exact that they permitted no reply, with her distant lips that kissed so seldom, so aseptically – perhaps the very kisses prescribed in the child-rearing manual – I believe I loved her for the woodsy perfume that emanated from her and took possession of her things forever, and for her soft, beautiful hands – hands that seemed fashioned to be, perhaps, so motherly – always dry and cold, that rested like fairy hands on my forehead during nights of fever. Now my mother, glasses and paper at the ready, follows me to the bathroom without interrupting her conversation, wrinkles her nose for a few seconds at the dense, rather cloying perfume, vulgar to a greater or lesser degree, emanating from soft little multicolored balls that tint the water and also invade everything with their smell (impossible now to perceive the more tenuous, variegated, and discrete perfume of thyme, woods, or lavender bushes), and wonders silently – as years went by she also lost the desire to fight with me – whether everything could be due to an innate coarseness, possibly inherited from my father, or rather, whether it might involve various forms of contrariness, a condition that I certainly inherited from my father as well, while the horrible perfume overwhelms her own discrete scent, and since she evidently doesn't wish to make any comment on the little multicolored balls that drive the third-rank concubines of Harum-el Rashid crazy, the Sultana, the one and only among a thousand queens, limits herself to wrinkling her nose, waving the newspaper as if my bathroom were infested with flies, and pleasantly venturing some observation about my dark skin – she says that even now, in winter, it is too dark – and my small bones – those narrow shoulders, those slim hips, those thin, gangly legs – because the queen, of course, has been brought to the harem as lady and mistress from far-off Nordic regions, and she is blond, fair, large, unquestionably Aryan. But the water feels deliciously warm and her voice lulls me to sleep – the voice has a pleasant tone although the things that the voice tells me may not be very pleasant – and on these mornings, I don't give a damn – Jorge loves me, Jorge has chosen me – that I am only a third-rank concubine in a palace which I am very soon to abandon without possible return. And later we would sit opposite each other in the dining room, she with her back to the light, her attention now centered on the newspaper, I before a big cup of black coffee – at that time, I too drank coffee without sugar, like you, Clara: it must have something to do with youth – bitter, black coffee, before a mountain of crunchy, golden toast – warm, recently made, with butter melting into it. And the sun poured in through the windows and made the canaries sing like crazy. I think that all that – the large, cold orange juice, served in a glass sprinkled with stars, the parallel rays of light on the ceiling, my mother's bursting in, newspaper at the ready, the bold struggle of opposing perfumes in the pink-tiled bathroom, the intense yellow of the canaries within the other paler yellow of the morning sun filtered through multiple white muslin curtains, the trivial conversation, always a little sharp, always looking for vulnerable spots, although in this period, half in jest – it is all tied forever to the memories of my months with Jorge, of my impossible escape on the Argonauts' ship, of my impossible abandonment of the lethal labyrinth, and it has left me this permanent nostalgia, this taste perhaps for fine hotels, for comfortable surroundings, for spacious, carpeted bedrooms, where the only thing I look for is the fleeting, silly pleasure of someone waking me with a large, cold orange juice, after pulling back the curtains a little, opening the shutters, raising the blinds three four five slats, while coffee and plenty of toast are placed on a little table next to the bed and in the next room you can hear my bathwater running.

I drive the car along the old highway skirting the coast. And the pleasure of the clean morning, of the spring air that enters violently through the open window, of the blue sea that ripples and mounts itself on successive crests of foam, is almost better today with that thin, aloof cat crouching on the other end of the seat, as far from me as the closed space of the car allows her, huddled next to the window, stubborn and shy behind the lit cigarette – Clara, almost hostile – it is odd that the pleasure of a car ride by the sea should be more intense with someone at my side than when I am by myself. Although her meow was the first thing I heard this morning at the other end of the telephone: "It's Clara." And then a long silence, tensely and almost painfully drawn out. Perhaps this may be what sets her against me now, because I amused myself by not participating immediately, by not speaking too, waiting for her to stammer any one of the excuses she must have been laboriously working out these past few days or the first one that occurred to her. As if I didn't know why she was calling, as if I hadn't known for quite a while – a long while that can be reduced to three real days – that this call was inevitable, that at some moment or other she would have to lower some of her defenses and end up dialing the numbers – all the numbers right up to the last one – after having dialed the first ones countless times only to hang up without finishing; and she would have to let it ring without hanging up either, and wait until I picked up the receiver and said "Hello"; as if I didn't know how many times she paced her room and the cigarettes she lit and stubbed out (as many as fit into these three days) before making up her mind. Because I have already figured out Maite's game and have decided to play – I imagine that the game would have arisen at any rate, even if Maite hadn't come to my parents' house to alert me, to stimulate me, or to warn me – and everything must evolve in an almost inevitable way. She had to telephone sooner or later, although it couldn't be much later, and she had to say in an anguished meow, "It's Clara," and I had to prolong a painful silence, more painful for her than for me, because it amuses me not to speak. As it has also amused me hardly even to look at her when I taught class these last three days, arriving exactly on time – almost late – and hurrying to my platform, with the words already on my lips, to rush out when I finished as hurriedly as if the relief map of Spain right at my back had caught fire or a firecracker had exploded under the desk. Leaving them all glued to their seats – stunned, openmouthed and incredulous – because they had never, ever heard anything as absurd in the university as my classes these past three days (the same three days that Clara spent in her room, except for class time, lighting and stubbing out cigarettes, counting her steps from wall to wall, lifting and hanging up the receiver countless times without having dialed more than the first digits of a number that she has known by heart for three days), about an Angelica ever thinner and darker haired, with greedy lips and burning eyes, who roams like a crazed Bacchante through unexpectedly tropical jungles, unmistakably Amazonian jungles, while great, dense vines block the tall monastic windows, and snakes and monsters hiss in the dark bower, while in the distance the hoarse cries of Orlando *innamorato* grow madder. I prolonged the silence, like a taut, aching thread that could hurt us badly if it broke. Though I already knew that I would finally speak, and I knew that I would bring her here to another of my ancestral wells of shadow, along this old highway, hardly traveled now since they opened the superhighway, on this journey by the sea which today seems even more secret, more magical, more intimately mine, with Aztec Angelica sitting here by my side, as far from me as the width of the car allows, so enigmatic, so hostile, so withdrawn behind her defenses that I burst out laughing when the wind unexpectedly gusts through the window, there is a brief swirling of long dark hair and reddish sparks, and a small, thin hand quickly beats the faded blue of her jeans, the upholstery, and puts out what remains of the smoking cigarette, the sphinx once again restored to flesh and blood and movement, because at any rate, she doesn't want to get burned. And I also laugh when she asks – it turns out that in addition to moving, the sphinx can even talk – if this is the Costa Brava. What could Oriental princesses, from either the new or the old Indies, know about my private coasts? And in a certain way her irreducible foreignness makes it possible to bring her here into these rites that she doesn't understand, and perhaps she doesn't even know that it is a question of rites, just as, three days ago, she didn't know that the pointed mound of creamy, thick whipped cream, the thick liquid oozing from the cherries, and the lemon ice cream next to the mountain of golden sponge cakes was also a rite of secret initiation, a pagan eucharist; she didn't know that we were in one of my temples, at the crossroads – in the magic mirror that opened onto all kinds of possibilities. I am leading her into an initiatory rite with no preliminary explanations, perhaps with the hope that she won't understand, or perhaps with the secret hope, with the forbidden desire, that after so much time, someone may understand something at last. Because this is definitely not a ride – at least, basically, it isn't a ride by the sea – but rather a passage (through time?), a complicated ritual – so delicate, so fragile, that it can be destroyed or broken at any instant – a complicated ritual that can take us to a far distant point through successive wells of shadow – a well within a well that is within another well (it has to be three wells as it had to be three days of waiting). That is, if Clara wishes and is able to follow me, if she moves with a great deal of care – because any error she commits, any slight clumsiness, the tiniest deviation from the exact tone, can break the spell; and I don't want to warn her, or give her edifying instructions or lend her any thread for the labyrinth, because that's the way the game is, and this is exactly what the test is, perhaps only because that's what I decided – if she wishes and is able to follow me, if she succeeds in discovering shreds of my life stuck like pennants on the branches of the plane trees and palms along the avenue, or tossed – forever motionless – among the waves that break on the beach, hiding in the market, in the stalls where I bought my first bunches of carnations for my grandmother and the stalls to which they brought the reddish, silvery, scaly, wriggling fish from boats that had just arrived at the shore. She will have to follow me – if she wishes and is able – from grotto to grotto, from well to well, leaving behind no thread to allow a successful, a graceful retreat, without even knowing behind which boulder, at which bend, under the waters of which subterranean lagoon, the Minotaur awaits her as lover or murderer – lover and murderer – to follow me on her own feet – if she wishes – to a distant time that no one shares, that no one remembers, that no one cares about. And in my first well of shadow – we have left the main highway and now the rite begins – there are high branches against a sky that is suddenly farther away – because we are beginning to submerge – nearby canebrakes, friendly old houses among huge trees with trunks so thick I can barely encircle them with my little-girl arms, and two or three of us could easily crouch behind them in a game of hide-and-seek, trunks with thin, brittle bark, so that if one inserts a fingernail into a crack and makes the irregular, waferlike piece fly through the air, dozens of terrified ants flee. My first well is green and moist and envelops us in a sweetish, vegetal, slightly decayed smell. Maybe the magical world of secret underground rites where Demeter plays, where Demeter dances the dance of death with the Minotaur, is close at hand now, maybe we only need to descend a little more – and it may not be too difficult, Clara, to manage to catch a glimpse of a timid, pedantic White Rabbit's tail, to find the kindly – the cruel – Snow Queen or three bearded dwarfs, who will return us to the surface changed into circus monsters, covered with indelible gold or tar, tirelessly spewing roses and pearls, or toads and snakes – what difference does it make? – it could as well be a rose and a toad, a pearl with snakes, because good and evil may not be so separated and far apart as in children's stories and – am I really a good little girl? – a worried look in the six eyes of the three teachers – because there are always three teachers, as in the best stories, always one or three or seven or twelve; there could never be two or four or six, with that stunted, perfect, closed roundness ("feminine," I read somewhere) of even numbers; the three dried-up, harsh – and oh, also so sweet and touching – teachers, look at me worriedly; what will become of this crazy crazy little girl in the future, this intense little girl who always seems to ask for the moon? – and they were absolutely right, they had ample reason to be worried, because nothing good in the world generally happens to crazy women who go around waiting for someone to give them a small piece, if not more, of the moon, fastened to a bouquet of red roses or on the tail of an alley cat – and the three teachers shake their three heads, and two small reddish dragon pupils burn in each head, maidenhood and monster tightly fused, maidenhood with dragon scales, and a moist, tight vagina – gradually a little less moist and a little less tight as the years go by – a vagina that is also another blind well, a vagina ignored, as if it did not exist and that shouts so loudly from this almost-nonexistence that its anguished howl can unhinge the universe: gloomy virgins who wait in vain for a slow, lazy, disdainful Saint George, capable of plunging his sword in the three wells and freeing the ladies from their spell; but perhaps Saint George has not yet discovered that the princess and the monster are one and the same, that the maidens and their dragons are one and the same, perhaps he is unable to hear that desperate, mute howl gushing from the dark, salty hole, from the burning wound between their legs. Grim, severe, gloomy, touching, timid, tender schoolhouse virgins. They shook their big, heavy heads, their clumsy heads in which good and evil – absolute truths, closed realities – waged a boring, interminable battle; they shook their big heads and looked at me sympathetically with their little red dragon eyes – but I knew that they had a dark, marshy well between their legs and that from this well gushed a desperate, lethal howl and flames, intense and long, that withered everything, and I knew that this well ached like an incurable wound, and they were probably not even aware of its existence as they waited for the miraculous lance that no Lancelot, no Saint George was to bring and plunge into it – the old women looked at me sympathetically, because they loved me in their way – as I loved them – and because I seemed like a weak, intense creature, as proud as I was vulnerable, doomed to attacks of a fatal rage, of a devastating passion that was to dash me inexorably against the cliffs of vice or against the no less rugged cliffs of holiness and virtue. And along this shadowy avenue from my childhood, among the same enormous trees with brittle bark where probably only the ants have changed in these forty years, hearing the muffled sound of the sea against the beach, sensing the whistle of the wind in the nearby canebrakes, where other new children are probably building identical playhouses today, I remember my grim virgins with incredible pity, with enormous contempt, with profound tenderness – those virgins who loved me whether I was an angel or a devil, in a constant struggle between my private angel and devil, destined for the highest or – and – the most sordid things, and I wonder what they would say if they knew that life has brought me back to this place at the end of so many twists and turns.

The house is empty. It smells very slightly of dust and closed space. The murmur of the sea and the leaves remains outside, the wind sensed rather than heard in the canebrakes. In my second well there is total silence – almost total, because several clocks ticktock insistently – and a tenuous light, because someone, although now there is no one in the house, raised the shutters, aired out the rooms a little, ran a quick dust cloth over the furniture and even arranged some daisies and carnations in the vases. They even remembered to plug in the refrigerator, and the ice cubes are ready. And there are provisions in case we want to eat in the house: fruit, salad, and cold chicken on blue and white ceramic platters. Clara laughs now, still timid and shy, but unmistakably amused: "Which of us is Beauty? And in what corner is the Beast waiting for us?" And we continue walking through the enchanted house, with its massive, potbellied mahogany furniture, wicker rockers, tall flowerpot stands, transparent curtains, flowered drapes, lace doilies beneath slightly chipped figurines. We continue on toward the nethermost part of my underground world, to the third well, a well within another well within another well, because this may be where we can meet the Beast, where the Minotaur can reveal himself, where every afternoon the Snow Queen and the White Rabbit play. And Clara is doubtless the Beauty in my story, and I am just an onlooker, perhaps curious, perhaps mildly interested, but not in the least involved, because I can't get involved in this plot taking place on the other side of a thousand walls made of glass or mirrors, because I am safely imprisoned – or so I believe – in the aquarium of my bygone time, still inside the fortune-teller's crystal ball or on the magic screen where future ages are reflected as drama in which I won't participate. We are in the inside patio, in the deepest and most inescapable point of my deepest well, in the exact center of the underground sanctuary, in the hidden chamber of innocent, perverse, forbidden rites. The amber, spring-morning light is tinged with green, with blue, as it filters through bougainvilleas and the vines of purple and blue bellflowers. The light hums in the thick dust, as it does in the shafts from stained-glass windows crossing the silent darkness of old cathedrals, and the same damp coolness is also here, the joyful certainty that life – that ordinary, jumbled, annoyingly noisy trifle that is life – has remained outside the doors, is still vibrating outside, giving us a breather until the instant we leave (because one always leaves patios and wells and old cathedrals). To submerge into this patio is like leaving the market square on an August afternoon in a small town and entering the deep, shady silence of an almost empty cathedral. One's eyes slowly become accustomed to the variegated semi-darkness, and now we barely make out the large basin in that corner. Before really seeing it, we heard the monotonous drip of the faucet into the still-invisible water. Just this monotonous, measured drip, and the unexpected sound of a bellflower shattering on the tiles, on the marble table, in the pots of hydrangeas. And here, among the flowerpots, I have seated Clara in a wicker rocker, as if she were one of my dolls, the longest-legged one, the thinnest, the least expressive of my dolls from earlier days. Under the bougainvilleas and the bellflowers, because I would like an overblown flower – dense, purple, fragrant – to fall ripely into her lap or in her dark hair. If that big doll dressed in blue could stop smoking for a moment and stay absolutely still . . . Unmoving and remote, still a bit shy, secretly amused, perhaps, and mocking, without a single movement – other than raising the cigarette to her lips – she lets me prepare the drinks, place an ashtray near her, put the plates, silverware, and napkins, the platters of salad and cold chicken on the marble table, and I don't know whether that wonderful naturalness with which she lets me do for her comes from a hundred generations of Aztec princesses – there were certainly no Aztecs in Colombia – dressed, bathed, combed, brushed, fed by dark, barefoot slaves, or if it is the docile and touching naturalness of a defenseless child, because she gives the unmistakable impression that if someone – I, for example, this morning – asked her to carry some plates or bring over a fork, they would shatter in her hands, or she would sink under their weight.

E very afternoon now, Clara comes up to the house on the cliff, above the changing sea of leaves that are still fresh and green. And on the first day she asks me laughingly – her shy timidity, that uncomfortable tension that constrains me and paralyzes her, momentarily broken – if I have many more, if I seriously devote myself to going around collecting empty old houses. Closed-up, empty old houses, with that smell of dust accumulated on the upholstery and the rugs, the curtains and shades becoming yellowed and moth-eaten, mildew and faded flowers between the pages of the books, out-of-date records that sometimes bring back a whole lost time, piled any old way next to the record player, and that filtered, amber-colored light peculiar to aquariums and cathedrals. And I laugh too – how delightful to laugh together for a few seconds – and tell her no, that on principle I don't collect anything at all, that I devote myself only to unique objects, although deep down perhaps Clara may be right, and what I keep and cherish and show to her may really be a valuable collection made up of two unique pieces: my grandmother's house by the beach, with the murmur of the sea, the periodic, harmonious whistle of the trains, the wind in the canebrakes (sensed rather than heard) and in the deepest and most secret part, the magic well with the bougainvilleas, and my parents' – my mother's – old apartment with the three balcony windows overlooking the cabalistic triangle above the changing – and also murmuring – sea of spring leaves. Two vegetal and aquatic houses, dark and whispering, where I lived a long time ago and where some part of me, a tenacious, malignant, deeply rooted, underground plant, continued mysteriously to grow, in order to see this unknown part of myself emerge now and sprout in the May heat – like a magnificent, carnivorous vine, like a voracious, dizzily growing vine – a part of me I thought was dead and that in the meantime was proliferating in the deepest abysses of forbidden depths. And in this museum-house, in this temple-house, in this tomb-house, in this house which is a threshold to the dream world, I am settling Clara-Ariadne, an Ariadne who may not serve as anyone's guide, but who follows me without any thread through the complex turns of the labyrinth, Clara the Aztec goddess – it is useless to recall that there were no Aztecs in Co-

lombia – Aztec goddess of bloody cults and purest heart, dark
Clara-Angelica whose sweet lips and honeyed breasts grew to
maturity in tropical forests, and for whose taste crazy Orlando
innamorato would search through innumerable honeycombs
to no avail: the only inhabitant of my uninhabited time, of my
bygone past, long-legged doll that I take slowly through the
labyrinths of my undiscoverable time. I prop her on the stone
balustrade of the balcony, with the wind stirring her long dark
hair against the tender green background of the leaves, Rapunzel's tower magically transferred from the dark forest to the
waves' edge; I seat her in the leather easy chair where Papa used
to read the newspaper; I keep handing her photographs and
letters, underlined books, books with sketches, books learned
by heart, and she is more than ever like a big, long-legged doll
dressed in blue – blue jeans, blue sweater – or I gently lay her
down on the carpet, a dim lamp lit in a corner and the amorous
lament of Isolde – mingled at intervals with the crazed lament
of Orlando – flooding the room in unbroken, rolling surges, as
rolling waves might chase and tumble over each other before
breaking on the beach or against the cliff, spreading through
the whole apartment, escaping through the open windows toward the noises of an outside world that was now nullified and
conquered. And in these soft, filtered lights, in these interiors
with music, my thin doll, so insignificant in class among her
fellow students – with her shy expression and her gray coat
belted at the waist – so insignificant and almost ugly on sun-
flooded streets, on café terraces, on highways by the sea or in
movie-house lobbies, blooms with a new enchantment: an in-
door doll, her fragility and clumsiness become solemn, touching, intimately different, while a moist brilliance dawns in her
burning eyes – her gaze so intense that I can't endure it, and I
feel disturbed, as in my early adolescence – and she stretches
her long, slender body – relaxed at last – a body, I imagine,
with dark, matte skin, fleshy like a fruit, with the slow grace of
a feline. I think that this new Ariadne has also been searching
for my labyrinths for a long time, although she didn't realize it;

and that like me, she is a subterranean, dark, plantlike creature, inclined to the strange, forbidden cults of Selene, to perverse Bacchic initiations, filled with the murmur of the sea and the canebrakes, predestined to struggle clumsily, languid and half-asleep, against the Minotaur's rough hoofs and Dionysus's heavy panting and bifid penis (in a certain way Theseus was always superfluous in this story): a futile parenthesis of hope between two magnificent misfortunes, and Ariadne passed from the labyrinths to the Bacchic woods in a lethal dream, from which she could not awaken at any time, never accompanied by the impossible, desertion-prone Theseus. Clara the cat, Princess Clara, more Oriental than ever – perhaps Lancelot has finally forgotten his love for the ungrateful Guinevere and might be the one who took her up to the tower by the sea where he is kept prisoner; perhaps it wasn't really Rapunzel's tower – she stretches and blooms on the Persian rug, where handsome warriors with long lances make their steeds rear up; her dark hair gets lost right in the mythic battlefield and curls around the hard, nimble hoofs; and perhaps it was for her sake that these strange men with almond eyes and drooping black mustaches fought a millennium ago without knowing her – I have always wondered, ever since I was a child, why these strange men on the Persian rug were waging such a fierce battle – the warrior riders who now make their horses prance on top of – under – the lovely body of the girl in flower, stretched out there as an offering, as a challenge, perhaps as the prize for the fiercest in combat, while she spreads out on the rug like a vine without roots – she doesn't need roots – she, who is so small, is enormous among the miniature warriors, a new Gulliver in the country of the little people, but a female Gulliver, a flower, incredibly delicate: her creamy, smooth skin, her long, dark hair, the faded blue of her jeans get lost and vanish, absorbed in the pinks, the mauves, the intense blues of the carpet, until all that remains alive in her are those burning eyes that disturb me and take me back to my adolescence, and an unusual, very slight, also disturbing throb in that long, thin, bare, defenseless neck:

he has become one with the silk carpet, an unknown tale a millennium ago, except for her burning eyes and the hidden pulsation of her throat. And in front of Clara-carpet, Clara in flower, vegetal, remote Clara, I open the costume trunk – couldn't this be a beautiful, perverse game of substitutions and disguises? – and I slowly put on my childhood sadness and discover that this is actually what I have come back to find in this stifling, dusty May, in this spring without spring in my clumsy city that knows little of subtleties and gradations: in this spring of examinations, of flowers to the Virgin Mary and the secret sprouting of the first leaves, an old sadness has been returned to me intact, a sadness that I believed I had lost forever – that I had perhaps even forgotten – which, safe from all deterioration in the costume trunk, was only waiting patiently for its moment. It is useless for Clara to question me – she is beginning to do so – about men or women I have loved, about the adventures that I have had or the work that I have done; it is useless to look for traces of the English lady who travels halfway around the world drinking tea – with milk – at five in the afternoon, distributing smiles and tips to the natives, sending me postcards with writing so large, so sure and possessive, that there is only room for a few kisses – aseptic and in like manner possessive – or sending gifts that are always wrong and magnificent – hand-embroidered antique silk tunics several sizes too large for me or Aztec earrings of wrought silver for my ears, which she, a very progressive and European mother, never allowed me to pierce – as it is likewise useless to search for signs of the other woman, Guiomar, at heart so like my mother and also so foreign – I am imprisoned between two women who are strangers to me, one at the beginning and the other at the end of my time – no matter how often she may visit American universities in search of precise references, write a few postcards in her tiny doctor's or scientist's handwriting, and send gifts that are exotic and of no earthly use to me because they are so utilitarian and sensible, useless to search for signs of these two women who are strangers to me and who are there, in broad daylight, self-satisfied, divine, Apollonian – and, like all things self-satisfied, like all things divine and Apollonian, a bit silly – each proud of the other, exchanging flattery and smiles over my head, and anxiously, spurred by a guilty conscience, hurling at me a fearful love that will never find me in my underground places and is fruitlessly lost in the labyrinths. And it is useless for Clara to ask me about the men I have loved, although there have been plenty, and although I must have loved some – at least one – a lot, and although there was one who was Guiomar's father and who, it seems, has been my companion – my companion! – for most of my life, no matter that he may leave periodically, en route to the shallow, familiar worlds of television commercials, but there is certainly no trace of them in the trunk: no costume for a sweetheart, or for a lover, or for a woman who has discovered love – because one day Ariadne met Theseus at last, one day a certain Valkyrie was awakened from her sleep by Siegfried – no costume for a faithful companion or for a most loving mother, not even a costume for a woman who is fulfilled or important or simply happy. In the trunk, I find only this overwhelmingly uncomfortable costume that constricts my chest and throat terribly – it already oppressed me as a child, and yet I must have grown up – have I grown up? – since then – a costume so heavy that it makes me stumble and hesitate under its weight, so monstrous that I think it could drag me to my death at any moment, so familiar and so intimately mine that it adheres to my body like a second skin, and nevertheless so beautiful, the most beautiful of all costumes, born of the solitary fantasies of a desolate girl who may already have intuited that one day she would meet and then lose Theseus, and that another day – much, much later – I would put on this costume to dance before you – or before her – a dance of the most intense agony under the lethal weight of a costume kept for years and years in the trunk – the costume for all the anguish, for all the fears, for all the sadness of childhood – and that I put on slowly, painfully, before you, vine-princess, new image of an Ariadne who prefigures all de-

, grim princess in flower among Lilliputian riders, y blooming, surrounded by the rolling laments of an ..10 was also betrayed, in bloom and magically fused in a Persian rug.

Clara – before entering into the game, before even guessing that any game could exist – looking at me curiously and with increased interest from one of the front rows in the classroom with the tall monastic windows – when I still didn't know that she was the one, didn't know which of those faces answered Maite's description, or even before Maite came to see me at my parents' house – Clara, revealing herself for the first time in Shakespeare, Homer, Peter Pan – slightly aggressive and playful at the start of the game – Clara, now defiant – defiant and frightened, or defiant because she was so frightened – holding one more subversive petition out to me after class – annoyed at heart that I would sign without reading it – following me along the Pasaje de los Cerezos, toward the blue mountain, on a rainy morning, aseptically dipping golden sponge cakes into coffee without cream or sugar, Clara – now definitely trapped in the game – finally talking on the telephone with a strangled voice or drowning in the interminable silences, Clara defenseless and sullen on the other side of the car – perhaps angry with herself for having given in at last, for having called me – and then taken out of her hieratic silence by a fluttering of dark hair and live sparks, Clara, the only doll in my scenery, sitting in the rocking chair on the patio with the bougainvilleas, the overblown flowers falling and shattering softly in her lap and hair, Clara leaning on the stone balcony over the forest of waves – could Lancelot have brought her to his prison by the sea, or could she be Rapunzel, Rapunzel, let down your hair? – Clara leafing through old books, looking at old letters and yellowing photographs, or stretched out among Lilliputian warriors, the sharp hoofs of the miniature steeds cavorting among the vines of her hair, where the juiciest and sweetest mulberries are hidden, Clara the attentive, interested spectator of my costumes, passionate listener to my stories and now, for the first time – what strange caprice could have made me bring her here? – surrounded by paper, not even cardboard, scenery – among shoddy characters. Beneath the seven fine feather mattresses, the princess, if she is a real princess, if she is the most princesslike of all princesses, will have to discover the trick and hold up a tiny, bothersome pea on high in her slender fingers. As we came in, she asked me jokingly whether this was a costume party and I explained to her – ignoring the taunting question – that our grandparents put on costumes for designated and almost always established occasions; that our parents, poor things, could hardly ever put them on – forty years of a costume-uniform made all costumes impossible – but later on, in the seventies, we reeled from costume to costume. The princess frowns and growls, "Not you," but she doesn't ask me who my "we" includes and whether a possible "we" really exists for me. And the "we" and I sputter in a false, flashbulb glare among the lit-up trees, unimportant second-rate extras from the worst Fellini. It is so bright in the garden that the house at the back seems dark, even with all the windows and sliding doors open, with crystal chandeliers, floor lamps and table lamps all lit inside – I wonder if a dark-skinned Vitti is reading Pavese in some hidden corner. And while I talk and laugh and dispense kisses one at a time and perhaps drink too much, I try to imagine what my grandparents' parties were like and remember that on a certain occasion – my grandmother told me – they were invited to one whose theme was the Depths of the Sea; and my grandfather went as Neptune, with his great trident and white beard, and my grandmother looked fragile and beautiful in a flesh-colored leotard covered with scales from the waist down. I remember that another time they took part in an Army of Devils where everyone, men and women, wore identical costumes, red leotards of a soft, velvetlike fabric that covered their whole body, with two little horns on the cowl and a long tail on the backside, a costume so apparently harmless, so plain and unimaginative – it wasn't even a pretty costume – so poor and shabby looking even on the old-clothes shelf – perhaps because I could only relate it to the moth-eaten Lucifer in Christmas plays that we always made fun of, that I had trouble understanding what made it so terribly sinful, although I knew without a shadow of a doubt that it was even much more sinful than the mermaid's costume, which was voluptuous, sumptuous, and pretty indeed and in which you could surely make out my grandmother's breasts; but the demon's costume was much worse: it was enough to see the stern, scandalized look on the face of the General's wife, her instinctive gesture of recoil, and especially to see how, at the exact moment when the General's wife began to carry on, snatching the outfits from me and stuffing them far back on the highest shelf, my mother and Sofía would exchange winks of amused understanding, stifling laughs behind her back and over my head, because my mother and Sofía got on very well at that time, whatever may have happened later on. And, as on so many other occasions, Sofía was the one who tried to explain about the costume to me, although I didn't understand it completely either, because I still hadn't learned the meaning of "promiscuity" (such a sonorous, pretty, suggestive word) nor did I manage to understand that what was wrong, what was so dreadfully wrong, was the fact that my grandparents and their friends were precursors of unisex fashions, almost one hundred years ahead of their time. And today at this costume party which isn't a costume party but which – Clara is right – seems to be, I discover a secret order beneath the apparent diversity, and it occurs to me that we put on our costumes in accordance with a common theme, which today isn't the Depths of the Sea or the Kingdom of Lucifer, as in my grandparents' Mardi Gras celebrations, but another theme with the same desire for perversion – capable of scandalizing people like the General's wife, and only people like them – and with the same touching ingenuity: the party seems to consist of a glorious or grotesque, in any case beautiful and comical, apotheosis of breasts: the Apotheosis of Tits. They are everywhere. Framed

74

by décolleté necklines, whose parallel edges plunge to the waist (quite a bit before reaching infinity) – white, trembling cupolas, fleeting appearance of mauve nipples – through the sides of backless dresses – repeated glimpses, frustrated at the vertex, obsessive in their quality of incompleteness – behind the transparency of chiffon or clinging knits – nipples that rear up and stand under scratchy fabric sensitive to the night breeze – under the thin cover of lamé – breasts in silver, in bronze, in gold, the sculptured ornament of divinities who are so very old and always young. I think we have brought our breasts to the party, and they are self-satisfied, silky kittens, terribly spoiled kitties in pink bows, freed from bindings and brassieres. And men prowl around them, disoriented and lost – relegated to such a secondary role – while the tits throng together, amused and resplendent, timid or quarrelsome, trembling with cold and champagne, and we exchange greetings nipple to nipple.

Clara hasn't brought any kittens to the party – at least not visible ones – no kittens or even the slightest desire to participate. My pea-princess with sensitive skin – there is no longer any doubt that she is a real princess, the most princesslike of all princesses – now looks at me mockingly from the edge of the pool. She sat down there, her back leaning on the ladder railing, her feet swinging almost in the water, surely she will end up wetting them. She is wearing her usual blue jeans and a heavy sweater in which she must be dying with heat – while all the rest of us are dying of cold with our exposed breasts and backs – although she knew we were going to a party and she clearly has other clothing at her disposal. But I didn't want to tell her to go up and change – why bother – and I brought her with me looking like a disreputable ragamuffin: only I know that she is the pea-princess disguised as a scamp and that under the wool that smothers them, she is hiding the most purring, the softest kittens at the party. And the princess-scamp smiles at me and beckons me to come closer; and here I am, squatting uncomfortably at the edge of the pool, my feet on the wet, slippery edge – besides wetting her feet, the silly fool is wetting her bottom – talking and talking – she who almost never talks – not even making the slightest move to get up, not even lifting her head or raising the volume of her voice so I can get up and still hear her – and even squatting at her side, I can't clearly understand what she is saying – with the same clumsy arrogance, with the same naturalness or the same insolence with which she lets people prepare her food, help her on with her coat, light her cigarette, or push her arms and legs inside the car before closing the door for her.

I submerge again into the costume party, into this "we" that is really only a fiction, because neither they nor I can ever be sure of truly being one and the same thing, and I always experience traces of a strange discomfort, a feeling of being out of place, and they experience a slight uneasiness enveloped in subtle distrust; I submerge into the costume party and renew my tender apotheosis of breasts, the exchange of smiles and kisses, while we take turns interrupting each other to say the most monstrous absurdities and blandly taking delicate wine glasses with champagne foam running down their long stems from great silver trays. Such profusion of champagne at a party is a great idea, as if they suspected my game and wanted to keep it going, finding a subtle analogy with our grandparents' bacchanals, although Clara, and I don't know how, has indeed managed to find a bottle of whiskey and a large stemless glass somewhere, and is serving herself and drinking by the edge of the pool, and surely because she is also drinking too much, she doesn't realize that she is dabbling her feet in the water and that her shoes and backside are wet, or if she does realize it, she doesn't care, because she watches me stubbornly as I stroll through the garden; she watches me, smiles, and raises her glass in a mocking toast, and drinks to me or to herself or to all of us; and I think that I never saw her drink, and that she may be drinking more than she should, but who doesn't drink more than she should at one of these parties, and without drinking, how would it be possible to tolerate one another, and to tolerate other people's inanities, to facilitate our own, and even to think we are clever and attractive and tremendously important as a group? – we are only a bad copy of the worst or the best Fellini – surely I won't find Vitti rereading Pavese in any corner inside this house – we are miserable remains of a race about to become extinct and that may never have existed as we imagined it; how would it be possible, without drinking, to close the ranks of the clan and maintain, like a sacred fire, that warm glow in our looks and smiles, that happy stiffening of nipples under the soft or the scratchy velvets and lamés that ride our breasts bareback, without reins and without saddle? how could we carry on the farce, because this party, like all of our parties, is a farce, even less real than the *House of Troy* of our youth, and we now play a different part, but with much less conviction than when we pretended to be young, carefree students who cut class and walked down to the sea, perhaps because with the years, our enthusiasm was lost on the way and perhaps because we don't have a big enough audience now – where are the old men sitting on the benches reading the newspaper, the fat women overwhelmed with children and shopping baskets, the grim porters at the Athenaeum? – here we are both audience and show, because the servants are only shadows, ghostly holders of silver trays that seem to glide by themselves through the garden; here the only possible audience is Clara, and for this reason she mockingly offers a toast to us from the pool ladder, she knows that we are performing poorly, that we are second-rate actors, and she suspects that I may have dragged her here to provide at least one spectator who is outside this pitiful play, because without a spectator, even though there may be just one, the theater no longer exists – and later I will have to explain to her that this isn't the reason, that I have really brought her to test her out and to discover whether she found the pea and was the most princesslike of all princesses – and I must admit that I, too, like to playact, like to put on costumes, like to submerge into this interminable succession of farces begun in adolescence: before adolescence there were no farces, just games, and games have been and always are sacred; we are born and we grow in the sacred world of games – where everything is real – to emerge later into this adult masquerade.

The house, as beautiful as a stage set without people, is empty and in semidarkness – they turned off the crystal chandeliers a while ago and only a few low lights remain. And, as when I sneaked into my mother's bathroom as a girl, I amuse myself at the pink marble dressing table, before the large mirror that almost covers the wall, by powdering my nose with the satiny cream-colored puff, by running the repoussé silver brush through my hair, by spraying my neck and cheeks with tiny drops of icy cologne that shoot out from the crystal atomizer. The intense, unfamiliar scent floods over me and I close my eyes for a long moment, long enough for someone to slip in behind me; I think it may be Clara, but I know it isn't, nor is Maite – who has been watching us all evening with growing curiosity – the one who has followed me up here: these hands resting weightlessly on my shoulders are not Clara's, this light panting, the breathing a little more rapid and labored than usual, that brushes my ear, my neck, is not Clara's, nor this other scent, also unfamiliar, but much more aggressive and intense, that now mingles with the one that I extracted from the atomizer. The hands begin a slow, graceful caress from my shoulders, almost a movement from a pantomime or a ballet, as if rather than touching me, they were sketching me in the air; they slide down my sides, brush my waist, stop for a few seconds, move up to my breasts and stop there with a slight tremor, apparently having reached their goal. Then, in sudden decision, they rise again to my shoulders and make me turn around. Now I am facing a pair of intensely green eyes – not Clara's and not Maite's, of course – two twin pieces of incredibly beautiful jade, in the depth of the abyss over which long, golden eyelashes flutter, tremulously frightened; I face a pale rosy mouth, a fragrant, moist pink that blooms in the lighter matte pink of her skin, because the pink color is toned down and filtered into an almost perfect imitation of flesh around the green stones and golden lashes; and the real and the imaginary find an exquisite meeting point in that delicate drawing-room doll (because the lady of the house is the person who followed me to the dressing table), and the matte pink of her cheeks is still more attenuated in her throat, allowing the bluish veins to show delicately, then regaining richer, warmer tonalities upon reaching her shoulders and breasts, to the violet tips of her breasts, like the tips of tuberose buds, a repetition, a soft consonance with the pink of her lips and the slightly warmer pink of her fingernails. She is a most rare and exquisite object, tremendously expensive, imported from far distant lands for the pleasure of the most powerful member of the clan, she is the most finely wrought piece in an ample collection of ivories and jades, of Gothic carvings and Renaissance arms, the most precious of all the treasures that fill this shoddy palace in which everything is expensive and authentic but in which nothing is real, a splendid piece of goldwork sculpted by expert goldsmiths, a magnificent gold and emerald nightingale brought here from very far away for the amusement and adornment of a false emperor, although this time not to console him for the loss of anything, since the lord of this house has no possible reason to be sad. A valuable plaything made of precious stones, who may even sing as well as a real bird, because in her hollow breast there is a hidden voice, all of it – the voice – of soothing golden and caressing pink colors, an opaque, melodious voice, that harmonizes delicately with the emerald green, with the matte marble pink of her skin, a voice programmed to rise to the voluptuous intensity of carmine pink, then to languish exquisitely into pearly pink, a voice that is allowed to know only one song, well recorded and memorized, a one-sided record that the emperor can comfortably start by pushing a button. But today something seems to have broken down in the complicated mechanism – and why just today, when I have come to this party with Clara, while Maite spies on the two or on the three of us? – the nightingale made of precious stones has certainly metamorphosed into a crazy bird, and if only she had kept quiet, but no, she has not; she is distorting the song horribly and now is whispering a blasphemous psalmody into my ear, a dark, meaningless psalmody – meaningless, at least in the world of Apollo and of the emperor – with a voice bleeding and turbid, like old clots of dirty blood, a voice that no skillful goldsmith could have installed in her breast, that no longer harmonizes with the soft ivory tones or with the purest green of the emeralds, although there too, in the deepest part of the translucent, cold stones a mysterious gleam is now growing; the faint rose of her cheeks glows, and on her pearly temples appears something that seems very much like sweat. The awakening to life of an inanimate being is monstrous, this second being that emerges alive is terrifying, as it takes shape line by line behind the evanescent features of the nightingale-doll, until she is swallowed and eliminated, as if it were devouring her from within in order to be able to grow toward the outside, her, this flesh-and-blood woman who is being born now, or that I am now discovering behind her masks, and who isn't even a beautiful woman. The hoarse croak envelops me – "Tell me that you feel the same way, tell me that you haven't thought about anything else since we met" . . . how ridiculous in an emerald nightingale! – and I feel myself dissolving in pink and pearl, in the sickly glow of mad jewels, in the sticky, cloying scent of the two intermingled perfumes, in the screechy, impossible song of the wrong record, while the tongue of the woman-bird, of the woman-snake, coils around mine, plunges into the deepest part of my throat, her lips draw at me like hot suction cups, and her terrible claws – where in the world could their unsuspected strength come from? – hurt my chest and throat, pluck monotonously, obsessively at my frightened nipples; and I keep telling myself that I must make her come to her senses, to return her as soon as possible – before Maite comes in, before Clara sees us, before the emperor realizes anything – to her magnificent outer shell as a sumptuary object, to the inert safety of stone and metal, to the luxurious immunity of her

thousand masks; I must warn this broken doll that she
low herself such misbehavior here, that her lord and
must never guess – I know the emperors of my land s
the lord who brought her from afar for the exotic decoration or
his drawing rooms and – though now this is more doubtful –
for the pleasure in his bed, must never discover, however much
he may shower her with attention and spoil her and heap her
with gifts and caresses, must never guess, however much he
may give the most splendid parties in the city in her honor
(which, let's be frank, didn't seem so splendid to Clara, because she was also from another world, and everything – cars
and whiskeys and jewels and servants – seems small and short
and withered and wretched in this world of ours), the emperor,
then, must never intuit that there is something in his magnificent toy that doesn't work the way it should, that there is an almost human face, a face that isn't even particularly beautiful,
behind so many masks, and within her breast is a secret record
that knows and whispers other words, words blasphemous to
him, and that her sophistication, product of such skilled goldsmiths from the Orient, can sometimes lead to forbidden or
unknown paths. Because my poor snake-woman, my defenseless bird-woman, programmed only to adorn beds and drawing rooms, would be returned immediately to the furthest borders in a carefully sealed package, unless something even worse
didn't happen to her. So I push her away from me very gently,
her hands still on my breasts, mine on her shoulders, give her a
quick, affectionate kiss, and rapidly slip away toward the garden – Clara is still by the edge of the pool and I don't think she
noticed anything – a bit amused at heart and a bit moved too,
because it's not every day that one can see the painful metamorphosis of a golden nightingale into a disheveled Bacchante
– she even smelled a little of wine, not of champagne – fervently
hoping that no one saw us at the dressing table or that anyone
might endanger the sad future, the brilliant future, of such an
elegant and beautiful bird, who, for her misfortune, was also
so inconveniently real and alive.

A long time ago – because time has begun to flow with a different rhythm and four or five or six days are now an enormity of time within our story – my story and Clara's – which perhaps may not even be the same story, but two absurd, parallel stories never destined to meet – because, who still believes in infinity? – or, rather than a story, a mere pretext for me to tell and relive old stories – a long time ago, then – exactly five days since the morning I brought her for the first time into the deep green of my enchanted well, to the constant, muffled noise of the waves, the canebrakes, and the intermittent whistle and clacking of the trains before they entered the tunnel, since the day when we looked for the Beast in the hydrangeas and the ripe bougainvilleas fell into my defenseless blue doll's lap, since that time, we planned this outing on the springtime sea, a clean sea without people, a sea still virgin, or newly virgin after the winter. But something has gone wrong with the game and now there are four of us in the boat, when this should have been an outing for two in pursuit of some of my old phantoms. Because the golden nightingale has climbed on board with us – insensitive to my resistance, which is, on the other hand, not irreducible or too difficult to overcome, I'm not sure whether because of a secret weakness for the nightingale or perhaps because of an evil desire to mortify Clara – has climbed into the boat metamorphosed into a black swan, doubtlessly because she has a preference for bird disguises, and although I think that a white gull's costume would have been much more appropriate, something simple for the morning, for the sea, she does look delightful with her long pearly neck and her jet-black hair pulled back on the nape of her neck, with her neck and arms emerging from a light cloud of thick, black ruffles. Indeed, her mouth is also bloodred, although she really seems more like the treacherous queen than the innocent princess playing foolishly with the doves, because this part-witch Odette unequivocally hates innocent, ingenuous, upstart, tropical young girls, and Odette has been pursuing me since the day of the garden party with clumsy, dense desire, which should have offended

or perhaps frightened me, but which amuses and moves
pathetic and defenseless at heart is this enchantress v
bird costumes and her innumerable masks. I hold the ruuu.
effortlessly, the sea is very slightly choppy, and we are the only
boat here – the fishermen's boats which still put out to sea are
already far away by this time – and I keep my eyes shut, although I see the black swan perfectly, petrified into a haughty
expression, a vacant look, her long neck emerging from the
ruffles, so cunning and beautiful that no one would guess the
presence of the disheveled, hoarse Bacchante in her, and I see
the thin back and wind-blown hair of my sulky, little ugly
duckling, also petrified, straddling the prow like a caryatid,
one leg on either side of the stem of the bow, too offended either to look at or to address any of the three of us, not the
treacherous black queen with the evil spells; not me, who betrayed her by introducing bird-witches into our sanctuary; not
even this young girl she herself brought along when she learned
that the sea outing wasn't going to be by ourselves as planned, a
splendid young woman who wears her youth like a profession
and her beauty like a banner – she would drive Julio crazy – an
aggregate of long legs, cute little nose, mischievous almond
eyes, beautiful tan: a calendar kind of youth, the kind in technicolor ads, the stereotyped youth believed in only by fools
and a few old people like the ones who watched us walk down
to the sea, so envious and so far from their own youth that they
had forgotten everything – the anguish, the loneliness, and
even the long nights of rage, confusion, and weeping – although none of that seems to affect Clara's friend; perhaps she
is an exception. I brought along an exotic, evil bird with her
hundred costumes – underneath is a dirty, infatuated Bacchante – and Clara has brought along that simpleminded em-
blem of youth and beauty, that perfect wrapping – what is underneath would be anyone's guess. Two absurd, crooked
pawns that we had up our sleeves are now tossed onto the
chessboard of two crazy queens, and here are the four of us, in
the big-bellied boat that cuts the slightly choppy sea so beau-

tifully – and if we were alone I would explain to Clara that no two boats cut the sea in the same way, that the keel of each boat forms a unique sculpture with the waves – the prow cleanly striking the water and dividing it into two bands of foam that slide rapidly along the smooth flanks, while the white foam jumps into the golden air and splashes the eternal jeans of my ugly duckling-who-is-today-almost-a-princess-white-swan, an Odile who turns her back stubbornly on us and – playing at caryatid – moves forward majestically with her feet almost submerged in the water – again – now it's an obsession – while the salty foam splashes the light, stiff satin ruffles of a black swan with a distant smile, perverse only daughter of the sorcerer who keeps so many formerly innocent maidens captive – I wonder if they have incestuous relations from which some strange monster is born – a black swan who perhaps invokes secret spells to enclose the clumsy, unfortunate duckling forever in her feathery prison – there is no doubt that today she is unlucky – she who is very soon to become the wife of some prince or the most beautiful swan in the whole lake: black swan and white swan splashed with golden foam, both hostile, stubbornly silent and antagonistic – although they don't look at each other – their splendid legs absolutely impersonal, even less human than birds, a fish out of water or a Pepsi-Cola advertisement at a gathering of birds – splendid, nonhuman legs also covered intermittently with brilliant little specks of foam. I keep my eyes half-closed, and the sun makes little colored stars behind my eyelids, and I know that if I pressed them lightly with my fingertips – as I did when I was a child, as all children do – the little stars would dance a ballet of metamorphosis like the glass pieces in a kaleidoscope, but I keep one hand on the rudder and with the other I grasp the side of the boat, and the sun and the salty taste on my lips and the constant, repeated slapping of the keel against the waves are so delightful, and suddenly queens' quarrels or birds' fights mean so little to me – and besides, I know that the search for any lost past or for any moth-eaten phantom has been spoiled from the start; phantoms being incompatible with ad-girls, emblem-girls, girls who flaunt their beauty and youth like a banner; beloved childhood phantoms being incompatible with perverse black swans, imprisoners of maidens – this means so little to me, that I let myself be carried along slowly, drowsy as a lizard, or like the idea we humans have of lizards dozing in the sun, detached from everything, although the three other women have begun to talk, breaking the stubborn silence at last, and the purr or the croak of their secretly aggressive voices blends with the waves, with the noise of the wind; it blends now with the sudden, harsh, savage shriek of the gulls, because the boat has slipped into a bay, and we are almost encircled by high, rough dark rocks, rising to a point above the water; and the water is suddenly still; it is dark blue, almost black, and the wind has also ceased all at once, and on the highest part of the cliffs, in a dense, unbroken line, tightly pressed side by side, gulls hurl their angry cry, insult us furiously from the black rocks whose base sinks into the black waters, stand out against a sky that suddenly seems dark and menacing, and I cast anchor, although the boat doesn't move in this dense, metallic sea, and when the motor stops purring, the shrieks of the gulls intensify, and I feel almost cold, and I lie back on the warm wood, in the sun – because there is still sun although it seems as if the day has grown dark – I lie back, closing my eyes again, and I think that my phantoms aren't really so far away, softly rocked as I am by the leaden, mercury-colored water, so silvery and so dark, with a sky from which it seems – only seems – that the sun has been blotted out over my head, and those savage birds, thousands of them, angrily insulting us from the cliffs, almost muffling the trivial chitchat kept up by a black swan, an ugly duckling, and a peacock, definitely barnyard or pond fowl, who are fighting furiously but without spirit, without attaining the terrible shriek of the enraged gulls, barnyard fowl in stupid, henlike competition, a competition that has ceased to interest me even if it is for my sake – because they are talking for my benefit, however much they seem to be talking to each other – this barnyard fight makes no sense in such a wonderful Wagnerian setting – until something makes me sit up, my elbow on the wood and my head resting on the palm of my hand, something makes me open my eyes and even forget the gulls and the phantoms, because on the motionless prow, against the black rocks, the emblem-girl has taken off her sweater and underpants with a quick, natural, simple movement, and she rises naked, her entire skin evenly tanned, more than ever like the cover of a magazine, a total picture, without the remotest suggestion of smell or touch, so tremendously impersonal, so young and so beautiful; and near her, the black swan is taking off ruffles and feathers with slow, practiced movements, emerging laboriously from multiple laces and embroideries, tiny exquisite, intimate garments, like little pieces of black foam, like the wardrobe of an elegant doll from another era – here the smells do spread, although, absorbed and devoured by the salty air that smells of sea, they barely reach me – and she lingers, shivers at the contact of an imperceptible breeze, stretches slowly and unsmilingly, and inch by inch, an unadorned, sumptuous body emerges: narrow thighs, long legs, small high breasts culminating in rough, coarse, almost violet-colored nipples, sumptuous, satin, cream-toned flesh, and the two women make a beautiful picture – one so natural, the other so artificial – splendidly adorned in their own nakedness, more covered than ever, safer than ever behind the armor of their nude bodies, standing tall in the almost closed circle of the black, menacing cliffs, under the angry cawing of the gulls; but my ugly duckling has turned her head at last and has lost her caryatidlike composure, and in her gray eyes there is a wounded glitter, a disconcerted, savage rage, poor gull trapped in strange nets, now more than ever vulnerable, more than ever a starving, lost kitten; but cornered here on the motionless prow, on the quiet black sea, she will unavoidably have to leap at my eyes or throat, because there is no doubt that she is a defenseless, wounded little animal, just as there is not the least doubt that she is a wild little animal, and her inevitable leap oc-

curs suddenly, a leap so brutally violent, so painful to herself –
because the aggression is against herself rather than against me
– that it leaves me astonished and touched: she hasn't gone for
anyone's eyes or throat, she has thrown herself into the dizzy-
ing void – and I see her thin back emerge, the translucent skin
covering the small bones; I see her white arms emerge, the head
with the dark hair, now tangled, as she holds her blue sweater
bravely on high, like a flag, and now she is shivering slightly,
tight-lipped and disconcerted, more than ever like a little girl
who doesn't know what to do; but we both do know that she
must continue, because I can't shout "I give up, it was a stupid
game, put on your clothes again," nor can she pull the sweater-
flag over her head again, and we must necessarily get to the
ending of this idiotic charade that hurts us both, and suddenly,
awkwardly, Clara yanks off her jeans, her brassiere – why the
devil does she wear a brassiere? – and her panties, revealing her
childlike, preadolescent body, her long dark hair falling to her
waist, white as snow, black as ebony, red as blood, not her lips
– so livid they are now blue – but her burning cheeks, with a
blush that she detests but can't control, and if the beautiful
young Miss Pepsi and the fascinating black swan have donned
their nakedness like sumptuous, magnificent finery, their own
bodies covering themselves – one can't exactly say that they are
naked in this new costume – now Clara's body, so tense and
pale in contrast to her dark hair, this body which is not yet a
woman's, not even an adult's, becomes so terrible, so disturbing in its ambiguity and its defenselessness, that it has concentrated within itself all the possible nakedness in the world; and
as I hear the three successive dives of the three bodies in the water, I lie down again on the prow, this time feeling a different,
more intense chill, searching for the comforting warmth of the
sun-drenched wood.

B elow her feverish, strangely fixed gaze, with her eyes
open too wide – I'm not sure if they see me or anything
else – trembles an anxious, innocent mouth that seems to have

intuited all kisses in dreams or to have learned them in other lives, past and half-forgotten, her salty, ardent mouth, with chapped, slightly rough lips stubbornly attacks again and again – in an intense, furious, desolate surge – and is going to crush itself against mine, while Clara's whole body trembles in uncontrollable spasms and her head rolls from side to side on the pillow, one of her arms encircles my waist with surprising strength – I am kneeling on the floor, at her side, by the bed – and the other arm clutches my neck, my shoulders, my hair, and, drawing my head toward hers again and again, toward her open, panting, thirsty, burning mouth, a mouth that kisses me and at the same time – or between kisses – utters a smothered moan, neither human nor animal, a hoarse moan like that of the sea or the wind on moonless, terrible Sabbath nights, when the spirits and the hot-blooded witches from the south roam loose, to the yowling of black cats in heat and the furious rubbing of lustful genitals against broomsticks. And I don't know whether Clara is really very sick or if she is only drugged and drunk, because she has spent, the four of us have spent, hours on end in front of the blazing fire, the flames indoors so pleasant after the morning on the sea; and the black swan has put on my grandmother's absolutely absurd, lavish old dressing gown – I wonder how my grandmother could possibly have dared to wear such clothing, even in private – a scarlet-colored velvet gown with lace ruffles, a wrapper that slides caressingly along the bird-woman's slender thighs and constantly opens, revealing her dark-nippled breasts; and the French girl, because to top it all off, Miss Pepsi has turned out to be French, has put on my grandfather's dressing gown, a navy blue silk with tiny gold fleurs de lis, belted at the waist with a cord of similar gold material; and the two of them have talked incessantly, have dried each other's hair, have rubbed each other with moisturizing creams, manicured each other's nails, all without ceasing their chitchat, leaving Clara and me out – finally – ignored, given up because we are hopeless, because I have lain down on the couch, as I did earlier on the boat, watching the reflections of the flames dancing on the ceiling, lazily drinking cup after cup of strong tea and listening to their chatter as if it were the sound of the sea or the canebrake, an agreeable, senseless sound to which I almost fall asleep and in which I don't intend to take part, nor does Clara, crouched next to the fire with a hostile expression, withdrawn into herself, at her side a bottle and glass that she continually fills and empties; though I am too tired to protest, or perhaps I simply wouldn't know what to say to her, how to scold a crazy girl who is drinking too much, and who, with the diligent gesture of a good little girl at the head of her class, wordlessly accepts and pulls on the cigarette that the others have prepared slowly, voluptuously, carefully heating the grayish little bar, mixing its tiny pieces with mentholated tobacco, rolling the cigarette with the skill of old peasants or old sailors, the ritual of the two women in front of the fire more agreeable than the pleasure of smoking itself, and I think fleetingly that I shouldn't allow Clara to smoke now, after having drunk so much; but how to interfere? and how infinitely lazy I feel, dozing on the couch, because I too have accepted the cigarette and smoked in silence, and, now relaxed, float in a delicious vertigo, ready to fly away, to climb on the broomstick of the most beautiful young witch, the one with the most lustful genitals and the blackest cat; no, not that, I'll put Clara on my broomstick – because, among witches, I may still be the most beautiful and youngest one, even if I am almost fifty – and all my cats can come with us; except that Clara is so angry with me, and when I turn toward the fire – and I don't know if minutes or hours have gone by – she is no longer there, she has disappeared from the room, where the chatter of the young-beautiful-French-girl and the swan-bird on the rug has been transformed into a purr of felines in heat like the witches' cats, the two bodies entangled in a strange struggle in which thighs, long legs, stiff breasts, yearning mouths, are jumbled together, and I have gotten up and looked through the house for Clara, until I find her here, trembling in this bed, with wild, unseeing eyes, rolling her head from side to side on the pillow,

her body shivering, and I don't know whether she is phenome-
nally smashed on alcohol and hashish, or if she is on the verge
of an attack of pure hysteria, or if, helped of course by the wine
and the drugs, she is refining and developing a play with some
trick to it, intended for my eyes only, nor do I know if I should
put cologne water on her forehead, fix her some camomile tea,
call a doctor, or give her a good spanking. And her stare becomes more and more fixed and vacant, and the trembling of
her whole body intensifies, as does the sea or mineral moan
mingled with incoherent words, and her kisses grow more violent, although I don't know if that rubbing and bruising and
biting my lips with her teeth and lips are exactly kisses, and
there is a nauseating smell of sea algae, of tobacco and wine;
and all of this is terribly irritating, out of place, and very uncomfortable – so embarrassingly adolescent – but I know that
even if her hands released me now, I wouldn't leave her; that
these sour, rough kisses, so clumsy or so skillful – who knows
– find me strangely vulnerable; and when this disturbing
princess from a dangerous and unknown planet, when my little
mineral-and-sea girl finally starts to cry – in an uncontrolled
avalanche of hysterical tears – all the red warning lights on my
ship light up, to a deafening howl of alarms and sirens – perhaps the beautiful young witch with the lustful genitals pressed
against the broomstick may not really be riding a broom but a
space ship en route to the impossible – and I have a foreboding
that if a single one of these warm, salty tears that pour down
my blue doll's round cheeks touches me, it will no longer be
possible to save the ship, the crew, or the captain. Because evil
plants are advancing and overflowing in a monstrous growth –
I don't know if the foreign girl could have brought them from
the unknown planet, or if they are plants that have been growing in secret for years in my own private underground places –
and they have already invaded the control room, the cabins,
the infirmary, the long corridors, with thick stalks that could
be roots or branches – I don't know if they come from me or
from Clara or which of us is actually going to be Theseus or

Ariadne – and I move clumsily among fleshy leaves wet with sap or dew, among enormous red flowers that smell of wine and sea; with difficulty, as if in a bad dream, a distressing – delicious – nightmare, from which I no longer wish to awake. The former flag-sweater is drawn up, like the corolla of some living night-blooming flower at the close of day, and my hands slide down her slender waist, trapped as in a bottomless marsh, one hand on either side of her waist, which has the same fragrant, slightly moist fleshiness of a tropical swamp flower. And her little claws – those terrible claws of a defenseless, cornered kitten – have released me now, because she knows very well that I won't be able to escape from these fine, white sands that are swallowing me up, that there isn't the remotest possibility that I will get up, say something trivial, leave the room, maybe lighting a cigarette or proposing a cup of tea; she knows that the cooing of the other two women – who have resumed their chitchat below in the living room – is now infinitely far away, where all the black swans from the past are dying, where all the black swans from any future time will be thwarted, because here – in this here and now – there is only room for a magical little blue girl who has climbed onto the broomstick, who has invaded the ship, who has filled everything with carnivorous vines – I am still uncertain whether they come from me or from her, but in any case, she has roused them – filled with luxurious red flowers, with bottomless marshes into which we both sink breathlessly; there is only room for this undernourished princess from a remote planet, a motherless princess, a princess never truly cherished, ignorant with the unlearned wisdom of centuries, a little girl so fragile and vulnerable that someone should really come to her rescue and save her from herself, that someone should cradle her, rock her, make her germinate with warm caresses, stretch her out in the sun, feed her thick, rare steaks, cups overflowing with thick hot chocolate and whipped cream, give her glasses of warm milk and honey to drink; perhaps the prettiest and youngest of the witches should do this; perhaps the captain himself, the pathetic captain who succumbs hopelessly among bottomless marshes and girl-flowers, and who now holds – who will hold all night long – Clara's pale, sweaty, thin body tightly embraced, safely trapped in my arms, which have started to rock it, to cradle it with a lullaby of tender words and soft kisses. Meanwhile, the tears have reached all the crew members, and all the ships en route to the impossible are wrecked or lost in space; and the only salvation possible for blue princesses or for girl-flowers is to sink into the deepest part of the marshes, to the very bottom of the soft, warm sands, because fleshy, perfumed, terrible, anthropophagic plants have taken over the ship or have flowered on the broomsticks.

I put the letter on the breakfast table next to the bitter, black coffee, the crunchy toast, the big glass of cold orange juice – one more attempt to sustain the old myths, although I had to prepare my own breakfast today, as I have done all these past days, and it is curious that I can easily forgo lunch or dinner, but not this ritual breakfast, and although my still beautiful mother doesn't march arrogantly through the room, in robe and slippers, newspaper and glasses at the ready, always prepared to goad me or try to annoy me, and although I myself will turn on the two bathtub faucets in a few minutes, this time I won't add the soft, little colored balls that dissolve and dye the water pink or green and blue, while a sweetish, supposedly luxurious smell, a technicolor version of the *Thousand and One Nights*, permeates the room, but instead, I will add the contents of tiny, exquisite little bottles with a French name on their golden label, bottles which appeal to me mainly because they are what I would have liked to add to my bath many, many years ago – when I was still unfamiliar with French oils and bought the little Myrurgia balls at the corner perfume shop – I put the letter – which the concierge has just handed to me – on the breakfast table, and, as I sip the strong, bitter coffee without sugar which I do like at this hour, and spread the golden, newly toasted bread with creamy, pale butter that melts and disappears and a thick layer of strawberry jam – another myth – I turn the letter over, not in too great a hurry to open it, and I imagine that she probably wrote it all at once, after starting it and ripping it up two or three times: these letters are always written that way: during the night, in a long, sleepless period that may have lasted until dawn, because she probably wanted to reread it a thousand times, and then she must have waited by the window, sick with impatience and anguish, until it was really daylight and she could go out into the still-cold streets, full of serious, ill-humored people hurrying toward inhospitable places where they would rather not be, and go to my house to hand the letter personally to the concierge, futilely explaining that it was personal and urgent, or perhaps not so futilely – since they have brought it up right away, before breakfast. The still-unopened letter smells of youth, of early youth still half-submerged into the heavy sleep of adolescence: an unmistakable, young-animal smell; it is odd that youth by itself, above and beyond any other consideration, clumsy, turbid, defenseless youth, the warm smell of tepid milk, could suddenly move me. Perhaps because I attained the necessary distance just a little while ago and now for the first time am definitely on the other side, because my nights are already so far away, the oppressive confinement of the room and the house, the dark hatred of locked doors, my heart beating against the walls – those nights of a well-bred adolescent girl, who doesn't go out on the street, who doesn't wander down the long streets to the sea at night, who doesn't yet know about those dark, almost private, often underground temples, upholstered in scarlet velvet or maroon burlap, where friendly or impersonal waiters serve you tall glasses of peppermint liqueur with lots of ice and light your cigarettes for you, where someone is probably singing a sad tango, or the latest rock record is playing; a well-bred adolescent girl who has not yet learned the resources, the tricks to facilitate the escape from herself and from loneliness, who does not yet know that this sadness, this anguish, and this fear can be conjured away, perhaps, with a few drinks, or with stupid conversation that takes up the entire night without filling it up, or with a more or less grotesque parody of love – at times almost tender, sometimes almost credible – and even if she had known it, she wasn't going to find drinks, conversation, or love, because at three at four at five in the morning, well-bred adolescent girls can't escape from their houses, because the streets and the night are forbidden to them, and they must stay at home, like prisoners, surrounded by their furniture and their knickknacks, the outings that now more than ever would have led them down to the sea, now limited to the distance between the mahogany wardrobe and the console with the mirror, or to a chilly foray – the apartments of well-bred girls are cold at night – to the library or to the kitchen, in search of a glass of cold water – drunk without thirst, because it isn't that kind of thirst – or for a new book – turning the pages without managing to decipher the words one after the other – all possibility of free space limited to the open window, which is where I am, with the light out so I can't be seen from the street – well-bred girls don't lean half-naked out the window at night, not even this little night the size of the window – taking deep breaths, freezing cold, listening to some guys talking on the corner in front of the door of the only bar that hasn't closed, and to dogs' barking far away – maybe they are as confined as I – until, all covered with distances and shadows, I go back into my room, shut the window, and turn on the lights; and since I can't rush out and wander through the streets, or mix with people, or go into these wonderfully impossible dens that we dreamed about as adolescents – dilapidated old barracks, rickety old barges now moored at dark docks, the sauntering of pale women in red, and sad adolescents, as sad as oneself, and around us milky liqueurs, tango or bolero music, and shameless words that creep lethally – and since I can't lie trembling in the arms of still-faceless men (although a constriction in the throat, a weight on the chest, something like a pain in the heart, isn't really sex – and my emotions had to follow a long downward path until they

94

reached places unknown to me then, because at fourteen fifteen seventeen, I didn't have thighs or a vagina or a womb, I still knew nothing about a possible wound between my legs, nor did I even feel my breasts: only a massive, irresistible desire to love, such a need to love, as ferocious and desperate as I imagined hunger or thirst could be, an errant, puzzling need to love, like an enormous boulder under which the girl that I had been lay dying); on nights like those, I would sometimes write a long, long letter – perhaps like the one I have in my hands now – a letter with all the loneliness and anguish of the night, impetuous, delirious, hesitant letters which were almost always ripped up before dawn; but sometimes, when day arrived unexpectedly but the night mists had not completely dissipated, and when the time came when a well-bred adolescent could finally desert the mahogany furniture, the gauze curtains, and the pot-bellied consoles with their mirrors, could escape from her bedroom and from the house to wander the streets hurriedly and breathlessly, to enter a doorway or the lobby of a hotel, and hand over the envelope – always marked "personal" and "urgent" and always somehow magically transparent – which filled us with embarrassment in case someone could read what was inside – to a sleepy concierge or a bored doorman who would look at us with sly suspicion or glacial indifference, then, on these unusually rare occasions, one of the letters would reach its destination.

And now, millions of years later, I am the one who receives one of these letters. And although I haven't been able to write a letter like this for ages, although now, whatever may happen, I could never, never write one again – because I grew, or matured, or rotted, or died, who knows? – I certainly don't have to open the envelope to know what it says, and the letter trembles in my fingers with all the cold of the night, and a fluttering of hoarfrost, that longs to return to any nest runs up my arms, tickles my neck, and makes me smile; and I leave the orange juice half drunk, and while I nibble at a piece of toast, I am dialing the telephone number – which I now know by heart – al-

fter the sleep-drugged kisses of the other night – kisses
the letter doesn't mention and which she may not re-
ber or even know about – I had decided to cut off this
y that, as far as I am concerned, is so silly, cunning, and
egotistical, and nevertheless may be obliquely dangerous, but
how to cut off a story that has hardly begun, when you are on
the other side of youth for the first time, when you begin to
fear that all stories have ended forever, when the world around
us is so shallow and everyone gets so desperately bored, and
only a painful and remote past still seems alive at times, still
seems to retain smells and taste and color, in a universe which
has imperceptibly turned gray, insipid, and odorless for us, in
such an imperceptible way that we haven't even noticed the
change, until it is already too late, much too late, and we are
immersed in an opaque, formless emptiness; and then, at that
exact moment – nothing, absolutely nothing from a conceited
husband who always runs away to possible and familiar is-
lands, from which he also always returns, from a distant, traveling mother who sends greetings in postcards, from a big,
grown-up, know-it-all daughter who never was or will be
capable of understanding, because she was born incapable: a
husband a mother and a daughter who hurl their love to me
into the abyss, as they would haphazardly toss food to the
wounded wild animals roaming in dark pits, a benevolent love
that never finds me in my underground places – in this hopeless
loneliness, there emerges from another world, from another
time, from other planets, a girl who brings with her all the
magic of sleepless nights, the warm perfume of dreams, the fervor of early, innocent passions, a girl with a thin body, a pale
face, long, dark hair, a bit of an ugly duckling, a bit of a big
doll, a bit of a lost, wild cat; and when the ugly duckling
brashly enters the garden and we know (even if it doesn't) that
it may be, that very soon it is going to be, the most beautiful
swan in the lake, when the doll dressed in blue sits down in
grandmother's rocking chair, in the deepest, darkest, and most
secret part of the patio, and a ripe bougainvillea or a mul-

berry-colored bellflower falls into her lap or her hair, when the defenseless, still-wild kitten hurls herself at our mouth in a desolate attack or scratches insistently at the windowpane with her paw, ready to curl up by the fire, perhaps for a long time, to purr and listen to all our stories – stories we believed were dead – ready to let us dress up in so many old costumes in her honor, in our own honor, and her quiet presence, the mere fact that she exists and listens to us and sees us, makes everything seem alive again; when this happens, who would be capable of driving such a duckling-swan out of the garden, of tossing a big doll into a corner of the attic, of closing the window on a wandering cat?

So here we are again, in the same ice cream parlor, which is almost empty at this time, because it isn't even noon, and there is no trace of chattering females who drink tea with petits fours, or of shouting, scolding, desperate mamas, ineffectually trying to make their kids behave as they climb and yell and swallow snot and hot chocolate at the same time – no mother, we must acknowledge to her credit, so beautiful, so blond, so white-handed and blue-eyed, so smiling and woodsy-smelling as mine was – just some harried man at the counter who burns his mouth drinking a cup of coffee. And we sit down at the table in the back corner, the one we like best, really the one that I like best, because Clara never said which table she likes best, because none of these things seems to matter to her; and I have ordered hot chocolate with whipped cream and yellow sponge cakes – although since I ate breakfast, I'm not the least bit hungry now, but this has nothing to do with being hungry, but with affirming in some obscure way something that may be important – and I pick them up one by one and I dip them in little by little, and the golden cakes ooze a thick, steaming brown, flecked with foam, while Clara sips her coffee, still without whipped cream, sugar, or any cakes other than the ones I hand her – this may also be an affirmation of something, which annoys me today, just as my way of drinking the hot chocolate may annoy her – and she obsessively lights cigarette after cigarette, obstinately silent so I would have to ask the questions. I think Clara sips coffee, drinks, smokes, dives into the water, does everything without pleasure, always in a concentrated, tense way, as if the bitter coffee or the cold whiskey, or even this tobacco – so delicious when slowly combined with spicy or very sweet flavors – as if the sea itself, or even my own lips, were only formalities to be gotten through, or rather, something that she must drain to the dregs, frantically, viciously, painfully, although possibly without understanding her own motives and definitely without pleasure. I think that not even there on the prow, one leg dangling on each side of the boat, the salty wind playing over her warm skin under the May sun, the sea splashing her temples and lips – those dry, slightly chapped, feverish lips – not even there did Clara have a moment of languor or abandon, and I also think that those kisses a few hours later, letting herself be cradled and rocked in my arms until dawn, may only have been anguish, grief, drunkenness, or momentary hysteria; I'm not going to ask about the kisses and the night, although she is hoping I will, and she did write me the letter and drag me here this morning, stubbornly maintaining her dark silence, just so I will be the one who asks and begs her more and more urgently, so that she can resist at first and then let out the truth bit by bit, as if unwillingly; but I'm not going to ask her, because I don't want to join the game she is forcing on me to such a degree, a game with rules she may not even know, and because I have suddenly lost interest in ascertaining whether those kisses (as sad as the cry of the sea birds lost far from the sea on stormy afternoons, as sad as the desolate slap of the waves against the rocks) were the result of bad wine, drugs, her tendency toward hysteria, grim scheming, or the beginning of love.

Clara wears her eternal jeans, a turtleneck sweater – not too clean – and over them, absolutely out of place, a splendid fur coat, too long, too big – the sleeves almost come down to her fingernails – with the lining ripped and hanging out on one side, but at any rate a silky, shiny, weightless, magnificent fur coat. It occurs to me that any moment someone will come up and ask where she got it, either borrowed without permission from the closet of some unsuspecting relative, or if perhaps a mistake was made in the checkroom, but no one says anything to us, no one comes up with a courteous but menacing air – because I imagine that in places like this, suspicious, troublesome matters are resolved with menacing courtesy, doubly menacing because of the apparent delicacy which conceals an impassive brutality – and we cross the lobby, both of us surprised and amused: I, at this gangling girl who secretly tries on her mother's evening dresses – who would have suspected it – and she, at the strange friend who insists on dragging her to incredible places – because what the devil are we doing in an opera house? What were we doing at a costume party without costumes, or on a boat with a swan witch and a French Miss Pepsi disguised as cops – on a cabalistic, nostalgic and – I wonder if Clara knows – ritual pilgrimage. Blushing, she looks mockingly at me out of the corner of her eye, as we walk down the large curved hall, on a faded pink flowered rug, under the dismally weak light from the pitiful bulbs, the light even more dismal on the dirty, bile-colored cracked walls – this combination of splendor and sordidness is characteristic of us – and she looks at me curiously, waiting for an explanation, for the secret key that can make this shoddy Visconti – or the apocryphal Fellini under the trees in the garden – interesting to her and justify my reason for bringing her here; she looks at me, waiting for a complicitous wink to assure her that none of this is to be taken seriously, that this is really a joke and we can laugh as much as we want at the fatuous men in tuxedos and the bejeweled, befeathered, décolletéed ladies, who are almost always ridiculous, and occasionally – as in the case of my mother – very beautiful. The trouble is that not even I know if this is going to be serious or a joke; I only know that one way or another I always come back here, because this theater is a pitiful parody, but, parody or not, it is my race's most authentic temple – a parodic temple for a race of phantoms; and we come here, more or less seriously, to feel that we are, to know that we are, a clan, perhaps to make believe – aided by the hostility directed against us – us? – that prevails outside, a hostility that is troublesome since it became aggressive, but which nevertheless strengthens the validity of tarnished myths, of cults in which even the gods themselves have long since stopped believing – perhaps to make believe, for just a few hours, that we are strong, beautiful, and important, that we are the best; or perhaps some of us, like me, return only now and then to confirm each and every time how mediocre, ugly, and irrelevant we really are. In a way, Clara, this is also a rite, but it isn't a private rite, like the ice cream parlor or the patio with the bougainvilleas: it is the rite of dwarf-people who many years ago changed from a young race to an old one, but without ever growing or maturing, without knowing fulfillment or achieving true splendor – that's why there is no Visconti here, or an authentic twilight of the gods, just the endless decadence of a dream which barely lasted an instant and which has been falling apart for more than a century – the rite of a class made up of shallow, petty people: everything about us is small and wizened, as if thwarted before birth, because a long time ago there were vigorous, enthusiastic children who discovered a few things – not too many – and may have believed that the world was their oyster, but the world gulped them down before letting them grow up, and vomited them out turned into grotesque – never tragic – old scarecrows, outliving themselves bitterly, uselessly: and such a long decadence, which does not derive from true greatness, just from a puerile, unfulfilled dream of splendor, is very strange. You are so right, Clara, to look at me with growing surprise and mockery, waiting for the complicitous wink that never comes, and you about to burst out laughing – even more mocking than that day at the garden party, sitting at the edge of the pool – because I don't understand either – I never have understood and I'm not going to start today – why I love all this in a certain way, why I associate

myself with a story I don't like and to top it off that ends
– collective stories that end badly should never be taken
one's own – why I always give in to the temptation of
proud of a mediocre past – even for a fleeting moment – and I
return again and again to the memory of those children at the
dawn of the race, so mighty, so ingenuous in their very malice,
their unbridled greed, their cruelty, so hopeful – children who,
more than a hundred years ago, built, among other things – not
many or important things – this absurd and – in my opinion –
marvelous temple. Because it is a temple the likes of which
filled the dreams of all the children in the world, with a great
deal of tinsel, metallic paint, scarlet velvet – in stories, you
know, velvet is always scarlet, as red as blood – with a great
staircase that you can ascend, majestically trailing sumptuous
brocade trains behind you, or rush down at the risk of losing a
glass slipper, because the race – even this miserable race of mine
– is mighty enough in its dawn to absorb a few Cinderellas
without too much risk, and the girls of four five six generations
have put on their costumes, with or without the help of some
fairy godmother, to see if they could find some romantic
Prince Charming here, a temple with mirrors and columns,
with golden, many-branched lamps, with veined marble, with
heavy curtains, with dark wood, and in the golden plasterwork
on the ceiling are pictures quite like the illustrations in my
childhood stories and an empty circle where the most magnificent chandelier from the most magnificent story must have
hung – I always suspected that there was one, but never veri-
fied it. There are many shoddy elements, I know, and much
imitation – isn't my class, the dwarf race that built this temple,
perhaps a mere imitation for a race? – but this doesn't matter to
children, and when the grandparents of my grandparents finished this temple, which like all temples that children build –
and who, if not children, would build temples? – was a temple
dedicated to themselves – however much it may have been assigned to high-sounding and, in this case, musical divinities –
and since they had built it for themselves and it was theirs, they

did the most incredible but most consistent childlike thing: they distributed it among themselves, they gave it out to themselves and to their children and to the children of their children; they gave it out for all eternity. And I am one of the daughters of their children. And this piece of property is mine. Now Clara does look at me in astonishment, because while the Methuselah-like usher whom I have seen here forever, generation after generation, inherited together with the theater, brings us sandwiches and a bottle of champagne — we had to gild the lily and go as far as we could go — and while I lock the door from the inside — so some intruder or some confused spectator won't bother us or steal the nutria coat — I go on to explain to her that all this, everything on this side of the door, is literally mine: I can sell it, rent it, close it up, keep it empty forever, make a rule excluding short, bald men with mustaches or ladies dressed in red — or simply exclude all women, as they do in another box — and I explain to her that each piece of furniture, from the little grained-wood table with carved legs to the sofas upholstered in blue velvet, including the English engravings and the duly autographed photos of divas, everything, everything, was bought, selected, brought here by my parents or by my grandparents . . . surely, Clara, there is nothing like this in your tropical jungles; surely, the temples there — which, undeniably, must be bigger and even more sumptuous and gilded, even more European — may occasionally have a single owner, a capricious, grandiloquent tyrant who erects them one day for his own glory or as a gift for the pleasure of a beautiful lady who lies on lace-edged sheets, dying interminably, but I am sure that there has never been a division of property so well organized, so inalterable, so touching, and so grotesque, so typical of my people: a people who laugh, cough, speak in loud voices, leave on the lights in the box — all of this during the performance itself — and who infallibly and Olympianly take off before the performance ends, because they are the ones with the money; and he who pays gives the orders, and all of this is theirs, including the clowns on stage who shout themselves

hoarse for almost no one – after all, they did get their m[c]
and it's not as if we have to applaud or listen to them be[s]
and in short, the spectators, not the singers, are the real s[how],
and the real performance always takes place in the halls, in the
lounge, in the boxes, or in the vestibule, because it is one thing
to finance certain controlled levels, certain assimilable degrees
of culture, and it is quite another – perhaps even dangerous – to
take culture seriously.

We have been drinking champagne – because although
Clara gave me a surprised, beseeching look, I didn't
want to give in and order whiskey from the bar – we have
drunk almost a whole bottle of champagne, in tall, slender
flutes of etched glass, the two of us hardly talking, sitting a bit
stiffly on the blue velvet sofa – the same sofa on which I sat as a
child, for years, for so many years, so many years ago, with my
legs hanging down, but not touching the floor, wearing a little
beige dress embroidered with tiny pink flowers and little
leaves, savoring the marrons glacés and mints as the lights went
down, and the way the house lights slowly dim, leaving only
some little red lamps lit, the brief silence that precedes the burst
of music as the curtain goes up, are still as delightful and exciting to me as then, or perhaps even more so now, after all these
years, with Clara sitting here by my side. And when the house
is completely dark, the music has been playing for a few seconds, and the curtain has been raised, and I have also put out
the lights in the box, I suddenly take Clara by the hand and
drag her with me to the long, steep staircase, lit only in red, and
without releasing her hand or turning to look at her, I boldly
start the descent – although this isn't a flight, but a descent into
hell – through the narrow bloodred, velvety tunnel, while
Eurydice follows docilely behind me, just a trembling, slightly
damp hand, a light panting, uncertain steps behind me, because she can't see the stairs in the dark and hasn't known them
forever, by heart, as I have, and I may be going too fast for
someone who doesn't know the way or our destination, and at

any rate, we have been going down this staircase for a thousand eternities, and although there is a little more light when we get to the bottom, she still can't see, and I have to grab her by the shoulders, push her and sit her down – again like a doll – next to me on the bench. We are motionless and silent in the reddish shadows, very close but not touching, and before us, very, very far away, on the other shore of deep, shadowy seas – surely impossible to cross – slender nymphs with winged feet dance around a papier-mâché prince – his eyes thickly made up, his lips red and his genitals bulking under his blue satin tights. But Clara – sitting stiffly in what must be an uncomfortable position, frowning, her eyes fixed on the center of light – has little interest in silly, innocent girls deserted on their wedding night by perverse, unfaithful princes, girls who with repeated fervor live out a love story with an inevitably unhappy ending, or perhaps this isn't about a peasant girl but about the silly, sweet little mermaid from my fairy tales, because everything down there seems diluted and distorted, like images at the bottom of the sea, or perhaps because this story, which is so stupid and so constantly repeated without possible variants – written once and for all with its unhappy ending – has filled my eyes with tears again, though Clara is evidently not interested in the story and looks unseeingly at the performance onstage, just as she cared nothing about my temple today – however it may have intrigued or amused her – or about the possible meaning – or lack of it – of this legend about old dwarf races that – like the peasant girls, like the mermaid – live out stupid stories that always end unhappily, a single, same adventure, with a single, predictable finale, nor could she possibly care anything about the feats of her perhaps nobler race of adventurers and lords, lost centuries ago in tropical jungles; the last straw would be for Clara, who has – or has not – made me into the stereotype of a strong, superior woman – only she knows why – to see that I am crying and to guess that the only things that will always make me cry are not disasters in India or atrocities in Vietnam, not even the absurdity of human nature, or Julio's desertions or my own incurable loneliness, nor this bottomless emptiness in which my life has foundered, but silly children's stories with unhappy princesses and deserted girls, stories of ugly ducklings, of panthers who die in the snow, of mermaids turned to foam. Clara doesn't know this; she continues looking very seriously at the stage – less stiffly, of course – without turning toward me at all, although a delicate hand, thin fingers, are lightly tracing a tentative path on the back of my hand, my wrist, my fingers on the railing. And I lean against the velvet back and half close my eyes – tears slide down my cheeks now, but my face is so immobile that even if Clara looked at me, she surely wouldn't realize that I am crying – and it is delightful to be here, in the dark, so far from the other spectators that I would have to lean far over the railing to make out their heads below, down there in the orchestra, to be here, in this safe, warm, velvety lair, as if my childhood bed and I – both invisible – had been moved to the very middle of the performance, and I don't know if all children – Clara included – dream as I did about a magic bed that carries them in the air above streets and squares, through fairs, circuses, and palaces, to the middle of the stage, tightly bundled up in quilts and blankets, safe and sound, right there, but without participating. The whole world flows and whirls incessantly around my small, childhood bed, while a long, slender finger – now it is just one finger – moves along, tickling my wrist. And although I am almost unable to see through my tears in the dark, I feel that the sylph girls surround me in their dance, that they have sat down around me, and that the queen of the night or the queen of the fairies has knelt on the floor at my side – but no, it isn't the queen of the night or of the fairies, it is only a silly girl, a crazy mermaid, the clumsiest undine in the pond. Her thin arms encircle my waist, and she puts her head in my lap; she is breathing hard, although she tries to control herself, and her hands are damp; perhaps the sweat and panting are due to the effort of dancing. She is a winged nymph with timid green eyes, and she has grasped me as if the very center of life were rooted in me – of all things! She has emerged from the waters, as mysterious and ambiguous as any amphibian, trembling like a frightened undine who is never to find her prince, who will never receive a woman's soul – why the devil would she want it? – and who must wander forever, turned to foam. Compassionately, I put my hand on her soft hair – which, oddly enough, is dry – and I slowly stroke her long mermaid hair, which almost reaches to where her tail begins, while she stops trembling for a moment, clings to my lap even more strongly, and then, both hands firmly on my waist, lifts herself up almost bodily, still supported on the ground by her feet or the scales on the tip of her fins, and leans toward my lips, as slowly as a dream – only in dreams or on sea bottoms could the action unfold with such slowness. What a pity her mouth doesn't taste of sea, of faraway fresh-water reminiscences: it tastes of cigarettes and champagne. But when she puts her damp head on my breast and the music languishes in muted chords, the purity of the dream is fully reestablished, with her almost weightless head now sheltered in the hollow of my shoulder, and her tiny, cold, wet hand just at my neckline, caressing such a small piece of my flesh over and over that finally the persistent light rubbing almost hurts me, and I feel a cramplike stinging, and place my hand over hers – my hand is so smooth, so beautiful, so delicate, that they always said it seemed – almost like mother's – like the hand of a princess or a fairy, but now, in contrast with Clara's, it seems like a coarse, huge giant's paw, and never until today did I have to compete in fairness and softness with the tiny hand of a nymph. So I put my hand on hers, trying to interrupt her interminable caress, but she doesn't understand, or perhaps I have expressed myself badly, because her hand does interrupt its incessantly repeated caress to change place, but not exactly to move away, and now it has crossed the boundary set by my neckline and it submerges and disappears under my clothing, and cautiously moves around to the center of my breast, like a curious, mischievous gnome who tries to rob the diamond blazing on the mountain peak despite his fear – such audacity is inconceivable in an undine, even in a crazy one who is in love – circling the hill again and again, always a little higher, not much, just a little higher, and sometimes, as he goes around and around, the height even decreases, and the little dwarf seems resigned to begin the descent back down, to renounce crowning the peak for today, but I know very well that he won't, I keep my eyes – now dry of tears – closed and wait without impatience: this tickling is delicious, this slow progress hindered by partial retreats, and now they are even kissing my neck, my ears, my breasts very carefully, they are biting my neck – this must be a crowd of gnomes, or a band of undines – ever so carefully so I won't wake up, because certain proud mountains don't like to be conquered or to have a little flag from some unidentified country – perhaps in this case from the fairy kingdom – placed on their peak; a little irritation, alarm, or displeasure would be enough to make the mountain move slightly and shake off the bold gnome who cautiously climbs its slopes, but these creatures from the waters and the deep places are cautious and weigh nothing, perhaps the undine chose the most astute and cunning of her gnomes for this virgin expedition through unknown lands, and now the kisses have ceased and the undine lies at my side, very near but not touching, while her emissary, the single, brief point of contact, gets closer and closer to the peak, and suddenly I hear the undine beginning to moan very softly, in a hoarse, drawn-out lament that I have heard somewhere before, the crying of a little girl in the very bottom of a well, and the moan chokes me as if it had burst from my own throat, it weighs intolerably on my chest, it claws me cruelly between the legs, it is nothing else, no, it is the moaning, and the gnome keeps on climbing, and the undine pants, so near yet never touching me, and then the gnome reaches the peak at last and, forgetting all caution – now unnecessary – ferociously grabs the diamond with its small, hard hand and sticks something – surely a flag – into the peak, and it hurts the mountain, but I don't have time to worry about the mountain's possible

to verify if the object was a pennant or only finger-
use at this very moment the undine's whole body be-
ible desolately, and the wound caused by the moan
⸱⸱cpens and lacerates me, the ferocious thrust of a red-hot
iron, and I stand up, and the gnome falls from the slopes of the
upright mountain, and I take the nymph in my arms, and I
squeeze her, I rock her, again and again I caress her long, silky,
straight hair, her wet cheeks, her trembling shoulders, and between kisses, in the brief moments when my lips separate a little from hers, I lull her with incredible, strange words, words I
never said to any man, that I never even said to Jorge, not even
to Guiomar when she was little and had not yet acquired those
hard eyes of a worldly wise woman, words which I myself
didn't know were in me, crouching in some dark corner of my
consciousness, quietly waiting to be uttered one day, not even
uttered, but chanted, sung, spilled out thickly and sweetly in
an unrecognizable voice that most certainly has to be mine, this
voice and these words hidden for so many years in the most intimate and secret center, to gush forth at last in this bloodred
darkness, in this den smelling of sea and young animals, in this
warm, velvety lair where I have been sitting year after year for
almost my entire life, in this temple of mine where I take on everything that I am and am not and that I love and hate at the
same time, while the violins – always out of tune – play trem-
olos, and swan princesses, girls deserted on their wedding
night, mermaids in love, flutter their wings, shiver, and die in
the arms of a cardboard prince, and the heads of the onlookers
are indistinctly far, so far away, and I am alone here, in this
dusty springtime in which I have felt so rapturous and so sad,
when for the first time I have been conscious that I am beginning to age, alone here with this big, thin girl, with this crazy
crazy girl with long dark hair and tempestuous eyes, who is
very still now, as if asleep – only the fleeting gust of a shiver ripples her smooth skin – while I stretch her out on the lustrous
furs – could that be why she brought them? – and unhurriedly
caress her silky legs, linger at that tender, exciting part of her

inner thighs, finally seeking the warm hollow where the algae nest, and although the undine left her pond a long time ago, a corner of the grotto is strangely moist, and the grotto is suddenly a living thing, a strange voracious monster from the deep that shrinks, swells, and contracts like those half-vegetable, half-animal organisms that live deep in the ocean, and then it softly yields, and the gnomes and nymphs disappear, and I no longer feel pain or hear any noise, because I have reached the very bottom of the seas, and here all is silence, all is blue, and slowly, carefully pushing the algae aside, I enter through the moist mouth of the grotto.

L ike Sicilian widows in mourning, the three of us climb up the tortuous, narrow, poorly paved streets. Here too the houses are very white, and all views end with the sea, a sea still near, because we have all followed the coffin out of the house by the sea – the house filled with the murmurs of waves and canebrakes, the trains' intermittent whistle, the house with its intimate, disturbing, magical patio, another sea grotto, where Beauty and the Beast search for each other and watch each other and pursue each other under the bougainvilleas, the house to which we brought my deceased grandmother yesterday, because it had been settled long since that she, or perhaps all of us, would be buried in the village – so the cortege has left, and there are lots and lots of people, but I don't see them, because like the sea, they are all behind me, and in deepest mourning, straight as arrows, without a single tear – how far this is from the savage howls of Italian widows in the movies now – alone at the head of the mourners, the three of us walk on toward the high part of the hill covered with vineyards and olive trees, toward the town cemetery where, oddly enough, I have never been nor did I even know where it was, but it is doubtless a sea cemetery, where my grandmother will lie facing the sea, among trees and vines, in the mausoleum that a great-grandfather I never knew had built on his return from the Indies. I climb the hill between my mother and Guiomar, because my mother had to cut short her trip to one of those strange cities from which she sends me colored postcards – lots of kisses, Mama – and precious, incredible gifts, and I suppose Guiomar had to interrupt some course or meeting at some terribly important American university, something very mathematical and exact, with many, many numbers and graphs and statistics, because Guiomar never understood that someone could waste her time in such dubious and imprecise learning as what we vaguely call humanities, a fraud, really – forget about Angelica and Ariosto – and here they both are at last, brought by the death of my grandmother, not by my unsuspected feelings of desertion, my unexpected anguish and loneliness in the face of what was only one more escapade – one of so many – of a husband whom I don't even love; here they are, one at each side: why have they situated themselves watchfully one on each side? It's as if they think that I am going to escape or do something terribly unexpected and eccentric, how curious that both my mother and daughter, in unison, are afraid of what I may do, it almost flatters me, after an existence, or what I have had of an existence, which comes down to the same thing, unintentionally devoted to calming all their fears and showing them that – aside from devoting some free time to literature, which is really an elegant distraction, since I haven't been so stupid as to take my work seriously – I will do nothing now, nothing more than carry on and suffocate and be bored and die of sadness some spring. Am I not here, so properly dressed in mourning, so straight and dry-eyed, so filial and, especially, so ladylike, such a worthy granddaughter of the deceased? I, such a link in this unbroken chain of women – because suddenly it seems to me that as much as men have moved around us and even have wielded the power, a masculine presence seems never to have existed in my family – follow behind the coffin, standing straight in my mourning, and I stay that way even in the cemetery chapel, on the front-row wooden bench, my tearless eyes fixed on the ground, so close to the coffin that I could touch it if I stretched out my hand – it is a shiny dark wood cof-

fin, with a lot of fittings, distressingly small – ar
can't kneel or cross myself or respond aloud to
the priest, much less look him in the eye while .
and I try not to listen to him, try with all my strength ı.
derstand what he says – about the patrician virtues ot .
grandmother – all of which are mere formulas to which no one
is expected to pay attention and which would be of no use to
me, or strengthen me in any way, which are, in fact, of no use,
except that I can't avoid them, because I don't have, like
Guiomar – as Guiomar firmly believes she has – a real struggle
on my hands, where in her persistence these formalities lose all
meaning, and she can even give in to them, nor do I have, like
my mother, this splendid, unbelieving cynicism almost exclusively found among popes and high prelates of the Church –
my mother participates in the rites like a Renaissance cardinal,
Guiomar as if she were dispensing kisses at a cocktail party or
handing tickets to the usher – and here I am, incapable of crossing myself, incapable of kneeling, incapable of responding
to the invocations to pray, infinitely uneasy and uncomfortable, but dignified and standing, without the slightest intention – my mother and Guiomar may rest assured and suspend
their solicitous, suspicious, affectionate vigilance of me, which
makes everything worse, more difficult, one on each side, like
nurses or bailiffs – without the slightest intention of undressing
suddenly and dancing the dance of death or of life around the
coffin, or of going to bed with the men at the funeral, poor
things, or even of lifting the priest's cassock or sticking my
tongue out at him or tweaking his nose. Tell me, dearly beloved, what would the people say . . . No, no one will have a
thing to say, because even though I feel a bit uncomfortable and
constantly suspect that I am out of place, that my place isn't
here or anywhere else, I have certainly learned to behave, have
learned the gestures – difficult apparently only for me – of ev-
eryday existence which I haven't managed to transform into
mechanical behavior. Neither dispensing kisses at a cocktail
party, nor handing tickets to the usher is a simple act for me –

do my mother and Guiomar guess that? – or at least not every day, because kisses can be too warm or too cold, they can be real kisses and not cocktail party kisses, aside from the fact that I never know very well whom to kiss or whom to give my hand to, or whether to give one or two kisses, and there I am, kissing the empty air, or the other person stands there with his cheek toward me, expecting a second kiss that is not forthcoming, and when a hurried, poor kiss finally is produced, that other person is already looking away: Guiomar is wonderful at dispensing precise, neutral kisses, with the perfect degree of warmth and affection, or of distance and coolness, without even having had to learn it, because she has always known how to handle herself, since she was a girl, with a magnificent naturalness as Olympian as my mother's, and it never occurred to either of them that the usher might suddenly argue with them, or that the aisle might be too long and too bright to walk without hesitation or without stumbling down that double row of spying looks. They are both magnificent: the same large frame, with long, slender bones, the same incredibly fair skin, transparent or reflective like crystal or porcelain, with the softness and slight fuzz of fruit and the fragrant smell of woods, and those eyes – both with identical eyes – large, blue, ruthless – Lord, how ruthless huge, beautiful, blue eyes can be! – eyes that I sense fixed on me until, like now, they look away, and which make me withdraw over and over again, forever, into silent, dark lake bottoms or sea depths, into the deepest and most secret recesses of my underground galleries, of my fathomless grottos.

I wanted to stay alone in the house, after so many damp kisses, so many tight hugs, so many heartfelt, empty words floating around me, I wanted everyone to leave in their cars, for me to be the last one here – to straighten out everything here, I said – and, although my mother and my daughter exchanged quick glances of consultation and surprise, they decided not to interfere and to leave me alone here – they will have time later, in the city, to lecture me, to convince me that

Julio is the best of husbands and that his brief escapades, always so brief, besides, are inconsequential for a man like him, and after all, surely I was used to them by now, so why be so angry? – and off they have gone together, as impeccable and fragrant as when they arrived here some hours before, no sweat or foam on their lustrous coats, two splendid mares who agilely and effortlessly jump over the clumsy obstacle that death sometimes puts in the way of the splendid promenade that is life, that is their life – beautiful, sleek mares with light blue eyes, while I stay here, panting and suffocating, feeling damp and dirty from head to toe, contaminated by the proximity of death, by being handled by the living, smelly with sweat and other people's saliva – dress wrinkled, shoes dusty, stockings twisted, and the unmistakable smell of anguish and fear mixed with the smell of sweat and kisses: I smell like a frightened animal. A disaster. And for the first time, I am the one who goes to Clara – the roles are finally reversed – and I dial her number with trembling fingers, getting the numbers wrong, having to begin again five or six times, and I hear the telephone ring there in her house, my heart in my mouth, invoking all the friendly spirits so whoever answers won't tell me that she has gone out, and I repeat – when I hear her voice at the other end of the telephone – I repeat her name like an exhortation, a magic word of two sonorous syllables, and I ask her to come, right away, immediately, to leave everything and come, because my grandmother has died and the funeral has been dreadful, and I am alone in the house, and I need her – I need you, Clara – it doesn't matter if you don't have any money, get into the first taxi, and I will wait for you at the door to pay for it. And assured now that Clara is going to come – I wonder what she thinks of this self-assured woman that she has invented, falling apart today, this imaginary, distant, superior woman (how I hate that image of myself), now reduced to a miserable little animal, and suddenly, with piercing certainty, I know that Clara, she alone among so many people, for so many years, knew what I was like from the beginning, that it wasn't necessary for her to follow me docilely to the deepest part of my wells or for me to put on my costumes for her, I have the sudden presentiment that at last someone loves me again in my sadness and fear, in my irretrievable loneliness; now assured that Clara will be at my side within the hour, I sink into a bath filled to the top with warm, perfumed water, I almost fall asleep on the watery feather bed, while dense steam fogs the glass, the mirror, the tiles, and I think that I might faint – I am really a bit nauseated – and die here, in this intense scent of a French oil called Love's Bewitchment, Pleasures of Venus, or something like that, and I decide that as soon as I get out of the water – if I don't die here – I am going to light a fire and burn this horrid black dress – I don't even know who got it for me or where it came from – those disgusting dark, heavy stockings, even the shoes and underwear – everything smells of death – and I think that I am not going to remember my grandmother as I saw her these last few months – I saw her very little, to be sure, but even that was too much, because I shouldn't have seen her at all, I should have gone off on a trip, or invented any excuse, or simply carried my ferocious, seamless selfishness to its ultimate extremes – a shapeless, hesitant figure, foolishly obsessive, forgetful, unbearably stubborn and reproachful, her bones deformed by arthritis, her mouth sunken and her eyes dull, so alien and strange – she didn't even call me by my right name – sitting in the wheelchair or lying down – later, her existence now reduced to surviving like a vegetable – on mountains of pillows, so alien and strange that it was impossible for me to associate these images with the mythic figure that she had been in my childhood and even in my youth, the most exquisite of all fairy godmothers, when she would sit on the patio of the summer house by the sea – her beauty so sweet and delicate, very different from the imposing, ever-distant and startling beauty of my mother or of Guiomar, much more like me, people always said we looked alike, and, although they never said this clearly, I was never so beautiful – she was a small, fragile woman with dark hair, she would tell me stories she had lived or invented from other times and sing habaneras to me, while she embroidered incredible raised designs, mixing pale colors from silky skeins. A delicate, tender grandmother who tells stories on the patio, among hydrangeas and bougainvilleas, to the golden trill of canaries, and though she was still pretty and still undisputably charming, it was difficult for me at that time to identify her with the arrogant, defiant, sacrilegious girl about whom my mother and Sofía spoke in a low voice, who scandalized the General's wife, the young mismated girl who went to masked balls clad, like everyone else, in a red unisex leotard, who took part in Bacchic parties, in outrageous dances, who let people believe she had numerous lovers and who talked of the incredible things she would do as soon as her husband died, a girl who may have seen herself as a strange combination of the Princess of Eboli and a sensitive lark, a slender, trembling gazelle, whose ill fortune had bedded her with a bull, or a bear, or perhaps an ox, at any rate, a clumsy animal who could understand nothing of her desires, and who even refused to grant her the small favor of dying while there was still time, when she could have donned her elegant, merry widow's costume and, astutely using her feminine charms and her masculine intelligence, led a splendidly dissipated life or perhaps could have found the right mate to make her happy, but my grandfather lived a long time, long enough for her youth, her emotions, and her beauty to vanish – how curious that in this chain of women, in this matriarchal family where in a certain way only we women seem to exist, the castrating, tiresome males always survive too long – with the result that when my grandfather finally died, he didn't leave her free, he merely left her a little bit lonelier – or perhaps very well avenged – and in any case I couldn't identify that gentle, mismated woman, the subject of the remarks of Mama and Sofía, sharing the fate of an ox because of a mistake, or stupidity, or the impatience of a matchmaking mother, or because she was too young and inexperienced, and with any possibility for happiness frustrated forever, any possibility for happiness dependent on the man's death – and he never seemed disposed to die – and who flung herself into a splendid, desolate carnival, dressed in a red leotard with a devil's tail and horns, because she was permitted to have – as were my mother or I – costumes and lovers and even orgies, but she wasn't allowed to be free of the ox who trampled her, who possessed her night after night in bed without understanding her, only death could have freed her, and the old man didn't die, while she – we – did go on dying a little each day, a bit every day. I couldn't identify that crazy, desperate, young married woman – not crazy enough, however, to break the yoke, or perhaps no one was in those days, hardly even in mine – with the small, charming older woman who embroidered with such fine multicolored silk among the hydrangeas and bougainvilleas – we had sprinkled the patio and the canaries sang deliriously in the afternoon – adored by all, finally respected by all, so beautiful at Sunday mass with her lace mantilla, so dignified and affable in the glove shop – with such tiny hands that they slipped effortlessly into the smallest gloves and the smiling clerk had to get out gloves almost in a child's size – in the flower shop, in the bakery, where workers, waiters – even the owner himself – hurried to wait on her, to open doors for her, to carry her packages to the car, as if they too wanted to make amends for something, perhaps for her beauty and her youth and her passion so stupidly wasted – because my grandmother no longer had lovers then – when I was born that phase had already concluded, lost in the mist of gossip and legends – and she no longer attended chimeric parties dressed as a mermaid or a devil, she didn't go to parties at all, but – until she was half-paralyzed, until sickness and old age turned her into this formless, vegetable being whom I should have refused to visit in loyalty to her memory – she always entered any room – public or private – with the absolute self-assurance of her own charm – like my mother or Guiomar, but nevertheless with a different style – she always addressed men, any man, with the absolute certainty that that specific man could have loved her, and she addressed every woman, any woman, with the pleasant condescension that one devotes to those who replace us because we have graciously desired to give them our post, but whom we could supplant at any moment, because my grandmother had finally chosen virtue, but she had chosen it as one more charm: she was a very virtuous lady – when she decided to be virtuous, her ambition made her more so than anyone else – and her life had turned out badly, but the certainty persisted intact – all the more intact because she couldn't really put it to the test – that she was by rights, like all the women in my family – the tradition broken in me, the only weak link in an otherwise unbreakable chain – the first among her equals. And as she embroidered wonderful branches and birds with fine silk thread in infinitely graded colors and told me romantic stories about the old days and invented others – she was always the center, always the protagonist – and took care of the flowers and the canaries, and gave orders to the servants, and was loved and admired by her friends, relatives, acquaintances, clerks, doormen, and even by strangers who crossed her path one day – at least she firmly thought so, and so did I, who certainly did adore her – there burned within her heart, like a living diamond, the certainty that any Oriental maharajah with herds of hundreds of elephants and a ruby the size of your fist on his turban, any sublime poet who amassed national or even foreign prizes, the arrogant soldier covered with scars and decorations – with such sweet eyes – who made his horse prance before her in the parade, or the bank president to whom she went to open an account to pay the telephone and electric bill, and who received her obsequiously in his office, all of them would, of necessity, have loved her unto death with unequaled passion, with undying affection, had it not been for the extraordinary, absolutely fortuitous and inexplicable circumstance that a woman like her should have woken up one sad morning in the bed of an ox.

Clara finds me lying on my stomach in front of the fire – a fire lit in order to burn clothing and shoes and also because it is still cold here on May nights, so close to the sea – on the carpet; through the now-closed balcony windows, the dark corner with the hydrangea pots, the purple bellflowers, the bougainvilleas, is discernible at the back. I am surrounded by dusty old books, and while she looks in my purse for money and goes out to pay the waiting taxi driver, while she takes off her jacket, pours a glass of wine, and sits down near me, I keep on running a dust rag over the covers, turning the pages of my childhood books, illustrations I colored in pencil and traced innumerable times on thin pieces of tissue paper which now escape from between the pages and slide onto the carpet. Atmospheric blue-greens from which big, evil noses and beautiful pale faces emerge: the slender princess – under some strange spell that I have forgotten, and riding on the back of a giant turtle, with a dreamy gaze and her heavy dark braid hanging down her back right to the shell of the ponderous animal – looks a lot like Clara, and I must be one of these older, haughty queens with stiff dresses of heavy, sumptuous material, wearing a huge crown on their heads, still beautiful, however, although perhaps a little wizened and hard, asking silly questions of mirrors that can't be flattering and truthful at the same time, or pricking their fingertips with little gold knives in order to let three drops of maternal, protective blood fall on light lace hankies – any resemblance between Guiomar and the stupid, helpless little princesses who care for tiny dwarfs in the woods or mount on Falada would be purely coincidental – perhaps that is why I never have been able to assume a normal archetypal image, so tranquilizing for a woman like me: envious and aggressive mother and/or clement, kind mother; I continue slowly turning the pages of my old books, while near me I feel Clara's impatience and annoyance invading the room like a thick, stinging gas so that I don't have to look at her – I have hardly looked at her since she arrived, just a quick glance and a gesture indicating my purse on the sofa – to know that she is impatient and irritated, all I have to do is breathe and her anger and impatience fill my lungs along with the air, they burst in my ears and temples like tickling bubbles, but nevertheless, I continue concentrating on my drawings, not even raising my head, because – first – that foaming, young-animal rage touches me, and – second – I must make Clara pay in some way for the fact that I am the one who called her today, she must compensate me in some way for the trembling of my fingers on the dial, for my drowning-person's voice calling for help, for this imperious, helpless need to have her near me, and perhaps it may be above all – and third – the pleasure of waiting, the pleasure of letting Clara and me and the air become slowly charged until the tension explodes, free of controls, capable of transgressing all limits. So I continue leafing through my books, and now I take another from the pile, without noticing the cover, and open it at random, and before me is an elfin boy with yellow stockings, shirt, and cap, and the face of a pretty girl, and at his feet, a little girl sits sewing in a white nightgown with a pink ribbon knotted at her breast – her little blond braids incredibly well combed for someone who was supposedly asleep and has just gotten out of bed, and – I realize now for the first time – her calm, sweet expression repugnantly possessive and maternal: the scene takes place in an intimate, homey interior, with a plush doll on a shelf with piled-up toys, a candle burning on the floor and the sewing basket next to the candle, everything very commonplace and familiar, in spite of the rather odd clothing on the boy with the little girl's face, were it not that outside, beyond the closed window, near the waning moon, there float strange, greenish, winged figures, and that we all know – Clara and I know – that what the little girl is sewing so carefully on the boy's moccasins is nothing less than his shadow, and this business of having lost his shadow has vaguely disturbing connotations, especially if it happens during the night of a waning moon and if tiny little green men show up outside the window. In fact, this image is what causes the foaming gases which have been filling the room to explode like a bottle of champagne shaken too long near the fire, and I burst out laughing and say softly, "Homer, Shakespeare, Peter Pan," and I take her hand – always fine, small, trembling, and sweaty – and pull her toward me in an almost brusque, play-fully violent movement, and I hold her tightly embraced, both of us lying on the rug in front of the fire, until at last she stops trembling, and it must have lasted for eternities because only embers remain of the wood in the fireplace, and it has been dark for some time outside the windows – you can't even make out the secret corner with the bougainvilleas at the back – but, although I vaguely think I should, I cannot make up my mind to get up and add wood to the fire or turn on the light, it's so nice this way, almost in the dark, and it's not at all cold and it's nice that everything is happening so very slowly, that eternities go by between each movement, because for the first time, we have all the time in the world – Don't hurry, I say to Clara, we have all the time in the world – and no one will interrupt us in my grandmother's old house, which is mine from now on, and tonight, with Clara at my side, I am taking possession of it, af-ter a fashion, because the house, Clara, my childhood, are sud-denly a single, tremulous, warm thing, so intimately mine, so much a part of me forever and ever, that I have all that remains of my life to discover and possess them slowly, and any impa-tience would be out of place, and, besides – I have also just real-ized – it isn't a question of possession: I don't want to possess them, I want to sink into them, I want to lose myself in them, I want to submerge into them, as in a still, warm sea, and there must be no possibility of retreat or turning back – especially turning back – and all that matters now is that Clara has stopped trembling, because I want her to unfold and bloom to-night without fear and without sweat, I want Angelica, sure and terrible, my fragrant tropical princess, to triumph over the anxious, frightened girl, and I rock her, I lull her, I console her for hours and hours – I console myself when I console her – for all the nameless fears, I restrain her softly – slowly, Clara, slowly, we have all the time in the world – because here, to-night, I don't want a repeat of that feverish aggression, that at-tack of a savage, defenseless little animal, that dark, terrible pleasure from before, and not until much later, when we are naked, her thin whiteness beautiful and no longer embarrassed in the firelight – now I have added wood to the fire, closed the curtains, fetched some blankets – with her dark straight mermaid's hair, only now, almost at dawn, do I allow her to clasp me with this dark, clumsy, desolate desire that almost makes me afraid, pressed against me, skin to skin, with a moan that ends in a mortal gasp, rubbing against my body, her legs wrapped around my hips like a death trap – easy, Clara, slowly, we have all the time in the world – until I free myself from the tight bond of her legs and arms – be still, Clara, be still, my love – I lay her on her back, force her to be still, hold her against the floor with both hands, and my mouth begins to move slowly along her delicate, throbbing throat, where her moans die, the throat of someone who is drowning and doesn't want to cry out – silence, Clara, be still, it is still night, we have all the time in the world – moving very slowly along her round shoulders which are trembling uncontrollably, along the delicately revealed bones of her neckline, over the small breasts, the pale nipples, biting from nipple to nipple until they rise crazily toward me, stiff under my feverish breath, under my hard lips and small, sharp teeth, and now her nipples seek my teeth and lips, and Clara's thighs are raised toward emptiness, also searching for me, because my mouth continues on her body, my hands immobilizing her, my own body still distant – slow, Clara, slow, soon dawn will come – and Clara's body arches in violent contortions, so pale and thin in the firelight, evoking somber images of terrible ancestral tortures, and now I do slide my body over hers, and I let her legs clutch me frantically – slowly, Clara, slow, my love, slow – and my hand softly opens the narrow path between her flesh and mine, between our two fused bellies, until it reaches the moist well between her legs, frothing jaws that devour and spew out all dreams, and I plunge into it as into the jaws of a wild animal, pulled on the waves of a whirlpool in which I founder, and the swaying of our locked bodies and the rubbing of my hand between her thighs intensify, and Clara's moan is suddenly like the howl of a white wolf with its throat cut, or raped at the first light of dawn – but this time there is no crazy trembling, there are no broken moans, because pleasure, sure and free of hysteria, gushes from the deepest part of us, slowly ascending in a magnificent surge of long, foaming waves – and afterward, Clara lies at my side, weak as a rag doll, still panting, but relaxed at last, her shadow finally recovered or freed forever from the crowd of lost children.

Clara doesn't ask me, Are you okay? Did you like it? How wonderful, Clara doesn't ask anything, she doesn't even say she loves me, weak and purring – she keeps her eyes closed and a fleeting Mona Lisa smile on her lips – she may even be half-asleep, because she doesn't stir at all when I get up but remains lying quietly on pillows and blankets, before the embers, like a satisfied kitten who has found its place on the hearth at last, who has ceased forever – or at least for a long time, or at least for a moment – howling at the moon from the rooftops and scratching, shy and desolate, at the windowpanes, and since I don't want to take Clara to the soft, low bed – so large it fills the whole room – where I have slept so many nights with Julio, nor to the tall gilded bed with a canopy and a cream-colored crocheted spread where my grandmother's body lay only a few hours ago – although I did refuse to look at this last image – I go up to the children's room – so many generations of children – and push together the two small beds of pale wood, which may be a bit too short for us. There are little English girls with hair nets and ankle boots on the curtains – distantly related to the blond children who run after hoops in the gardens of the ice cream parlor – and the large plush bear – a bit moth-eaten, but always mythical – that will watch us benevolently from the top of the toy closet. In one of the chests I find a soft, sumptuous golden fur, made to cover the legs of a Russian princess or the Snow Queen herself on her silver sleigh pulled by six white reindeer: one of those pleasant, beautiful, absurd objects that I buy from time to time – sometimes on days when I feel too sad – without knowing why I want them or when I am going to use them, and on a certain occasion, I bought this fur throw because of some long-forgotten sadness and now it turns out – unbeknownst to me and especially to her, lost in the heat of her Colombian jungles – that it was for Clara, to envelop her pale flesh and her dark hair, to frame her feverish eyes and bruised mouth – her lips are swollen and a reddish-purple bruise is coming out on the lower one – to rub her sleeping nipples warmly with the soft golden fur of my enchanted fleece – they don't hurt yet, but I know that tomorrow, at the university, in the middle of the street, in my house by the sea, they will burn like two wounds under her dress, they will make her groan at every step and hate the contact of the brassiere, the sweater, or the shirt, hate all contact that is not the contact of my mouth, of my own breasts on hers, of my hands – to encircle her warm thighs, to tickle her curly, moist, dark pubis playfully with the blond fur of my enchanted fleece. I take her in my arms, all wrapped up in the fur, and I carry her up to the bedroom, and she puts her head on my shoulder and an arm around my waist, she purrs meaningless words – perhaps in the language of fairies or cats – and I yield under a brutal avalanche of tenderness that cuts off my breath and stops my heart, because love is surely as terrible as an army on the move, and tenderness is as cruel as death, and I, too, begin to whisper strange words, words which don't have meaning either and which belong to an unlearned language, and I remember that I experienced something like this before with Clara, but this time I don't want to stop, because the words spill out in endless intoxication, and I know that all barriers have fallen and all defenses are down, and here I am, helpless in my tenderness, helpless before the terrible attack of this tenderness a thousand times stronger than death, here I am, defenseless and naked as never before – even in the most remote and intimate of my never-told pasts – dissolving in words, flowing completely from myself in a torrent of words, words which Clara surely couldn't understand – not even if she were attentive and awake, instead of languishing half-asleep in my arms – words that of course she doesn't listen to, words which I may have intuited so long ago for Guiomar when she was a child, that I may have guessed when she was sleeping, when she couldn't look at me with her wide, blue eyes – implacable even then – words that I was about to begin at times when the little girl was sleeping on the floor or on a couch and I had to carry her asleep to her crib, but which I didn't say to her, which never even managed to emerge, that I didn't even formulate in thought, because this language doesn't originate first in thought, next to be turned into sound by the voice: it is born from deep inside, and is already a voice, and the mind, disconnected from the process, listens to it in surprise, not even in fear or shame, because we are suddenly on the other side of fear and shame – way beyond them – and it is obvious and clear that at any moment I will have to die, because tenderness has pierced me like a hundred diamond pins, tenderness has trampled me and swept me in its path like the most terrible of armies on the move, and I am melting, dissolving, bleeding in words, so sweetly dead that I can hardly manage Clara's weight – she who weighs nothing – but fortunately we have reached the two twin beds, and I deposit her there and slip a pillow under her head – without her even opening her eyes, like Guiomar as a child – and I cover her with the sheet and the fur throw – it's cold with the window open, and I want to keep the window open because the room smelled musty and because it is essential for us to hear the sea and the wind in the canebrake and the train's whistle as it goes into the first morning tunnel – and now I tell her softly not to wake up, to sleep, and I lie down next to her, at her back, and she parts her lips at last, moaning, "Don't go," and I know that my hands will be able to repeat the same soft journey over her body a million times, that I will be able to whisper the same silly words into her warm neck interminably, to listen to her sleep peacefully, with an occasional sigh, while I wait for death with the dawn.

I wake up with a start, because for so many, many years I haven't been able to sleep like this, my body linked with an-

other sleeping body, breathing in unison, lulled in a same tor-
por, in identical moist warmth, both bodies naked, for such a
long time that I had lost the recollection and even the memory
of it, and when I lay down next to Clara yesterday, at her back,
almost at daybreak, and she softly murmured, "Don't go," and
then when she half turned in her sleep and curled up close to
me, her long legs and thin arms like vines, Clara-octopus enveloping me, Clara-octopus encircling me all over, then I
thought that I was going to spend the night awake, listening to
her breathe, feeling her sleep, watching her face slowly emerging in the morning light, and nevertheless, I must have fallen
asleep almost at that very moment, and now I wake up startled,
still not believing it possible to have slept so much, and Clara
laughs at this abrupt awakening – like a cowboy on the run
who sleeps with his six-shooter in his belt, in the shelter of a
tree under the stars, she says – and she clucks her tongue
against the roof of her mouth with that tender little noise one
uses to calm children who wake up frightened in the middle of
the night, although the night is now long gone and I didn't,
even in dreams, hear the whistle of the first morning train –
how could I have slept so soundly? – which probably went by
quite a while ago, as the second, and third, and even the noon
train must have done, not too far from the open window
through which a watery, dense sun now enters, so like the
golden sun of my youthful awakenings – my golden moment
of splendor between the end of my adolescence and meeting
Jorge – while Clara laughs, a little embarrassed, now I don't
have to look at her – I lean back on the pillows again and half
close my eyes – to know that her hands hold a big glass full of
cold orange juice, and that somewhere in the house – it necessarily has to be in the back patio, under the bougainvilleas – my
clumsy doll – having recently acquired unsuspected domestic
skills along with her soul, along with her shadow, has set out a
sumptuous display of thick hot chocolate and golden toast.
And Clara is on the bed next to mine, sitting up very straight,
with her legs folded under her, wearing a faded sweater and

some shorts, also faded and blue, that she probably found in a corner of the children's closet. Her tremulous mouth is smiling, and her serious, vibrant voice becomes finer and softer, deliberately clothes itself in velvet and turns into a caress as it comes to meet me, and when, at my gesture – I have held out my hand without even opening my eyes – she rushes toward me, rather like a torrent and comes to rest quietly on my shoulder, curls up in my arms like a tame, affectionate cat, expectantly awaiting the slightest gesture of consent in order to leap softly, cautiously into our bed or our lap, when she purrs softly, rubs her cheek against the hollow of my throat, and kisses me on the eyes, and her purr is simply my name alone, the two syllables of my name pursuing and outrunning each other to infinity, and there are no sharp claws or teeth, because even the wildest and shyest of felines – or perhaps precisely only the most savage and wildest felines – can, one fine day – one terrible day – blunt its own teeth and cut its own claws, and turn into a kitten that is all soft fur, all moist eyes, all rubbing and meowing, and although the purr now leaves the singular monotony of my name and combines it in innumerable alterations with the word love – love, love, love of mine, my love, my sweet love, beloved love, my only love – I know – and for that reason I suddenly feel so frightened – that when Clara says love, she is alluding to something very special – sinister and dangerous – something that has little to do, nothing to do, with the love that even women like my mother and Guiomar, like my swallow-grandmother – with all her romanticism! – may ever have felt, nothing to do with the love affair that a malicious and trivial Maite planned for us, with the love that, only a short while ago, an unhappy black swan looked for in me – apparently the emperor has finally detected her false note, the discrepant note in her elegant melody, and, as I feared, sent her back to her remote lands, in an unappealable exile – with love like the kind that Julio has placed on me for years and years, or like the love mouthed by successive, now faceless lovers, love composed of bargaining and vanity, of obstinate insistence on finding ourselves magnified in the other, of obstinate insistence on wielding power and on affirming ourselves, of canceling out our frustrations and all our fears, a cruel yet banal game of sex and power, or of power through sex, a perverse narcissistic game, an implacable game of multiple mirrors, always in search of one's own image and always holding ourselves back, always putting the other to the test, giving up only the strictly unavoidable territory, always keeping the last card – a trick card – up our sleeves: no, the monstrous process that has begun in Clara and is to drag her to the end – because perhaps the most terrible part of this process is that it always reaches its own end inexorably – beyond the farthest limits of any possible happiness or any possible suffering – this process has nothing to do with anyone else's love or even with my own. Clara has suddenly let down all her defenses and has lucidly – crazily and lucidly – renounced any attempt at a game. Clara slips into my arms so defenseless and alone, so absolutely mine, that I feel a strange anguish, the same anguish as the other morning on board the boat, when her body contained and summarized all the possible nakedness in the world, and, just as on that morning, I would like to cover her, to protect her, to warn her of the danger, to make her go back – as if a return were possible – to keep her in the protected, exact enclosure of our calculated pretenses, of our reservations and precautions. And I hold her very close, I kiss her eyes – only to make her keep them closed so I won't have to see this helpless, unblinkingly steady gaze, in which it is useless to look for Clara now, because in her eyes I am the only one who fills this world – and I think that it may be possible to conjure away the evil spell and, if indeed at the end of so many tiring journeys I have unexpectedly found a beautiful young man waiting for me, without knowing it, in the deepest part of the grotto, this time I will never harm him – no matter how terrible and precise the oracles may be – not even inadvertently, not even by accidentally losing my balance and falling on him, with a murderous weapon in my hand. Because Clara, in the patio with the bougainvilleas and blue bellflowers and the gentle, soft dripping of the water into the basin, where my kisses can no longer keep her eyes closed, this Clara, who has managed to overcome her doll-like clumsiness and prepare hot chocolate – although she eats absolutely nothing – has in her eyes the look of those beautiful Oriental adolescents who love lost travelers, for their misfortune, survivors of a thousand shipwrecks, travelers who have landed on the island and broken the seal on the grotto and are going to kill the young men on the very day of their fifteenth or seventeenth birthday – she has the look of mermaids in love who intrepidly walk over the sharp steel blades of innumerable knives in exchange for a woman's soul – a soul that they don't need and which would be of absolutely no use to them, since the Prince Charmings who inhabit the land never understand anything, they are oblivious of romantic, crazy mermaids, since from the beginning they have set their sights on silly little princesses – the same look that naive country girls bestow on their deceitfully disguised lovers who always, always, always desert them on their wedding night, the look of a tremulous undine who whispers very softly, "since I fell in love with you, my loneliness begins two steps away from you" and who will shout uselessly and stubbornly, "I have deceived you with Bertran," because all the creatures in the lake know already – they knew before it happened – that he is the one who betrayed you, poor, handsome, silly Hans, losing himself when he lost you: the stubborn, fixed, rapturous, excessive looks of adolescents, of country maidens, of sea and lake mermaids, never the look of a man or a woman, never the look of complete, mature beings – perhaps maturity consists only, basically, of no longer being capable of looking that way – mysterious, disquieting, terrible looks of beings still unformed, larval, growing, of underground or aquatic beings, the look that Ariadne gives Theseus at the exact moment when she decides to sacrifice the Minotaur and leave his labyrinths forever, a look unrecoverable after the desertion, a look which Dionysus would vainly seek for himself with burning desire. Looks woven into stories that always have sad endings. The same look that Sofía had.

When Clara woke me up this morning – almost at
with a large glass of cold orange juice in her har
smiled and asked me if she looked like Sofía, and I ar.....
no, she didn't look at all like greedy, lively, sensual Sofía, with
her delicate body, perfumed skin, carefully plucked brows,
fleshy lips, and abundant silky copper-colored curls which she
gathered on her head in a knot, especially when she returned
from the beach, a Sofía who seemed "very French" to my
grandmother, who seemed absolutely bad to the General's
wife, and who had managed to win a joyous complicity from
my mother – who was, on the other hand, almost always so
correct but so distant with the help – because she was doubtless
the prettiest and most affectionate of all the young ladies hired
to care for me, who had come and gone from the house, the
Sofía who put snowy hands – almost as cold and soft as my
mother's and infinitely more maternal – on my forehead on
nights of fever or of fear, and who sat on the edge of my bed
and, before I fell asleep, told me fascinating stories about men
and women she had known and which I almost always believed
were stories about herself, only camouflaged under different,
made-up characters – the General's wife didn't approve in the
least of those stories about men and women, or even of Sofía
sitting on my bed, of our being so inseparable, so equal, such
friends – stories much more fascinating, infinitely more magical and more difficult to assimilate than the stories about
golden-haired princesses, handsome princes, good-looking
but stupid warriors, and talkative rabbits that I read about in
books or that other people explained to me – but which nevertheless have lasted more intensely through the years than
Sofía's stories, so mysterious and suggestive at the time – and
what was so contradictory and disconcerting about her, what
perhaps made me misjudge Sofía for all those years, was the
daring, devil-may-care airs – which she put on, I now believe,
just as I put on so many costumes – her apparent self-assertion
and knowing what she wanted in life – and you could already
see what she really wanted – and she even looked like a woman

in every sense of the word – "a woman with a past," the General's wife assured us, and, in spite of her childlike air and copper-colored curls, Sofía certainly must not have been very young when she came into the house, not a girl in any case, or an adolescent, no matter how sisterly and equal we felt when she sat on the edge of my bed and told me stories in the third person that I knew were hers – and all through that soft, intimate, drawn-out summer – why are the best summers of childhood so intimate, so soft and drawn-out? – my father (who usually didn't stay at home and hardly set foot in grandmother's country house, where Mama – always efficient and always absent – organized her only daughter's vacation with the help of maids, generals' wives, and nannies) stayed in grandmother's house that year – I don't know what he used initially as a pretext, perhaps he had been sick or thought that there he could finish one of those studies he always wanted to undertake but never finished, and very likely never even started because other pressing activities, which shouldn't have been so pressing, never left him a free moment, and I invariably remember Papa thinking up projects that he didn't have time to undertake or complete, although they were the really important ones, while he busied himself with other matters which seemingly didn't interest him at all – my father, as I was saying, settled himself during that summer on the back patio with the bougainvilleas – he had never liked to go on walks or to the beach – in grandmother's wicker rocking chair with the flowered cushion, with a pile of books and papers next to him on the marble table – the same one where Clara has now placed the breakfast and where we ate on the first day I brought her here – and, between his teeth, a beautiful copper-colored wooden pipe, which emitted a thin thread of clean smoke that had the smell and taste of honey, that summer, when Sofía sat on a low stool, her hands in her lap, her cheeks a little paler or a little more blushing than usual, and I played with our cat's newborn litter a bit further away, next to the basin – because even though I loved the sea so much, that summer I didn't feel like swimming or boat rides either – and that summer I didn't realize that in Sofía's eyes, the eyes of a woman in every sense of the word, of a woman who even had a past and infinite stories to tell, there was growing a terrible look, terrible for her – a look whose source and total meaning are only too familiar to me – a look that day by day made her a little younger and infinitely more vulnerable, that not only delivered this defenseless woman to that weak-willed, tired man who for years had allowed too deep, too unbridgeable a gap to develop between his idea of what the world should be and the reality of his own life, his thoughts too remote from his actions to be able to turn back and perhaps recapture it: not only delivered her to that prematurely and irreversibly old man, but also rendered her defenseless before the resentful, petty maliciousness of the General's wife, before the perverse, bored slander of the town where people of my class, of my mediocre race of aged children – never, never adolescents – killed the summer months, as best (or rather, as worst) they could, defenseless, above all, before the marble goddess of serene whiteness – my mother was fair even on the summer beaches – of unyielding harmonies, the distant goddess who so infrequently – always fleetingly – burst in upon the magical intimacy of the threesome in our grotto, while Sofía got up hurriedly, inopportunely blushing – how could I not have realized what was going on? – and Papa, somewhat annoyed, took the pipe from his mouth for a few moments, and then there were a few kisses, some candy, and certain remonstrances and advice, so routine and innocuous, spoken but not intended to be listened to by anyone, like prayers in church, that magnificent deity who would arrive unexpectedly from the temples of Apollo – Apollo meant absolutely nothing to any of the three of us – but who at any time could turn – who, before my astonished eyes, did turn one day that same summer – into the most disheveled and uncontrolled of Dionysian Bacchantes, into a shrieking, angry harpy, who screeched and screeched at the top of her lungs like some filthy rat whose back was being broken with a quick whack of a broom –

although no one was doing, or even saying, anything to her – in a childish tantrum – for which I would have gotten a good spanking – waving her arms frantically, her features – not at all Hellenic now – contracted in a grotesque rictus, her mouth spitting foam, her eyes – her big, light blue eyes – now narrowed and cruel – the eyes of a furious wild animal, of a cornered rat – while she insulted all of us – even the General's wife, who was without doubt the one who had organized the scene, and was now standing in the wings half relishing it, half horror-struck – insulted all of us in language that I had only heard from fishermen or the most common women in the marketplace, language meant to be dreadful but which there, and especially in my mother's mouth – where could such a refined person have learned such words? – seemed merely grotesque to me, a farcical parody, just as what she said was likewise grotesque, absurd, and out of place, because the Olympian goddess – always above good and evil, always creating and accepting her own exclusive norms of conduct and disdainfully rising above the common opinion of mortals – screamed, until she lost her breath, that we had made a fool of her – all of us, including me and even the General's wife – and what would her friends say? and what must the neighbors have thought? and during all this time, which was very, very long, while my mother was divesting herself by the handsful of style and class, of that damned air of class distinction – because no one ever dared to doubt that my mother was a real lady, as much of one as the best pea-princess, and I wondered what damn good being such a lady could be if, when the time came (and what a time, because there was no reason for such a fuss) you acted like a rat – that damned air of class distinction with which she crushed and sickened me since I was a girl, that goddesslike serenity that can't even allow itself excessive effusion and tenderness – not even with her own daughter – while my mother screamed insults at us all, I was waiting – so intensely that it hurt – for Sofía to burst out laughing at last, waiting, above all, for my father to grab that shrieking fury by the neck – the way you grab wild animals – and put her out the door or send her to her room without supper, after slapping her good, but nothing of the kind happened, and my mother went on and on until she ran out of breath – and she had a lot – until she finally ran down, and my father listened to her with an air of fatigue – one of so many injustices of life, he seemed to say – listened to her as if he were only half hearing her – his pipe had gone out and he held it uncomfortably in his hand, not knowing what the devil to do with it – listened to her as if he didn't have all that much to do with this annoying matter, and Sofía also seemed only to half-hear what Mama was saying, it was as if she were listening attentively to my father's words, as attentively as if her life depended on them – to the words that my father did not say, because he hadn't even opened his mouth – because I realize now that Sofía was also waiting, and what I don't know is whether she was hanging on the words that my father should have said and didn't, or on a secret inner speech that my father was delivering only to her and that only she heard, but it was apparent that the goddess-rat didn't have any direct power over Sofía, that she couldn't reach her, or offend her, or hurt her, and that on the other hand it would have been very simple for Sofía to silence my mother in an instant, very easy to interrupt that disgraceful, seemingly interminable scene, at least very easy to try to defend herself, or move to the attack, but Sofía seemed paralyzed, attentive only to the reactions – to the lack of reaction – of my father, to the words that my father was not saying and it was these words, made necessary by the very logic of the absurdity of the situation and nevertheless not said, not my mother's repetitious, ridiculous torrent of words, that were destroying her, because at first, Sofia's eyes had a combative, burning look, an untamed, passionate look, and this look died little by little, became more and more opaque – how terrible to witness the slow dying, the unhurried murder of a look – until it was reduced to a sad, dying ember, the same look that must have fluttered in the astonished eyes of the adolescent into whose chest the fatal knife has just been plunged by mistake, or in the eyes of the mermaid when her prince finally announces to her that he is going to marry the most vulgar, commonplace, and ordinary of princesses – but the realization that now she will never obtain a woman's soul isn't the worst of it (at this point, humans and their souls have lost any possible prestige for her): the worst and saddest thing is discovering that like his princess, Prince Charming is also the most ordinary of princes, that, in short, everything has happened for nothing, just as, for the undine, the loss of Hans is not terrible, but the fact that he lost himself when he betrayed her stupidly with a cruel, pretentious girl he didn't really love, a cruel murderer of her bird friends – or in the eyes of country girls deserted on their wedding night – here, too, their anguish may seem to be for themselves and their own abandonment, but on a deeper level it is for the sad runaway bridegrooms, who will have to dance with their shadows throughout the night, and then expire at dawn – or in abandoned Ariadne's eyes when she wakes up on the island of Naxos and discovers that the seemingly invulnerable Theseus has also fled, because even flawless heroes, even those who are capable of facing the Minotaur himself at the limit of their audacity – the Minotaur, who is so tender in his secret, betrayed labyrinths – even the most charming and valiant princes, even the travelers who have survived a thousand shipwrecks, all experience fear when they encounter the unimaginable in their path: the terrible look of total love (Theseus flees, not from the worst storms or the angry threats of the gods, Theseus flees from Ariadne's love, terrible and dangerous as an army on the move), a love felt only by certain adolescents, a mermaid or an undine, gullible maidens, perhaps Ariadne, lost in the dream of her labyrinths – Ariadne never to be found again by Dionysus on the island of Naxos – and although they all – Theseus and the others – may have wandered, although they may have believed that they wandered for their whole lives in search of love, when they find it like that, in this unimaginable degree, this degree of completeness and of abandonment that seems inconceivable, almost monstrous, to them, such a burning, sharp, dangerous love, so disposed to wager everything and take supreme risks – because even innocent, sweet Gretchen with blond braids can end up administering an overdose of sleeping potion that causes her mother's death, can end up drowning the newborn child in a ditch, can end up causing her only brother to be killed in an unequal duel, and what was poor Faust going to do with that angelical creature who had metamorphosed into a monster because of her love and who, after so much blood and so many crimes, after so many transgressions, now inspired a chill of repulsion and even of fear deep, deep inside of him? – when they find it, they all necessarily assume an expression of fear or of rejection, and they feel they must destroy it and escape, or destroy it simply by fleeing, they feel the same fear that my father must have felt that morning on the patio with the purple bellflowers and the bougainvilleas, now so many years ago, not fear of the flashing eyes of an enraged Athena – although he almost certainly believed that he did, and even I, for a long, long time, thought that my mother's abrupt, dreadfully violent eruption into the patio had been conclusive and terrible, and much later, perhaps only now, did I understand that also Mama, with all her screams, her rage, and her embarrassment, was there to do what everyone, and on this occasion concretely my father, expected her to do – my father felt fear of the look with which Sofía, simply and neatly, put the destiny of the two of them – my father's and her own destiny – in his hands, the same fear that Clara's look inspires in me today, which I vainly try to dispel with kisses, because I don't want to run the extreme risk of having to destroy it ultimately as my father cowardly destroyed Sofía's look that morning with his silence, betraying her and losing himself forever – perhaps betraying her so as to lose himself forever – renouncing irrevocably the possibility, not of recovering the woman, but of finding himself again.

My father chose for the three of us, or perhaps he had already decided before the story began, on that first morning when he stayed there chatting with Sofía and I realized that we weren't going to the beach but didn't care, when he stayed there with an unlit pipe between his teeth – he relit it from time to time, but that morning it went out again almost immediately – and a pile of papers on the marble table between him and the woman on the stool, my father chose clumsily for the three of us, reducing my mother's role to a rat's part – the only one possible, the only one that had been assigned to her in the story – in which she would lose her Olympian calm and dignity for several hours, because in a certain way, my father wanted her like that: a goddess capable of turning into a harpy, just as it was my father who condemned Sofía to the desolate acceptance of defeat – a defeat that she didn't understand – voluptuously giving himself one more reason to feel sorry for and to despise himself – nothing pleased him so much – to indulge and cultivate his image as a tired, weak-willed, and beaten man, and it was really very much like Papa, almost always so cultivated, so fond of symbolic gestures, to offer us that coup de theatre, to impose on all of us that truly magnificent finale – the end of the third act in a play with only three acts, because the fact that my mother threw Sofía out of the house the next morning was an incidental piece of information, an epilogue which the spectator could disregard with no harm done, an insignificant footnote, of which my author-father apparently didn't even seem to be aware – the end of a third act that unfolded within the framework of the great party with which the idle vacationing bourgeoisie ended the summer vacation, the famous party at the casino, which we didn't think would take place that year, because I had never ever seen it rain in such a torrential, excessive way – the rain began shortly after the rumpus on the patio with the bougainvilleas – and the river overflowed, the ground floors and cellars of houses were flooded, and streets flowed like rivers, in which incredible things floated; cars sank and got stuck in mud swamps, and avalanches of water carried some of the beached boats out to sea, but everything was ready, and the party had to take place at any cost, so with considerable delay, we all began arriving at the casino in little groups – how I hoped we wouldn't go – remotely strange figures, covered with all kinds of old jackets and raincoats, with umbrellas that the wind turned inside out and thick, heavy shoes or gum boots, taking them off with joking and laughter and panting – emerging in silk or tulle dresses, golden sandals, complicated hairdos of tight curls, with high topknots and silky locks – and the four of us went because Papa made the women agree to act as if nothing had happened, once he had regained control of the situation, the powers of command, which he hadn't assumed on the patio that very morning only because he didn't wish to, he made the women put on the dresses they had gotten ready, fix their hair, and make themselves up carefully – I want you to look very pretty, I want you to be the queens of the party – and the two women arrived at the casino, one on each arm, occupying, as always, the best table by the dance floor, while our friends' children – the young group in that summer colony, somewhat older than I – sang songs popular at the time, danced supposedly exotic dances with a false modesty that made them twice as suggestive, and finished up by staging the same jokes as every summer, while I felt that everyone was watching us – those sons of bitches – and that the attention was divided equally between the performances on the dance floor and what was supposedly going to happen at our table, and my mother was the most beautiful of beautiful women again, undisputedly first among those who dreamed of being her equals, the queen of the party (my father had said it jokingly, but he was really quite serious), was absolute mistress of herself and of the casino and of the world, her magnificent eyes incredibly radiant and light blue, as if she hadn't been crying right up to the time Papa ordered her to get dressed and fix herself up, and like a goddess who benignly hands out flowers and hydromel at the assembly of the few chosen ones, she dispensed applause and smiles, and the warmest smiles, the most affable words, the most glowing looks, were for my father, who was sitting next to her very naturally, very quietly, very calmly – he had said all he had to say, and what he had kept quiet, he knew he would never again have the chance to say – a Zeus who was slightly annoyed – just slightly – as if his only worry in life were to make sure the two women's glasses were filled with champagne and to keep his pipe from going out – that first morning, in the patio of the bougainvilleas, it hadn't mattered to him at all that it went out again and again, while he pontificated radiantly and Sofía listened to him with astonished eyes – but tonight, yes, tonight it seemed vital that his pipe not go out, and my mother dispensed her sweetest words and her warmest smiles to Papa and Sofía – there was Sofía sitting up very straight in her party dress, like a dressed-up doll – Clara, Clara! – her face expressionless and pale, her hands strangely cold – not with the good cold of my nights of fever, the kind cold of my nights of fear, when she put them gently on my forehead, not those hands which held out a large glass of orange juice to me every morning: now they were cold in a different way, as if dead, and they didn't respond to my furtive touch – but worst of all were her eyes, those beautiful brown eyes which I don't believe had shed a single tear, dry eyes, impeccably made-up – implacably dry and made-up – and so frighteningly empty – eyes in which there were no longer looks, but the atrocious emptiness of a single, murdered look, terrible eyes like the place where an irreparable crime has been committed: Sofía's eyes no longer saw anything, just as they had ceased to admit those of us who clumsily tried to draw near and enter as so many other times; they had become a smoothly polished, seamless surface, so irrevocably shut – although the lids stayed open – and so definitely empty that I didn't understand how the world could continue to revolve impassively in its orbit in the face of that terrible reality – how could a few drops, a storm, a summer shower, reflect the cosmic magnitude of the catastrophe? – I didn't understand how a party could take place and how our friends could spy on us only with malicious curiosity, instead of watching us with horror, I especially didn't understand how my father could continue filling glasses and my mother con-

138

tinue dispensing smiles, and when the show was half over, the direction of the wind suddenly changed, dragging off all the clouds in an instant, and a superb round moon, like a balloon filled with blood, came out, and perhaps a stage set so reminiscent of García Lorca was a bit excessive considering the scene that my father was preparing for us, but I wasn't aware of much of anything, intent as I was on Sofía's eyes, on her icy hands, on her rigid expression, nor did I pay any attention to the pretty, chestnut-haired girl in a floating, turquoise blue tulle dress who came out onto the stage with an enormous basket overflowing with wax roses – it was one of those divinely grotesque schemes, divine because of their grotesqueness, which people of my class know so well how to organize and use to fill up a summer vacation, because for three months they had talked of nothing else but those horrid wax roses and the more or less exorbitant price they would be selling for (there had been a great controversy about the price, and they had finally agreed on an excessive amount, a very, very high price – set not so much to reach the amount necessary to construct the lateral chapel altar in a church dedicated to some saint or other, so that the parish priest would finally leave us alone about it and choose another topic for his Sunday sermon), the exorbitant price was not so much for this purpose as to make sure that only the most powerful men in town would be able to afford a rose for a wife, for a sweetheart, for a sister, and when they fixed such a high price, for once vanity triumphed over their inveterate stinginess – and I didn't even notice that my father had gotten up as if propelled by a spring as soon as the girl came out onto the stage, and when I finally saw him, he was already up there, right in the middle of the dance floor, next to the girl with the roses, and every light had been turned on, lights so powerful that they more than canceled out the reddish moonlight, the spotlights all converged on them, on that single point, and everyone in the casino realized what was happening long before I did, because a dense, incredulous silence finally alerted me that something very unusual was happening or about to occur, and that in our honor – in honor of Sofía, the deserted undine, in honor of my goddess-harpy mother, in honor of the summer vacationers whom he had finally managed to leave gaping with astonishment, but especially in his own honor – my father was giving the great coup de theatre of the evening, because without losing his air of indifference, Papa quickly and elegantly crossed the floor to the girl, said a few words to her, filled her hands with bills – or perhaps he may only have handed a check to her and I am fantasizing – took from her the entire basket with all the roses in it – not a single one of the wives, the sweethearts, the mothers, the sisters of the local patricians would ever acquire one of those roses that were so ugly, but so talked about – and, still imperturbable, still natural, even slightly smiling, though his shadow of a smile could have been the effect of the spotlights, he turned and came toward our table again, and now we all knew – at least my mother and I and even Sofía knew – what was going to happen, and that my father – as a beautiful, theatrical gesture meant for himself, or as a sarcastic, disdainful joke on that bunch of jerks in tuxedos and stuck-up bitches who had spent the entire summer in idle, malicious gossip at our expense, or perhaps as a ritual punishment, a symbolic but necessary punishment, for the goddess whom he had forced to become a harpy for a few seconds, and who, although he had wanted her to be like that, nonetheless had to be purified before resuming her place on Olympus, a goddess whom he had to put in her proper place, no matter how wild and out of control he had wanted her to act some hours before, and above all – I want to believe above all – as a last, sorrowful, guilty offering to a look he had murdered – we all knew that my father was going to deposit the absurd basket full of roses on the lap of Sofía, who was on the verge of fainting.

I have finished the repertoire of my stories – although it is only a feeling, since the stories are almost infinite – I have the feeling, then, of having finished the repertoire of my stories, stories that are almost always very similar, and that I renew, revive, and repeat in the face of each possibility of love, as if loving were only finding the best of pretexts to recall, or perhaps to invent, to take dusty old memories out of the closet, to open the costume trunk and to put on the costume of ancient sorrows – at bottom the same, single sadness – the costume of innumerable, renewed periods of loneliness that constitute a life, before an untried and perhaps – oh, miracle of love – even remotely interested onlooker, as if loving is a pretext for offering this precious image of myself once again – you are exaggerating, says Clara, you aren't so narcissistic – yes, Clara, I am so narcissistic, although quite possibly I don't even like this image, which I nourish and spoil, as my father spoiled and tended his image to the end, his image of a weak-willed, tired man, a bit cynical and perfectly capable of aesthetic infamies – quite possibly I don't even like this image of myself – for offering this image in a sad mating ritual which, unlike those associated with many species of fish and birds, is much grayer and infinitely less showy, and I have already put on and taken off all my feathers, with their crests and plumes, I have fluttered my translucent fins and multicolored tails in warm tropical seas, I have poured upon Clara the bittersweet tide of memories, in the abysmal depths of my grottos – Clara, the most attentive and exceptional of all my listeners, because Clara isn't (I have never wanted to say this) one more in a long line of lovers, and until Clara, absolutely no one came so close to sharing and taking on my unrecoverable past, so close to accompanying me in impossible, definitive loneliness – the bittersweet tide of memories that still live, but which may never have been the way I recall and tell them to her, I have related the furthest, most intimate of my stories to her – except the one that I have never told anyone until now, that I stubbornly refused to discuss or comment with anyone, the poisonous one lying hidden in the deepest part of my marshes, throbbing and burning like a wound that never heals, the story that expelled me, that destroyed and nevertheless condemned me forever to my labyrinths, and perhaps I have never told it to anyone, not even to Clara, because I am incapable of reducing it to a story, of putting in order and reducing to story form that lethal, interminable injury that in reality marked the end of all stories and started a gray period consisting only of data, facts, and quotations – I have told my stories, I have put on and taken off my costumes, I have exhausted all the recesses in my labyrinths and grottos, and now I am at peace – or almost at peace – with the ghosts of a past that I have lovingly reconstructed for Clara, or for myself, taking advantage of the pretext that Clara offered me, or perhaps I hoped that when I raised my past from the dead once again, raised it at last for a different listener, it would die once and for all, would stop wandering about like an unhappy, sleepless specter, would rest in peace under the flowering almond tree in the cemetery, because the ghosts are vanishing and the past is collapsing around us gently and softly, leaving me empty and calm, while, in this landscape of ruins and remains, Clara – a laughing Clara who asks, when I finish the story of Sofía, "Why are you telling me these things? What are you trying to frighten me with or what are you trying to warn me about? About you? About myself? You know that I will risk it anyway" – Clara flourishes and relaxes among the ruins; I see a different Clara emerging in grandmother's old house, through which we seek each other and caress each other without respite, but also without impatience or apprehension, with new, recently learned gentleness, everything surely imposed by this smiling, expansive Clara who – having annihilated the ghosts of a past – seems to have taken sure command, because there has been no repeat of the desolately violent caresses of the first days, as dreadful as the croak of sea birds lost inland on stormy afternoons, or of the tender brutality on that afternoon when Clara came to the house and we made love in front of the dying embers in the fireplace, because now days and nights blur into a single act of infinitely protracted love, a love that Clara invents for me second by second – she had to invent it, since neither she nor I knew that it could even exist – a love devoid of programs and goals, as tender and clumsy and delicious and wise as that of two adolescents who might spend centuries engrossed in loving each other, a love unacquainted with paroxysm or weakness – there is no before or after – because where pleasure should culminate and desire die, a subtle, voluptuous live ember always remains, and even when we are both asleep, our bodies continue rocking, cradling each other, entwined and seeking one another, and we love each other in dreams or in an interminable doze, although I don't know whether Clara has truly ever slept in all these nights and all these days – she assures me that she has – because when I wake up, there are her wide-open eyes always spying on me, watching my sleep, her hands and her mouth are there for me, initiating the caress, her legs ready to encircle me, and the fact that I may feel sleepy or hungry at times – that I could feel any other thing that isn't love – constitutes a touching but rather incomprehensible weakness for this crazy adolescent, and she lets me sleep or brings me food with a condescending, mocking expression of consent, as if acceding to the necessities – so different from ours – of a small child or an earthling who has fallen, poor thing, with all his dead weight and limitations into a land of undines or Martians, and I am not sure whether she has slept a single hour in the days and nights that we have spent loving each other throughout the empty house, even though, when I ask her, she may assure me that she has, and that only to stop me from bothering her and wasting my time on silly things, and only so I will devote myself entirely to the only important and, especially, the only real thing – loving each other – she hurriedly and indifferently swallows the fruit juices or big glasses of milk with honey that I prepare for her, and only in the face of my insistence does she finally consent to call out and order meat, eggs, bread – solid, disagreeable nourishment for the exclusive use of a famished earthling, because the undine will stubbornly continue living on milk and fruit juice, apparently more compatible with love – although the exterior world – all that remains outside the door of this house – should not exist, and step by step, Clara's will is turning grandmother's old house into the impregnable castle of Sleeping Beauty, and her desire causes a dense, thick growth of hedge and underbrush to encircle the walls, where the aspirations and curiosity of any violator of our solitude will die; it turns this house by the sea into the monster's palace, in whose rooms and secret gardens the love of Beauty and the Beast triumphs (and now I know that we are both Beauty and we are both the Beast), where no one dares to interrupt or cross the bewitched fence where the white rosebush blooms, the palace inhabited only by invisible servants – I told the cleaning woman not to come these days and the dust is accumulating on the furniture, but it doesn't seem to matter either to Clara or to me – because when someone really feels "my loneliness begins two steps away from you," then the only solution is to wait for a thick wall, for an impenetrable forest to grow around the two lonelinesses magically fused into a single company, and there is nothing to do but wait for eternity to begin right now. And while Clara abolishes external reality with her constant, passionate insistence – if a reality really exists, if anything external could exist – while she keeps away this so-called world that exists on the other side of hedges and walls and that is alien and perhaps hostile to us, while she bites her nails and gloomily watches over my short, infrequent phone calls to Mama and Guiomar – the indispensable ones to keep them from coming to the house – calls in which I try to explain that I wanted to stay here for a few days to recover from grandmother's death or to clear up what they call my "problems with Julio" – what could they understand by my problems with Julio? – while she keeps the telephone off the hook for hours and hours, and she tells Maite – when the poor woman finally gets through – that I am not home or that I have died, and watches the mailman pass by the garden fence with infinite distrust – but Clara, Clara, who would think of writing to me here? – while she gets rid of the shopkeeper and the cleaning woman (who has finally come, surprised that we don't need her) with feverish urgency, as if their mere presence on the threshold already constitutes a danger, as if she had sniffed out a hidden fire in some corner of the house and had to run and put it out, and dismisses them, thrusting exorbitant tips into their hands, though at other times she forgets to pay them – and they find themselves on the street without an inkling of what is happening here – while she does all of this, she is meanwhile constructing a different reality: a reality based on words, situated in an unknown place in time and space – on the other side of the silk cocoon in which she wraps me – because this is what Clara is doing: weaving a silk cocoon around me – she is building an impossible future for both of us, an improbable future that opposes and prolongs my implausible, perpetually reinvented past – which sleeps in peace at last under the flowering almonds – a future to which we will both fly very soon, transformed into radiant butterflies, a future that could as well be located in the suburbs of Marseilles as in Colombian jungles, and which at times seems to unfold in Paris or in New York or even in Barcelona, but in which we are invariably together, endlessly together, always loving each other and turning this love into a magic lever that can transform the world, because – Clara has decided – this exceptional love, this love which occurs only once every thousand years, can't end in ourselves, it must also embrace all oppressed people, all sad people, all people downtrodden unjustly, all the lonely people in the world, this love must be capable of carrying us up to unsuspected heights, it must finally lead us to transgress all limits, to violate all norms once and for all, and then to reinvent them, and I am afraid – terribly afraid – that in her fantasies, Clara imagines the two of us in guerrilla uniforms, which certainly wouldn't look bad on her, composing immortal sonnets or the definitive study on Ariosto – between armed raids and terrorist bombs – and caressing each other with caresses newly learned during the respite from combat – our hands still smelling of fresh ink and homemade gunpowder – the old dream of seeing art, love, and revolution joined.

In addition to regularly ingesting animal proteins and falling asleep, idiotically, at the least opportune moments – for example, while we are being told, at five in the morning (because Clara has broken into speech, breaking her stubborn, hostile little-girl silence) what making love under the stars could be like, with the smell of dynamite and fresh poems and tropical fruits, around us the trilling of exotic birds and the hiss of the snakes that inhabit the Colombian jungles – we earthlings also need a change of scene at times and a breath of fresh air – a different air from that of the patio with the bougainvilleas – so Clara, distrustful but certainly understanding, consents to go out on the boat with me at dawn (without swans or French girls, of course). We escape furtively with the dawn: I, because I don't even want to imagine what the people of this town, who have known me and have been spying on me disapprovingly since my childhood, could be saying about us, and I prefer not to give more fuel, more concrete images, to their malicious gossip; and Clara, because any contact with the external world – and everything that breathes outside the cocoon that she is slowly but implacably weaving around me, around us, is external – seems obscurely dangerous to her, capable in a certain way of breaking the spell (of breaking the cocoon). Only when we are already on the boat, the moorings released and the motor going – an enormous, absurdly large, round, red sun rising into the sky from the sea, emerging from the sea and leaving a bloody trail behind it in the waters: this scenery is excessive for my taste and much more in tune with the theatrical sensibility of my father – I discover that it wasn't really the stifling atmosphere of the house and the patio, not even the stifling feeling of the silk cocoon or boredom that spurred me to leave, but the whim of once again placing a now different Clara in an old landscape, and we move silently over a sea of blood and lead to the cove with the crazy gulls, and again I throw the anchor in the center of the almost circular bay, where the sea is very deep and dark blue, as on that other day, and where the lunar crags rise steeply to the sky, but today the gulls who crowned the pinnacles have disappeared, and the water doesn't move, and there is total silence when I turn off the motor. And after Clara-girl-flower, so beautiful in her one-piece shiny black silk swimsuit, her straight, loose hair falling to her back – then floating around her – has dived into the sea and I after her, and we have swum, chased each other, caressed each other – the touch of her long legs, of her slender arms, of her narrow hips, of her sweet mouth in the dense, icy water feels so strange – we climb aboard the boat again, and she sits on the warm wood, barely warmed by the early morning sun, as I lie down on my back, wrapped in the towel, my head sheltered in the space that one of her slightly raised thighs forms with her belly, and I feel her throbbing against me, living and warm, as if a conch shell were close to my ear, my head twice rocked by the slight undulation of the sea under the boat and the girl's rhythmic breathing, and I feel that I am sailing – floating – in one of those rare moments when everything becomes peaceful and life flows along gently, and with incredulous surprise I confirm that now, for the first time after so many, many years, I am absolutely happy again, and as I close my eyes, and salty tears – also gently flowing, with no convulsive sobs – mingle together on my cheeks with the other dense, salty drops which fall on me from Clara's hair, and tears and sea water mix together, flooding my throat, and rush down the narrow cleavage between my breasts, and I am not too sure whether Clara has really asked aloud, "What did happen with Jorge?" because it is very possible that she didn't even open her mouth and that nothing has broken an almost total silence – the only sounds are the muffled murmur of the sea against the sides of the boat and Clara's breathing close to my ear – I think that perhaps, in a time of wonders – almost feeling companionship, almost feeling peace, are wonders, to be able to cry with love is a wonder, a wonder that Clara's face is leaning over me, that her dripping hair raining over my body as over a desert land burned by a thousand summer suns, that her hand on my naked belly can seem so very much like happiness – in a time of wonders, I think that perhaps it might also be possible to bring the wound to light, now at last to reduce what has happened – what has been for so many years an anguish without limits – to the reasonable limits of a story, that perhaps I could make up a story with Jorge in it, one more story in the series of stories, only much more intimate and infinitely more painful, and offer it to Clara – so she can file it and put it in order next to the others, the series of my life complete at last – offer it to Clara for this inconceivable, absurd happiness that she has stubbornly invented for me, that she has forced on me, beyond any possible merit or hope, offer her this story, or the clumsy fragments of a disconnected, pitiful story, just as I might give her a lost, wild kitten, that I had just found on the street starving and full of fleas, because throughout the length and breadth of a thousand years of loneliness, she alone has determined and been able to break the isolation, to enter into my dark labyrinths, she alone deserves that I surrender to her my deeper self – trembling, miserable, and sick – a self that is all the more hurt because it is deeper: this final reality, which lies buried and lethal under all my appearances and my half-truths, under all my disguises . . . *in principio era il dolore*, right, Jorge? – in the beginning was sorrow, and the ending – I wonder whether I have reached the end, whether I am very near the end? – must resemble a definitive, seamless easing of my pain – on that day, strange as it is to think of it, even you will stop hurting me – in the middle, unfathomable abysses – much deeper, much wider than human capacity seems to be able to contain – in which pain and a loss of feeling alternate or combine, but at times, very, very few times, in the very abysses, in oceans of unhappiness, a few fleeting – very, very fleeting – moments of happiness occur, like this moment in which I have taken refuge in Clara as in a nest, and her whole body becomes a cradle, becomes a sea shell, becomes a warm lair for me, and I suddenly have the absurd illusion (of all the illusions this is the one that will have to be paid for most dearly, the one that will exact the greatest tribute in tears and in blood, but I don't want to think about this now), the wholly absurd illusion that I am not completely alone and that anything – even loneliness, even sorrow and fear, even the very story that I lived through with Jorge – can be shared sometimes.

I begin The Story of Jorge for Clara like almost every story is begun – as if that way, under the guise of a story, it might hurt a little less: Once upon a time there was a king and a queen. . . . The queen was fair and blond, with enormous, fearless blue eyes, royal, flashing eyes (the eyes of a goddess or a sorceress), and hands – also magical – that convoked the secret perfumes of the woods. And the king had a mysterious, distant, exquisitely tired demeanor, and his eyes were as light blue as the queen's – although not as withering and lethal – his hair was also very blond, and he smoked in pipes of dark, beautifully grained wood, English tobacco – almost everything that the king used was imported and almost everything was English – that flooded the rooms and the patios with the bougainvilleas with a whitish smoke that smelled deliciously of honey. The king and the queen did not love each other – it was apparent that they did not love one other, because love between the two of them, even love coated with sophisticated Anglo-Saxon conventions, would have been somewhat out of place, somewhat commonplace and bordering on bad taste (bad taste was the supreme crime in that kingdom) – but they supported and respected one another: they looked at each other with satisfaction, each reflected in the other, and said sublimely foolish things like, "Really, beauty in human beings begins in the bone structure" – how different from "My loneliness begins two steps from you," but undeniably, both had long, elegant, harmonious bones – or "There is nothing like having blue eyes" (in fact, Papa's were gray-green, but this nuance didn't modify the situation too much). And being blond and fair, having light blue eyes and a long-boned frame, was connected in a very strange way to smoking English tobacco that smelled of honey, to living in large houses, full of light and of beautiful objects, to attending the opera and the theater and concerts, to buying pictures, to commissioning oil portraits – my mother dressed as an Amazon, with an ivory-handled whip and a setter stretched out at her feet – to filling mahogany bookshelves with leather-bound, gilt-edged books, to collecting antique firearms or little ivory figurines, to buying a new car every year, to having pretty houses by the sea, houses with back patios full of bougainvilleas and purple bellflowers, houses noisy with trains and canebrakes, and above all, to surrounding themselves with mountains of people ready to flatter and to serve them. My mother the queen went into stores, coffee shops and restaurants, the hairdresser's, the dressmaker's or a taxi like a goddess capriciously dressed as a woman under whose coarse clothing her Olympian radiance shone unmistakably. And my father the king – always remotely complacent, pedantic, and bored – discoursed on art, philosophy, politics, and morality, as if he were naming things recently created by him and placing them in their exact spot – in our world it was terribly important that things be kept without change in their exact spot – for the rest of eternity. Nevertheless, they both had that condescending and glacial amiability that I imagine in gods. Furthermore, the two of them went about the island, as did all their peers – because the story, Clara, takes place on a small, poor, gray island, lost and overlooked in the immensity of the ocean, although its shallow, miserable residents don't know this, an island that seemed to have been condemned to grayness and mediocrity forever, or at least for quite a long time; and if the king and queen had been taken from their island, they would not even have seemed so handsome or so tall or so blond, nor would the houses have been so large and beautiful, nor the cars so new and so long, nor the firearms so antique, nor, extrapolated from the island, would their aesthetic and moral pronouncements have retained the least validity either, an aesthetics based on good taste and the morality of petty shopkeepers and traders – they went about the island as if the world belonged to them (a peculiar form of existence tenaciously attributed to gods). Until the day came when the king and queen had a daughter, and not even all the fairy godmothers in the fairy kingdom would have been able to turn her – however much they heaped gifts and more gifts on her cradle with the best will in the world – into a real princess,

into the most princesslike of all princesses, into a pretty, graceful, and elegant princess – this sometimes happens to even the
most radiant, proud, and golden families – a dark, thin, small-
boned creature, pale, not fair or ivory-skinned, and to top it all
off, her dark brown eyes were crossed, although that certainly
could be corrected with time and without fairy godmothers – a
girl with an unrenounceable vocation for sorrow and all the
fears in the world on her shoulders – a creature – and everyone
saw it immediately, even the king himself, everyone except my
mother – absolutely beyond hope, so different from the other
whelps of her race that people wondered on what fateful day of
what leap year, on what Sabbath night when all witches roam
loose, she could have been conceived, and the innumerable
teachers and nannies who passed through the house – except
Sofía, because Sofía deserted to the enemy, as it were, stood by
me, and sealed a secret pact with the shadows – the nannies –
although there were no other children but me in the house, and
it might have been different if I had had a brother, or I might
well have ended up by killing him on the high seas and scatter-
ing pieces of his body over the waves foamy with saltpeter and
blood, one never knows – what is certain is that the school-
teachers and the various frauleins and mademoiselles and
señoritas who attended me at home didn't even know quite
what was missing or what they could try with me, because I
learned my lessons quickly and thoroughly for them, was very
quiet, docilely put on the clothes my mother bought me and
even grudgingly attended the parties that her friends' children
organized, and what could be done if sometimes I understood
stories and lessons backward – I often made a fuss about who
were the good ones and who the bad ones, I infallibly took the
side of the losers and the persecuted, and I might well cry in-
consolably at the supposedly happiest endings – what could be
done if clothing truly worthy of the most princesslike of all
princesses looked hopelessly bad on me (surely because I was
not only not the most princesslike, but I wasn't even a little bit
like a princess), and if at parties – in the nurseries of the very

houses in whose drawing rooms my mother radiated her light and her perfume as the undisputed first among her equals – I always ended up taking refuge in some corner, in the darkest one – a friend of shadows and moonless nights – or, in the best of cases, playing in the kitchen with the newborn kittens or even leafing through the books in the library? Sometimes I did risk expressing myself, and the result was general consternation and astonishment, because when I spoke, which was seldom, there was such uncomfortable and dismayed silence that even I understood that I had said something absurd, although I didn't know what. Nothing of what I felt, nothing of what I thought, fit into that closed, insular world into which I had been born and which was the only world I knew at that time. "And" – Clara asks or declares – "Ariadne built her labyrinths." Yes, from the time she was very little, from the time when she read her first stories under the shelter of the table in her father's study, on the soft, dark-green rug – or perhaps even before – Ariadne secretly began to dig her labyrinths. Ariadne had always sought dark allies for herself – perhaps because she had been conceived one Sabbath night in a leap year – beings, like her, who couldn't survive in that steely order, in that aseptic, resplendent world, beings who for that very reason knew how to direct her flight toward Never-Never Lands, where together they could find a little underground house, a true home for lost children, a warm, closed refuge where excessive sunlight or the terrible glances of blue eyes could not penetrate. And a playmate appeared there, born of Ariadne's terrible solitude, the Minotaur, and the two grew up together in the moist depths, where strange carnivorous, purple flowers sprouted, and there were bottomless marshes of warm sand, there were reptiles of a most beautiful green, with scaly bodies and endless tails, reptiles that had never risen to the surface. There Ariadne and the Minotaur played, grew up, and loved one another for years. Until one day, Theseus arrived. Yes, Clara, then Jorge arrived. Because Jorge – like Theseus – didn't belong to my parents' world; he would never have wanted – in fact he refused – to sit in this grotesque assembly of men-gods, he refused to be assimilated into this deformed race of prematurely aged children: Jorge didn't have luminous blue eyes or fair skin, and I am almost sure that he didn't possess a beautiful bone structure, but Jorge came from very far away and didn't belong to the perverse race of the servile, he didn't belong to the shapeless group that bowed and groveled around a few chosen ones: Jorge came from very far away, from other continents, and made fun of our ridiculous playacting, of those Pygmy quarrels – intent as he was on a vast, authentic struggle – he laughed at structures that had crushed me, that had made me suffer so horribly for so many, many years, laughed at the world I feared and detested, but which I had never seriously doubted, because I thought it was superior and therefore immutable, the world that had rejected me and relegated me to dark labyrinths – do you understand, Clara? – Theseus laughed at those false gods out of an operetta, at our aesthetics based on good taste – aesthetics consisting of antique firearms and ivory figurines, of still lifes and watercolor landscapes, of portraits of ladies in Amazon outfits with setters at their feet – he laughed at our wretched peddler's morality, at our castes, and although on certain occasions he would become indignant – because my parents and the others, I repeat, went about as if the world belonged to them – in general, at least during a first phase, they only made him laugh, or feel sorry for them, or be very angry: Theseus looked my mother in the face – he didn't even bother to look at Papa – his serious unblinking eyes fixed on her blue eyes, and he laughed, but not maliciously, he laughed, I believe, almost sadly, as if saying to himself or to her "What a waste of a splendid woman" (because even Theseus must have thought that my mother was a splendid woman, if only potentially), and then the structure in which I had lived imprisoned shook from its foundations, and there was a movement of panic and disbelief in that cardboard Olympus, because the unimaginable had happened, Clara, the unexpected had happened, something that I had been waiting for unknowingly for a thousand years, my humiliated pride asleep for a thousand years but never annihilated or conquered on its fire-encircled crag, waiting for the only one among all the heroes who could pass through the wall of flames and awaken it, Ariadne dreaming for a thousand years in her secret labyrinths, not really knowing whether the Minotaur was a product of my dreams or if my whole being was a dream that the Minotaur had dreamed during a night of fever, each one of my desires and fears my brother Minotaur's dream, until one day Theseus arrived, Siegfried arrived, and he was the strongest, and the flames went out at his step, the mountains and peaks subsided, the labyrinths crumbled, and he took me by the hand – because he was the strongest – and I let the palaces of the gods burn behind me without sorrow, I let the underground grottos crumble, and I let the Minotaur die – he didn't die in combat at Theseus's hand, he died of sorrow at my absence, little by little, in tiny, successive deaths, or because Jorge was annihilating him in me, and I was the one, yes, perhaps I was really the one who finally caused its definitive death in the deepest part of myself – and I followed him on board his ship, but I would have followed him even walking on the surface of the sea, because if he had commanded me, if Jorge had asked me, if Theseus had stretched out his hand to me in the midst of the waves and said, "Come," the waters surely would have held me up, I would surely have walked on them to the very end of the universe, and my parents no longer existed: not their shallow world, not that race of dwarfs into which I had been born by mistake, not even the subterranean places of refuge that the Minotaur and I had so lovingly built together to be our lair, because at last I was moving forward with him, and he was leading me toward freedom, toward the final encounter with myself and with men – not kings, not servants, not gods: men among men – because we advanced toward lands without borders where people had to be better and different . . . because life, as you say, Clara, can be different, and I believed it then – I believed because I loved him, if you could only understand, if you could only imagine for a moment how I loved him – and even now, even now, during sleepless nights, I keep on believing that life could have been different. . . . Life was going to be different. . . . Now Clara has delicately collected my salty tears with the tips of her soft, slender fingers, and she gently places a hand over my eyes, between my eyes and the sun, and speaks as softly, as carefully, as tenderly, as if she were addressing, as if she were caring for a critically ill person, a sick person who is a single wound, and with her voice like balm, Clara finishes so that I won't have to go on – because it hurts her or because it hurts me too much – so that I won't have to say it, to spare me the extreme suffering of saying: "But Theseus deserted Ariadne on the island of Naxos."

Now Clara follows me through the house like a shadow – the rediscovered shadow of a women who lost her shadow a long time ago – she curls up at my feet when I am sitting in the rocking chair on the patio with the bougainvilleas, her head languidly on my lap, huddles by my side on the living-room couch in front of the fireplace that we haven't lit again since the first night, because summer has arrived, this time suddenly and definitely, while on the record player French songs from the fifties and sixties play over and over again, one after the other, ones she knows that I like and that she imagines – with a hint of jealousy – may evoke painful, forgotten nostalgias in me, when actually these days – days situated outside of the natural flow of my life – cunningly snatched by Clara from the implacable passage of minutes and seconds, since in a certain way Clara has won the impossible battle against time – these days I think about nothing, my mind strangely blank, I don't remember anything now, only a very sharp stab of pain, an unbearable nausea, the day when Clara – where the hell could she have gotten these records? – makes me listen to the bitter, scratchy voice of Pasolini, as scratchy and bitter as Jorge's, "in principio era il dolore" and then "io ho sbagliato tutto, tutta una vita," while Clara watches me compassionately, almost frightened at what she has done, suffering, I believe, as much as I – no, it isn't possible for her to suffer that way – but as if she were administering the healing, bitter medicine to me only for my own good, and perhaps the beloved-hated voice of Pasolini may really be the marvelous lance that can heal the wound at last, and Clara climbs into my bed with catlike agility and softness and stretches her body out next to mine with an unusual ability that I only remember in one of my cats, a calico alley cat with fierce yellow eyes, who stubbornly stole food from the kitchen and never accepted anything we offered her on a plate, not even by me, although she certainly did take food delicately from my hand and kept her big, adoring, golden eyes on me in an unyielding, immutable gaze, a cat named Muslina, who lived and died many years ago – an unusual ability, in some cats and in Clara, to press against my body, keeping the maximum skin surface in contact. And the truth is that Clara's skin has become silky, like a cat's, her whole body seems like a big, clumsy, warm cat, who gets under foot when I walk, leaps into my lap unexpectedly, sleeps pressed against me, curls up next to me, with this terrible gentleness of tamed wild animals, this total meekness of animals born not to be submissive – or to be so only in love – and who, when they abdicate everything, when they surrender everything, without haggling and without calculation, without possible retreat, can't bear for the other not to accept this terrible abdication and surrender naturally and joyfully, for Clara's eyes – which have turned more golden day by day, with the dark, liquid yellow of wild honey – follow me and spy on me like the devoted, restless, disturbing eyes of Muslina, hanging on my most insignificant gesture, on how startled or annoyed I am, fixed on me even when I sleep – especially when I sleep – because second by second, as if her life, as if our two entwined lives, depended on it, Clara keeps watch over the slow growth of this cocoon enveloping me, which is almost completed now, a cocoon that is so delicate, so fragile, yet so wonderfully resistant, that now nothing can drag me to the marshes of a past that is vanishing day by day, now nothing can make me retreat, and when the last silk thread has been woven and the seamless cocoon encloses me, perhaps then Clara can rest at last, perhaps then she can go to sleep by my side, give up her restless vigilance, doze until the day (by that time sure and inevitable, foreseeable and certain as the order of the seasons) when the ancient prisons will open by themselves and I will be reborn, transformed into a butterfly, until the day when I will be able to fly again, and even begin with Clara this existence that she is prefiguring and inventing – looking for an apartment for us both, getting money from her father, making me prepare classes for the university – I don't know whether I believe in this existence or not, because no one has ever explained to me how wings could grow again on the birds of my race, no one has ever explained how a wandering, yellow-eyed cat, a solitary, shy cat, can sometimes weave the warmest silk cocoons around the beings it loves; and perhaps if love, if this love is intense enough, if the cocoon that she builds for me, and that I allow her to build, is resistant enough, and if both of us truly want it, perhaps then this marvelous story that Clara has made up for me can yet be real enough to wipe out so many years, all those tenaciously wrong years, real enough to make me revoke my decision not to live, and perhaps because she believes that the cocoon is really finished, or perhaps, more probably, because part of this spell demands that I alone must spin the last thread, the one that finally closes this capsule from which I can be reborn as a different person, that I alone must overcome the final test, Clara – who has stubbornly placed herself between me and all calls, who for days has watched over my answers to Mama and Guiomar, who has said a thousand and one times that I am not at home, and who has kept the telephone off the hook most of the time – now holds it out to me with the gesture of someone who is holding out a poisonous snake to her best friend, her arm stiff to keep the receiver as far away as possible from her own body, and she is paler than ever, and for the first time in these last days her voice is hard and quavering at the same time, her voice stops being a balm or a friendly meow, it is the same hostile voice from the days when we met – she always becomes aggressive when something hurts her too much – as she explains to me – as if any clarification were necessary, as if we both hadn't been expecting this call, dreading this call, from the first afternoon when we shut ourselves up in Grandmother's house together and began to invent a future for ourselves – "It's Julio." He has delayed calling more than expected, more than feared, surely because it took longer to find out that I was here, but finally the alarming news must have reached him from my mother, or Guiomar's remarks, or the malicious gossip of any one of our friends – if what we have can be called friends – and the escapade – mine, not his – must have seemed serious enough this time for him to start toward Ithaca from the most unlikely spot on earth, abandoning fabulous business deals in which I don't believe and one of the many equally fabulous girls in whom I can't manage to believe either, although I know that business deals and girls do exist, although I have even been furnished proof that business deals and girls do indeed exist, because the money flows in, flooding us like a tiresome river of gold, and because all our friends know, and make sure I know, that not even rare, sophisticated, imported nightingales that are then returned to far-off lands by the emperor, not even black swans, can compete with blonds or redheads with long straight hair, with Afro-style hairdos, always broad-shouldered and long-legged – they also have the kind of beauty that Mama looks for, the kind that begins in the frame, although surely their loneliness doesn't begin or end two steps from anyone – who appear on magazine covers – often wearing very little or no clothing and with a very odd smile, which may be the only thing that makes me pay some attention to them and that intrigues me, because these girls, at least in the magazines, and particularly if it is a cover picture, smile as they pout with their cute, square little mouths – how odd to have a square smile – girls that Julio shows off in movie studios, on fashionable beaches, in the casinos of high society, younger, more blond or more redheaded, slimmer, their little pouty smiles also squarer as the years go by and oddly enough, in spite of all the proof, which, on the other hand, I neither seek nor care about, Julio's business deals and his women never seem, have never seemed, even remotely real to me, and even Julio himself, in the immense majority of moments that have made up our shared life, has never really existed for me, however much, as now, I hear his voice on the other end of the telephone, saying that he will be waiting for me at the door in exactly ten minutes, repeating over and over that he loves me – of course he loves me, with the impossible love of a nonexistent knight – making me promise to see him – and how am I going to see an invisible person? – but jokes aside, I begin to feel afraid and look at Clara, with a final, remote hope that she will oppose it, that she will hang up the telephone for me and we will run away together to some place, without luggage, but Clara isn't even looking at me, and it is obvious that I am going to have to pass the final test by myself, that I alone am going to have to weave the final thread of the cocoon by myself, because Clara assents with a vague, resigned gesture, and I say good-bye to Julio, finally hang up, and devote my remaining ten minutes swearing to Clara, repeating to her in every possible tone, and in some impossible tones that now emerge from my desire to calm her, repeating with kisses and caresses – that she doesn't seem to feel, just as she really doesn't seem to hear me either, absolutely withdrawn into herself and paler than ever – that I will be back by dinner time, that I want her to set the table on the patio with the bougainvilleas and purple bellflowers, because the night will surely be very beautiful, a night with an almost full moon in its fourth quarter, to open the best wine we can find in Grandmother's cellar – a good French vintage – that we will have one of those absurd, delicious banquets that Clara has prepared for me some days – the days when she gave in to the incomprehensible hungers of a starving earthling – at times like ethereal collations for gnomes and others like monstrous banquets for Viking princes who have just conquered a fortress in Normandy after arduous combat: never a meal on a human scale, that we will dine under the moon by candlelight, surrounded by the whirring of moths – and, I promise you, Clara, not a single one of those moths will burn its wings – then go to sleep, like every night remaining to us, curled in each other's arms all night, lost in the same dream.

Julio's body very close to my body – that is, Julio's impeccable suit, his silver temples (the term *silver temples* seems to have been invented expressly for Julio), his faint smell of English cologne and American tobacco – very close to me, because he has gotten out of the car – one of those dumbfoundingly ostentatious cars that seem made to require some comment, and about which I never know what to say, because all that occurs to me, and this happens to me often with Julio, are lines from some television commercial, as if he and I, and the car, of course, were characters in an ad – he has gotten out of the car as soon as he saw me come through the garden fence, and now he whispers my name several times over, his mouth pressed against my ear, and even the two syllables of my name, so sonorous and beautiful when Clara repeats them to infinity, now sound false to me, make me think that I have the name of a character in a cheap novel, and nevertheless, I am afraid that Clara will unavoidably see us from the window or the door of the house, and I am afraid that this whole cheap performance – which Julio is putting on for my benefit, but also for the benefit of my invisible companion, of the strange rival he doesn't know, because Julio takes for granted that she is watching us, and I know that the desire to humiliate her and, in a certain way, to provoke her, is part of his game, just as I know that drawing the girl into a suggestive, banal game for three people enters into his scheme – that is the word he would use, for even in his schemes, Julio inevitably falls into the most hollow banalities – I am afraid that this whole production might confuse Clara and even seem slightly real to her, this possessively protective gesture with which the man puts his arm around my shoulders, speaks into my ear, opens the car door, settles me inside the car as if I were a little old lady or an invalid and couldn't arrange my feet and purse and skirts on my own, and gives me one final, light kiss before climbing into his seat and starting this strange, chrome-plated, rocket-shaped gadget (not toward the stars, I hope). And I don't even have to look behind me to know that the back seat of this sputnik is filled with velvety, red, long-stemmed roses which he won't have allowed the florist to touch, or arrange, or sprinkle a single petal with artificial dew, because Julio never invents anything, he never improvises, and he learned a long time ago that I like roses that way – bloodred, dark red, with long stems and petals that aren't retouched, and I don't have to look among the roses today – an excessive amount, there are too many roses – to know that I will find a card there, and I know before looking at it that it contains the three ritual words – so empty of meaning that to say false wouldn't express it – because it is even possible that Julio does love me, but in him these words or even this very love for me, just like my two-syllable name or the flowers, vanish into the meaningless "I love you." And Clara will never understand, and, except for very brief instants of intuition or lucidity, even I can barely understand how my life for the last almost thirty years – that is, the totality of my life as a so-called adult, of a would-be woman – could have been lost in such sordid falseness, how I could have fallen into this trap, and especially how I could have stayed in it, a monstrous and gigantic trap, no, not even that, a minuscule, ridiculous mousetrap, with its little piece of moldy cheese – when I never liked cheese – because this trap, not even allowing for the accidental circumstance that I am the one who stays in it, has never ceased to seem grotesque to me for a minute, a crude trap made up of sophisticated, latest model cars (sputniks that will never carry me to the moon), of luxurious, uninhabitable houses, although they appear systematically photographed in Japanese magazines, of course, and seem unbeatable sets for shooting television commercials with mature, silver-templed men, Italian clothes, English lavender water – imported, the best – filter-tipped cigarettes – at least my father smoked a pipe and, let's be frank, it is quite possible that he never approved of this wedding and that Julio seemed a perfect fool to him – cinematic embraces, words whispered in my ear, mountains of red roses – Julio has never found out that I have a secret fondness for tuberoses and that in my underground places magnificent orchids bloom, perhaps because I have never allowed him to discover something so intimately mine – endless cards written in ink more or less faded with time on which one reads – on which one could read if I had kept them anywhere – invariably "I love you," each card and each bunch corresponding almost exactly to the demise, by natural causes or at the hands of excessive scandal, with the resultant outrage and interference of my dear mother – who, from time to time and always in the least opportune circumstances, decides to take an interest in my affairs and to take charge of my drifting life – of friends, even of Guiomar – You are going too far, how can you do this to Mama? – with the resultant calls to order – a real screw-up, Julio, we all do what we can, but let's not overdo it – at any rate, each one of these faded cards, each bunch of roses – always very beautiful and always excessive – corresponding to the death of one of his adventures with blond, red-headed, chestnut-haired girls, girls whose hair is straight or full of little curls, girls with eyes and skin of every imaginable color, but invariably young, invariably beautiful, invariably endowed with long legs and a little mouth that seems square on their front-page smiles, younger, prettier and shinier – the cars are also increasingly ostentatious and spectacular, more like covered wagons from the Old West or interspace rockets – in proportion to the passing years, in proportion to the growing number of times he serves on panels of judges at festivals and his list of film credits increases, and rave reviews accumulate – which a secretary who is also blond and long-legged pastes into leather-bound scrapbooks – and the certainty grows, deeper and more incontrovertible – although he won't confess it to anyone – that he will never make "the" film now, "his" film, which will remain unmade for eternity, though it doesn't worry me much, because – and this is something that my mother never guessed, she who was so discerning, so clever in taking the rudder and managing the threads of our lives, nor Guiomar, so practical and so wise in human relations, nor the friends who call me by turns (Maite almost always at their head) to sympathize (at each new affair), or to rejoice (at each new breakup, with the resultant card in the bouquet of roses), or to congratulate us (at each new stellar triumph of his career, a triumph on our dwarf scale) – the funny thing about this trap is that I chose to get into it together with a man I not only don't love, but whom I don't hate or truly despise, a man whom I no longer judge, because millions and millions of years ago – so many that I have no memory of any former time, and I can't be sure of its existence or nonexistence – he ceased to interest me to such a degree that I don't even feel curious enough to understand his reactions, and of course no temptation to try to know him, and the films that he directs – always with a pretty and, if possible, famous young actress, always on a subject that aspires to be the latest thing but is really what was fashionable in London or New York ten years ago – seem neither good nor bad to me – just very boring, not even remotely credible, even by the logic of the absurd – and Julio knows very little about the logic of the absurd – as if devoid of flesh or deprived of a spine, as if they have nothing to do with men or women, as if the films themselves don't quite exist, just as these starlets who should hurt me and whose names or faces I don't even manage to retain don't exist, because they really are of no interest to me – although no one, least of all Julio, can or wishes to believe it – and I am convinced that they are merely a smile with a square little mouth, depilated genitals smelling of Badedas, and actually, Julio doesn't really exist either, except as an institution, an institution of national importance, the invention of a few critics and a public that perhaps need him to justify and assure themselves on some points that are of no concern to me either, and as a matrimonial institution – on a more social than private level –

that my mother and Jorge invented for me together – that Jorge didn't know Julio personally isn't important – because Julio has been only this for me: a constant and painful and ever-present performance of the life and of the death that Jorge chose for me, and this ridiculous trap, this grotesque mousetrap in which I am suffocating and where all hopes and all future projects have died, this trap in whose bars not even I myself believe, but from which – Clara, Clara! – I am never going to escape, was what Jorge chose for me on my behalf, Jorge built it for me when he unforgivably deserted me on the island of Naxos, when he deserted me without the possibility of finding me again halfway between my impossible labyrinths, which had been my only refuge, and in the ruins of which the Minotaur lay dying because of my love, and that other, more utopian world, of which I had no other proof than Jorge's words, which brought out unknown desires in me; I will never know now whether that world could have been real, whether it exists, whether it once existed for someone somewhere – although you, Clara, also believe in it, and your world of an undine in love, this world where people would be better and different and even more beautiful, and where human relationships, all human relationships would be based not on force (how could I ever have believed in that?) but on reason and justice, seems very much like the world that Jorge was gradually constructing for me from pieces of his projects and my dreams – because I was too young, too weak, I came from a race of dwarfs who had become old without reaching adulthood, I had found refuge only in dreamed-of labyrinths, love only in the Minotaur, and Theseus fled like a coward, with that final, cruel cowardice of which perhaps only heroes are capable, taking with him the maps and the ship, and it wasn't certain, Clara, whether Ariadne could have followed Theseus by sea, whether Ariadne could have gone on alone by sea without Theseus – nor was it certain whether she would have thrown herself into the sea to die, into the sea which is death – whether she could have walked on water, perhaps because Theseus never said,

"Come with me" before his desertion, Theseus went away treacherously on his ship, without the possibility of returning, without leaving behind a good-bye or a message, a "Come with me," and Ariadne, a silly little princess, the least princess-like of all princesses, whom they had taken from her nest without even teaching her to fly, stayed behind, deserted in no-man's-land, at the mercy of the first god, of the first monster – the race of men began and died with Jorge – who arrived at the island and wanted to rescue her, and when Julio arrived, I didn't exactly choose him (or I chose him perhaps for inverted reasons: because he couldn't understand me, because I wasn't going to be able to love him, because he wouldn't follow me into grottos or labyrinths, because he was a worse and more insignificant death, a worse, more cowardly, much more painful suicide), not even my mother chose him, however much she sang his praises from the rooftops and constantly talked about him and about her daughter's good fortune – what an incredible piece of good luck, after the scandal created by the existence, the mere existence, of Jorge from start to finish – though I proudly showed him off in our court of pygmies (I had of course been returned to my small island, to my parents' house, to the race of dwarfs, all hope of taking flight now lost), my mother hadn't chosen him nor had I: Jorge had chosen him for me in the most magnificent and destructive of his sarcasms, Jorge, whose murderous jokes would have destroyed him in any one of our brilliant ceremonies, our sacred cults, who would have despised him with infinite condescension, had chosen him for me by not taking me with him on board the ship, by denying me any right to choose for myself whether to remain or to follow him – he hadn't said, "Come with me," because if he had said it, if Jorge had said it, I would have suddenly had a woman's wings and would have walked on the sea, and the sea would have held me up – he had condemned me to the worst mediocrity, to unmitigated banality, or perhaps Jorge didn't want this for me, perhaps I went into, and stayed in this trap so long – a whole lifetime – as revenge, the most terrible and most useless kind – useless since neither this nor anything can reach him now, the sailor safe on board his ship which will never return – and in short, when Jorge deserted me without pity on the island of Naxos without leaving behind a message or a good-bye, especially without leaving a "Come with me," he made it plain, definitely and once and for all, that whatever road I took from that time on, into my future without him, even if he had really chosen it and had indirectly forced it on me, it was no longer his business and was of no concern to him.

We are still together, in the currently fashionable restaurant, sitting at the table that Julio has permanently – a permanence that will last as long as the fashion does – reserved in his name, in front of a foie gras that seems tasteless to me and a Burgundy that will give me a terrible headache tomorrow, trying not to listen to the words that Julio stubbornly repeats in my ear – it is one of his incurable quirks – and I don't dare make him stop by telling him that none of this matters, all that business about my love being more intoxicating than wine, gentler than all perfumes, that I am a garden enclosed, a spring shut up, a fountain sealed, the only one among the chosen women, the queen on whose account virgins and concubines will be despised – and why don't I make him stop talking today? although I should have done so long ago, almost thirty years ago. Why not explain to him here and now, that none of what he has been repeating for centuries ever interested me in the least, not even the first time I heard him say it, because before meeting him, I had read the Song of Songs for myself, and besides he always quotes it badly? Why shouldn't I get up today, here and now, before I get too drunk, and leave the Burgundy and the French foie gras and the red roses for good, drop this grotesque role of official wife of a supposedly important pygmy who isn't of the least concern to me? Why not get up without even saying a word – I know very well that there is only one way to leave a man: get up and go – and run back to the garden with the bougainvilleas? Why not begin the solitary apprenticeship of flying today, perhaps with Clara beside me, why not try at last to walk on water without anyone's holding out a hand to me and saying, "Come with me"? Why shouldn't I write immortal sonnets, or at least why not try? And why not be a guerrilla fighter in Amazon jungles or make love with whomever I please, under the stars or in the urban jungle, why not begin today some struggle, probably impossible and surely useless, but alive and real, certainly better than this mediocre performance by an "I" in whom I don't recognize myself, this imitation that I reject, this revenge that Mama and Jorge planned for me? Why not accept today, once and for all, the fact that the elderly English lady who roams across continents and disdains natives and sends postcards with huge writing and absurd gifts, has very little in common with me and has been left behind – with her love or lack of it – for good? And why not accept – but how can I accept it? – the fact that Jorge has been dead for thirty years and that he chose his own destiny by and for himself, but not with me in mind, when he left me in such a cruel and incomprehensible way, without a good-bye, without a note, the silly princess deserted on the crystal island, and since I chose not to follow him then, since I didn't throw myself into the sea which is death, and go after him, in short, since in some way I chose to continue living in a world without Jorge, why not leave this half-life starting today, this slow, cowardly suicide, leave it to those who condemned me then, perhaps to punish him? Why not try a real life, at least for the years I have left? But I don't get up, I hold the long, cold stem of the crystal wine glass between my fingers – this and the color are the only things I like about Burgundy – and I say aloud that Clara must be waiting for me, and Julio answers that we can telephone and send the chauffeur to get her, and adds – I think this is the moment, Clara, my love, when we lose the match – that if this would make me happy, he wouldn't mind if you came to live with us for a while, and it is like the moment when my father put the absurd basket full of wax roses on poor

Sofía's knees, and for the first time during the evening I feel apprehensive that I may not ever be able to get up – among other things, because I am going to be very drunk within a very short space of time, without even liking Burgundy – and that you, Clara, may possibly spend the whole night alone on the patio with the bougainvilleas, waiting for me – until what time? At what instant will the suspicion be born, at what instant will the certainty be confirmed that I have betrayed you, that I have betrayed myself? – waiting for me and hating me, while your dinner for gnomes, your fairy feast, gets ruined, while the candles slowly burn down and one after the other all the moths fall to the ground or on the tablecloth with their wings burned, and when Julio takes me by the arm and drags me almost bodily to the car and settles me in the seat – now I do need to be settled, now that I have been reduced to invalid state in these few hours – it doesn't even occur to me to suggest that he return me to my grandmother's house, because there's no reason now, and I don't want the bitterness of seeing the two of you together – him, so pleasant and silver-templed, so understanding and charming; you, looking at me with your astonished eyes, the eyes of a betrayed mermaid – and I let him take me wherever he wants (what does it matter now, if the night, at least this night, is irremediably lost for both Clara and me?) and Julio puts me into a strange glass box, with an intensely white floor, everything so large that it seems made to a giant scale, a giants' operating room where a monstrous operation might be going to take place, a sinister amputation – of myself, I think – but no, it isn't an operating room, however much it may seem like one, nor is it a movie studio recently built for him, as Julio does his best to explain to his wife, who is too drunk to understand him: it is a box for dead butterflies, a collector's box of astral dimensions, all white and glass, as my body is also white under the spotlights – all the spotlights have been turned on inopportunely – while Julio arranges me on white cushions, on white quilts full of white feathers, and as he licks me, touches me, sucks me, slobbers on me, bites me, I no longer feel anything, not even sorrow – not for me or for Clara – because I know that now everything will unfold inexorably until the end, and – although this may not be a studio – it is like a film that has already been shot and that someone – I, perhaps – has watched indifferently many years later, and not even this time has his film turned out to be even slightly credible, not even this time has he been capable of creating flesh-and-blood men and women, and in this film, which certainly is really neither interesting nor credible, the collector manipulates me, handles me, places me in different positions like a jointed doll: a display of juggling and postures, although it is useless, because the script is indelible and the characters in the story aren't very real, but at the end I am the way I should be, stretched out on my back, eyes staring at the white ceiling, his body pressing down on mine, his arms and legs gripping me in a vise, and it isn't possible to fly or to walk on the sea, it is no longer even possible to move, and then, in a brutal thrust, his penis penetrates me like a red hot needle, no, like a ball of fire through a hoop, like an arrow that strikes the exact center of the target, without the archer's using his eyes or hands, and it is such a spectacular move, so circuslike, so precise, that you feel like applauding – what a shame I can't move or free my hands – and I think that perhaps the collector feels proud of this much-repeated feat, and that perhaps those girls he puts in the casts of his supposedly avantgarde films and whom he helps get on the covers of intellectual porno magazines, may admire him or may also love him for this, perhaps their depilated genitals that have been recently bathed in Badedas like this attack, and perhaps, unlike me, they aren't poor dying butterflies, a poor enraged butterfly – in another world, Clara once said that I was an enraged butterfly – who can't even flutter her wings, while the hard, gradually faster, sure, rhythmic strokes nail her once more and forever to the dazzling white bottom of the big glass box, and I can only remain motionless, eyes staring at the ceiling – uninterrupted, unrelenting white, without damp spots, without old coats of paint that recalcitrantly appear, without moldings of flowers in which the old fairy friends of my childhood show up: implacably white – my lips pressed together and my throat contracted so that I won't cry out, won't cry out with pain, but above all, before all, so I won't cry out with pleasure, this indecent pleasure which will come at last, hysterical and twitching, inevitable and loathsome like death itself, loathsome like death, another form of death, because my own death is what is riding on top of me, what is holding me clutched between his legs without possible escape, what is penetrating me in repeated, brutal thrusts, more and more brutal, it is my death that fills me, inundates me, overflows me, this deadly Julio mounting me like some poor mare broken once and for all, although not by him, not by this circus-exhibition he-man, he wasn't the one who put the bit, the bridle, the saddle, the stirrups on me, he wasn't the first one who drove in the spurs until my flanks burst, making me give in, you are only a mask, Siegfried rides me treacherously in the guise of an incompetent king, Siegfried who woke me for nothing – who awoke me for death – from my deep sleep on the crag, Jorge who dragged me to this death, who chose Julio – without knowing him – so that what could have been everlasting life would be perpetuated in the form of death, and life was only perpetuated in Guiomar, never in me, never for me, and now once more, while my death rides me and destroys me, while I keep my eyes fixed on the lid of the implacable box that closed over me long ago, while I struggle bravely not to cry out, in this hysterical substitute for pleasure, I only succeed in thinking confusedly, painfully, of all the mermaids who would forever roam the beaches in useless pursuit of a woman's soul, of a certain undine so foolishly deceived, of girls deserted for no reason on their wedding night, about a young, dark adolescent with Oriental eyes who has just been killed by mistake, about Ariadne deserted on the island of Naxos.

I wake up in a large, soft, low, really very comfortable bed, that is supposedly my bed, the double bed that at times – so many times, too many times, all too many – I share with Julio, and I wake up in a strange apartment that seems like the set for an American film of the twenties or a succession of photographs from architectural magazines, but it turns out to be my apartment, although I don't know it is mine and I almost get lost in it, because it is Julio's apartment, and Julio shares with my mother – among so many other things – the taste for superfluous and superficial changes – not the great change: never *the* change – the taste for what is new and shiny, and I gave up trying to reason with the architects and decorators long ago – as I also gave up finding dark, complicitous corners in these houses, establishing secret underground alliances, and perhaps it may be precisely to this end that Julio and my mother condemn me to these impossible houses – and I allow doors to be opened where formerly there were none, partitions to be moved, absurd carpet-covered platforms to rise from the floor, the few pieces of furniture that – perhaps because they had lasted a little longer – had almost begun to please me – to disappear without a farewell, and periodically I allow myself to be settled in a car and removed to another location – it isn't necessary to have the furniture moved, because they never make use of anything, just me, I'm the only thing moved, probably because I'm worth more than the furniture; I am moved from duplex to town house and from town house to apartment – while in exchange, Julio and my mother condescend to allow me to keep my two hidden wells, they agree not to sell the apartment where I lived with my parents as a child, and they accede to not changing one single thing in my grandmother's old house by the sea: it is necessary to leave some last refuge for defeated phantoms, a last den where mortally wounded wild animals can lie in their final agony. I wake up with a disagreeable start, while the maid that Julio or the housekeeper or someone has hired for me, hands to me – how ironic! – a large glass of cold orange juice, and explains that the master has left very early – he goes off to create an inspired work, coolly, after having spent the night crucifying butterflies – that he absolutely insisted I not be awakened until noon, and that Maite has called several times. And, holding the glass of cold orange juice like a useless talisman, because it will be of no use to me and can save me no pain, I hear the exultant voice of Maite, this voice that she assumes only for great occasions – or rather, to relate monumental scandals or great catastrophes that don't affect her – and a triumphal Maite – I can't even hate her, because it isn't even simple wickedness, at least not the kind of wickedness that I understand, that I can practice, it is sheer stupidity, the sheer silliness of my island of dwarfs – informs me that our Clara – our Clara? – is the new lover, or at least has spent the night – I imagine it was the last part of the night (at what moment did Clara become desolately aware, intolerably certain, that I had deserted her?) – with the emperor. I hang up the telephone without even saying a word – what could I say? and what does Maite expect me to say to her? and what does it matter now if they think I am half-crazy? and I remain huddled, very still, between the sheets, very, very still, in a desperate effort not to think of anything, not to feel anything, especially not to imagine anything, very, very still, as if in that way I could at least put off the arrival of pain for some moments, because it doesn't hurt yet, I still notice almost nothing – a very slight nausea, a certain bewilderment – and I am still more afraid of these pains that don't appear immediately and fully, all at once, with exactly the right intensity and at the proper moment, these pains that make you wait and allow you to cherish the illusion – so false – that if you are still enough, detached enough and empty of thoughts, perhaps they may pass you by without touching you, without warning you, perhaps they may never really start, and so you lie very still to forestall their arrival, to try not to let them see you, to make them forget you, and at the same time with all your might you want them to arrive right this goddamn minute, this lousy, stinking minute, to get over this tremendous uncertainty which is even worse and crueler than the pain itself, to have the suffering at last with you, within you, to become acquainted with it and to know its quality and what materials it is made of, to know what the pain you are going to suffer this time is going to be like. I remain huddled and motionless in bed, my legs pulled up to my chest, as in my first menstrual periods in adolescence, when traces of blood had already appeared, but the pain had still not begun, and I would sit down on the floor, on the green carpet where I read my first stories, my back against the leather armchair in Papa's study – that honey smell from his pipe permeating everything – knees to chin and arms around legs, waiting for the intolerable, certain moment when a monstrous, raging hyena would devour my insides for hours and hours without letting me die, without my being able to die, or like the day in the kitchen when I was still living with Julio, and I spilled a pot of boiling oil on my hand, and my skin wrinkled up in a few seconds, like old parchment brought close to the flames, like a fine kid glove pulled off the wrong way, pushing and gathering the skin upward from fingertips to wrist, but for a few seconds – and surely they were the worst – I still felt nothing, only the panicky fear of a pain that I hadn't experienced, but that I knew would arrive punctually at its appointment and that I imagined would be intolerable, the terrible wait for a pain not yet begun, still faceless and nameless, it is dreadful that the most serious and deepest pains in my life never appear suddenly and then gradually disappear – who could have invented that silliness that time cures everything, it's not even comforting – but they make me wait a long, long time, so long that at times I can't pinpoint the exact moment when they began, and then they progress vaguely, sneakily, slowly growing and invading me, never decreasing or weakening: *in principio era il dolore* and this pain will only end in dreamless death. Because the afternoon that I went into Jorge's apartment – we hadn't seen each other all day, and it had been a glorious, almost magical day, one of those days with clean air, a high, blue sky that changes to an intense red in late afternoon, one of those days when one can feel the sea at the end of the streets, when all the streets in the city seem to open onto a present, omnipresent, but invisible sea, a sea that has little to do with death, one of those days

173

when my city seems so beautiful to me, even though a race of dwarfs may have built it, and people seem unexpectedly cordial to me, and I linger buying flowers, huge bouquets of tuberoses, perverse orchids that vaguely recall my labyrinths, buying beautiful, useless objects, sitting on the terraces of bars to order drinks with suggestive names served to me in large, sugar-rimmed goblets with different kinds of fruit hanging over the edge; and that afternoon I had bought a meerschaum pipe for Jorge, a very beautiful pipe, whose bowl rose from an intricate hat full of buds and ended in a woman's swelling breasts, and it was the end of the month, and there was no money, and it had been a crazy thing to do, and I opened the door laughing, all day long I had been laughing to myself, anticipating the pleasure of telling Jorge that the morning had been wonderfully glorious, that all time and the entire universe were wonderfully glorious, since he existed and he loved me, telling him that the sky had turned very red after having been very blue, that people were nice and really didn't seem so hostile, so petty, so cruel, that at best it wasn't certain that hell is other people and I was laughing as I thought about all the things I would say to him in a moment, as I was opening the door and it was hard to manage with my key, my purse, and the huge bunch of tuberoses in whose scent, as in my childhood dreams, and in spite of Jorge's desperate, smiling protests, we would make love and really, the day had been glorious because I knew, I thought I knew, that he was waiting for me that afternoon, and I would tell him that the day had seemed wonderful to me, and I thought, I thought I knew, that he would wait for me every afternoon and every morning of my life, as he had waited for me every afternoon and every morning and at all hours from the day we met, when he tore me away from my dark labyrinths and between the two of us we happily killed the Minotaur, when he woke me from my deep sleep on the fiery crag, a sleep which may have already lasted too long, and sat me behind him on his horse and took me out into the light, into life, into the beautiful days of my city in springtime, because that year, spring was indeed present, and I learned to discover the magical moment when the first shoots of the trees appear, tender and pale, when I learned to decipher the arrival of the first swallows, and together we gave names to trees and birds, and that unique spring day, that unrepeatable, unrecoverable day, I had seen so many exciting things that Jorge had taught me to see and that I was going to tell him now, after he lit his meerschaum pipe and I had put the tuberoses in a large blue pitcher, had taken off my dress and shoes, and had sprawled by his side on the bed, seeing the last traces of the still-reddish light of that superb afternoon through the open window – as soon as I entered the apartment, because I finally got the key to turn in the lock and the door opened – and long before – I mean a few seconds before – I went into our bedroom and saw Jorge, if that was still Jorge, if anything there still remained of Jorge, I knew with absolute certainty that something terrible had happened, but I didn't begin to suffer, as if my capacity for suffering were too small for that reality that was about to crush me atrociously and absolutely; and this capacity had to grow and enlarge to give way, to make room for that virgin, unknown magnitude of pain, for that pain never intuited or imagined: I didn't feel anything, as if my potential for feeling, for being moved, for suffering, had been suspended, put off to some remote future, while I did what had to be done with the speed and precision, with the efficiency of an automaton, and really, there was no longer anything that could be done, there was no longer anything left that I could do in the world, but I called the family doctor, I sent for an ambulance, some friends, friends of Jorge that I would never want to see again, who sobbed and hugged me, secretly shocked by my impassive face, the lack of tears, perhaps secretly suspicious that I had never loved Jorge as they thought, and I didn't even feel anything when I touched his body, when I took his pulse which didn't throb, when I listened for his heart – as I did so often in our love games, my ear against his smooth, warm, bare chest – and only when – before the doctor and the friends arrived, before the apartment was filled with strange people who made empty gestures and said senseless things to me – I began a search that became more and more frantic as I realized it was going to be useless – a search for a note, a letter, a sign, something that would mark the road I was to follow or that at least would signify a good-bye, only when the absolutely inconceivable idea exploded like a firecracker inside me, the idea that he had betrayed me, when I began to understand at last that he had stolen me from my parents' palace for nothing, that the Minotaur's death had been in vain, that the fiery peaks had been extinguished uselessly and for nothing before the hero's stride, and he had awakened me for nothing from a centuries-long sleep which, in its way, was happy, or at least not unhappy, which could have lasted forever without his interference, only when I began to understand that it was a lie and absolutely untrue that he had believed in a different world or that he had wanted to teach me to fly, and if he had believed in a different world, it was in any case a world in which I didn't exist, or existed very little, a poor plaything for ambitious, tired heroes, for petty heroes who, halfway there, turn back and desert you sleeping on the island of Naxos, because I was beginning to understand that I had been deserted horribly, without ships or directions or compasses or sea charts, long before I had time to learn to fly or sail or walk on water, and no one had said, "Come with me," I was beginning to understand that he had decided for himself alone, without any companion, without any partner, had made a choice that excluded and humiliated me to such a degree of humiliation that I hadn't foreseen it even in the worst moments of my childhood; Jorge had played the last hand behind my back, without giving me a single card, or the wretched piece on the chessboard, or five minutes to speak in my own defense or in defense of us both and ask him to stay or to let me go with him, and there was only the question whether he had chosen this for himself and for me, without consulting me, with that kind of enlightened despotism with which one decides the fate of children and animals, or

whether he had chosen only for himself alone, without even remembering that I existed, the question remained whether, as
he was swallowing pill after pill, he was condemning me to
crawl back to my island of dwarfs, to my parents' palace, condemning me to marriage with Julio, to my farce of love, to my
farce of work, to my farce of life, to my remorse and my nostalgia for an unrecoverable Minotaur, for undiscoverable labyrinths, or whether he had simply forgotten me completely –
runaway princesses, the least princesslike of all princesses, silly
princesses, don't count for anything in the destiny of heroes
who choose the solitary feat of self-destruction – whether I,
not to mention the entire rest of the universe, had simply
ceased to exist for him as he lay down on his back and closed his
eyes before the most beautiful late afternoon of that spring;
and only then, slyly, slowly, something came to me that wasn't
exactly pain, something that seemed a lot like hatred, because
the terrible certainty sprang up that if he died – and I knew that
he was going to die – if Jorge died before giving me the opportunity to express myself, to take some small action, to play a
part – even though it might be to spit out my disappointment
and contempt for him with terrible words, even though it
might only be to slap him repeatedly until someone took him
out of my hands – if Jorge died forever without allowing me to
argue with him or to take part in the game, the solitary hand he
had decided to play with death without me, then there would
be no salvation or flight possible for me, because I could never
walk on water now even though someone might someday say
to me, "Come with me," I could never learn to fly alone to
Never-Never Land, deserted on the island of Naxos without
wings and without oars, but Jorge had fulfilled his destiny,
though in a terrible way, he had chosen and taken his destiny in
his own hands, with supreme freedom, with complete efficiency, but he had left me forever deserted on something worse
than the crystal island where the dead wander, he had condemned me to a terrible no-man's-land in which I was never
again to find or recognize myself, and all that – that rancor and

that hatred and that certainty of having been hopelessly betrayed, left on the sidelines of death and on the sidelines of life
– I don't know if I can call all that exactly pain, it wasn't something that could slowly deaden with time, something that
could lessen day by day, month by month or year by year – and
it is absolutely false that time helps to overcome suffering: real
injuries are timeless – on the contrary, it was going to become
more and more inflamed, gradually less and less bearable, like a
malignant, slow-growing cancer for which no painkillers are
possible, located where there can be no amputation, since it af-
fects the very core of our existence, something that would
grow with me until my own death and with which I would
have to learn to coexist forever, in a certain way and only up to
a certain point.

All the sadness in the world rains beyond the windowpanes, as if fall were beginning, when we are really
just starting summer, and I am surprised to see how brief my
adventure – my adventure? – with Clara has been, twenty-five
days, twenty-six, twenty-seven at most, the adventure – I can't
use the word *love*, as if prevented by a secret pain or a hidden
shame – that now ends in this hotel room, where, scarcely
looking at me, she walks back and forth near me as she packs
her suitcases. Because Clara, too, has decided to return to her
island of dwarfs, to her parents' cardboard palace, but I think
that she isn't crawling back in defeat nor is she returning forever: Clara isn't going back to them, she is simply escaping
from me, her ability to walk on water intact or almost intact –
although I may not have said, "Come with me" – to explore
new underground worlds, to learn to fly and grow wings, perhaps because I – even while betraying her – gave her the opportunity that Jorge denied me, the possibility of arguing, of
taking action one way or another, of taking a stance and of taking revenge, the possibility of hurting me by spending the
night with the emperor – Clara with the emperor: Clara jump-
ing nude from the prow of my boat, using herself to take re-

venge on me, always giving aggressive answers when she is hurt, because wild street cats, genuinely solitary and hunted, who become lap kittens for love of us, always react ultimately to pain, to our desertion and to our betrayals, by putting our eyes out or hurling themselves into space from an eightieth-floor apartment on Fifth Avenue – or by hurting me in this final interview; "I would like to see you before I leave," her voice over the telephone impersonal, sure and firm for the first time, not quavering, a voice, of course, that carefully avoids pronouncing my name – that would hurt us both too much – just as the motions with which she is packing her perfect suitcases are surprisingly sure, firm, and precise – as she carefully prevents our glances from meeting – suitcases out of a contest for the perfect housewife – who would have said that my clumsy blue doll would know how to pack suitcases like that! – and it is becoming very clear that there isn't going to be any explanation, any reproach, that she isn't going to say anything, that the only thing she wanted was to have me here, watching her arrange her things in the suitcases, seeing it rain beyond the panes, in this room that, no matter how elegant the hotel may be, I will always remember as sordid, smelling of drainpipes and dampness, with a gray wall on the other side of the window and the rain. Clara has me here, without even looking at me, almost without saying a single word – just that she doesn't want me to go with her to the airport, that she has already called a taxi and it is probably waiting below for her – and we both know that we still love each other, and we both know that there is no way out of the situation, no way out except for her departure, and not because my night with Julio or her night with the emperor means so much, but because I would always betray her again, over and over, in order to betray myself, I would hurt her again in order to hurt myself, I would kill hope in her again in order to annihilate all possible hope once again in myself, because there no longer exists for me – and perhaps it doesn't exist because minute by minute I choose it not to exist, renewing the irrevocable, permanently updated decision that I

made on a certain spring afternoon, so many years ago now –
the slightest possibility of learning to fly (nor do I want to
grow wings any more), of following her beyond the narrow
frame of any window and setting out together on the route to
Never-Never Land, and I understand suddenly that I knew all
of this with almost total certainty from the very beginning of
our adventure – of our love – that I never managed to fool myself or perhaps even to fool her, and right now, beyond any sorrow and knowing that a dreadful nostalgia will soon begin, I
discover that Clara's departure entails an immense relief for
me, and when she is on the other side of the world, out of my
reach once and for all, making – I hope – guerrilla warfare and
love and literature with others in her Colombian jungles or
wherever she wants to and can do it – in spite of the nostalgia – I
will once again be able to sink without problems into this light
sleep that is my life, my no-life, in my enchanted forest or my
aquatic depths or my fiery peaks, while a domesticated, moving zombie efficiently takes my place, doing even better than I
would, at gala dinners and movie debuts, at the university, in
my nights of love, if the prolonged mounting of my dead body
by an unknown man are nights of love, while it speaks and
moves and even thinks for me, much better than I myself
could, and my mother and Julio and Guiomar will meet happily and conspiratorially behind my back to breathe a sigh of
relief and remark that I have happily overcome a new spring
crisis, that I look good, that I am very pretty, that we could go
to New York for a few days, or buy a new Afghan hound or
perhaps change apartments, and they will happily drag me here
and there without it mattering to me at all, without it hurting at
all now, because Clara will take with her, I hope, what still remains of my capacity for suffering – although she may leave me
the nostalgia – and I can no longer be hurt by the loss of this
last, ill-timed possibility of returning to life, this crazy, wonderful possibility called Clara, who is still here, within reach of
my hands and my words, of my kisses and my "Don't go," but
who acts as if she has already gone, because, contrary to what

happens with pain, true absence really begins a little before the material emptiness of absence takes place, it begins at the very moment in which we really understand that the other one is going to go away and that we are going to remain without her, and Clara is still here only to inflict on me the last minutes of punishment, the last minutes of anxiety – I prefer not to think that she could be waiting for me to tell her, "Don't go" – before letting me rest, letting me sleep, letting me die, before we both leave this horrible, smelly room that has only a gray wall on the other side of the rain and the window, leave here with her con-test-suitcases, and leave me free, forever drained of any hope, of the heavy temptation of life, of the false illusion that any companionship is possible, leave me in peace once and for all. And only at the last moment, when the boy has already put the luggage in the taxi, and she has paid the bill, and given out the tips, Clara gives me a light kiss on the cheek, smiles with the sad smile of my same old Clara, her self-confidence and aplomb gone for a few seconds, and with her mouth very close to my ear, she whispers – I don't know whether as the final slap of punishment or as a sign of pardon, but in any case as un-equivocal proof that she has understood me to the end: "And Wendy grew up."

Margaret E. W. Jones

Afterword

Esther Tusquets (born in Barcelona, 1936) has had long-standing connections with the literary world (she has been the director of Lumen, a Barcelona publishing house, since the 1960s), but her first work – *El mismo mar de todos los veranos* – was not published until 1978, when she was forty-two. Since that time, she has produced a steady stream of creative literature. There have been three more novels: *El amor es un juego solitario* (Love is a solitary game), 1979; *Varada tras el último naufragio* (Beached after the last shipwreck), 1980; *Para no volver* (Never to return), 1985. Tusquets herself calls her first three novels a trilogy; however, all four works are autonomous, although they are bound together by common themes which center on a middle-aged female protagonist who must come to grips with the meaning and future direction of her life; in all four, an important relationship develops at a time of crisis, allowing the woman the possibility of refocusing her life. Tusquets's collection of short pieces (*Siete miradas en un mismo paisaje* (Seven looks at a same landscape), 1981, de-scribes seven different episodes in the life of the protagonist,

Sara, presented in nonchronological order: major themes are family relationships, friendships and allegiances, the awareness of social and class distinctions. A book for children, *La conejita Marcela* (Marcela, the bunny rabbit), appeared in 1980. In addition to writing fiction, she has contributed occasional articles to newspapers.[1]

When *The Same Sea As Every Summer* was published in 1978, Spain was beginning to experience a type of freedom unknown during the previous thirty-six-year dictatorship of Generalísimo Francisco Franco – a freedom, for example, that allowed controversial or critical material to be published. Thus, to understand Tusquets's criticism of Spanish society and the innovative nature of some of her material, one must be aware of the cultural premises of Franco's Spain – the Spain in which Tusquets grew up. The end of the Spanish Civil War (1936–39) abruptly truncated liberal policies associated with the Second Republic (1931–36); severely repressive measures ensured the swift implementation of a new ideology based on conservative national and Catholic values. All areas of Spanish life were tightly controlled in order to foster these policies and to suppress heterodoxy. The government prohibited works found on the Roman Catholic Index and censored criticism of the ideology and practices of the Franco regime (including its views on public morality, historiography, and civil order).

National policy also affected civil and human rights, and permeated social areas. The close relationship between church and state made divorce illegal, homosexuality a crime, and adultery illegal – for women. Women's rights, which had begun to receive attention under the previous government, suffered considerable setbacks; work restrictions emphasized that a woman's place was in the home; the legal status of women responded to a concept of patriarchal authority (females passed from their father to their husband as legal "minors"). Such restrictive measures characterize the early postwar period, but the necessity for economic development and Spain's growing interest in rejoining the international political scene prompted

186

the government to present a more moderate and open image of itself. Signs of dissent also began to appear: even the Catholic church called for reforms and change; regionalist movements began to gain impetus; the work force rebelled against the syndicates established and controlled by the government. This unrest led to a reform of the Spanish Civil Code in the 1970s. Franco's death in 1975 and the country's elections in 1977 (the first in forty years) propelled Spain into the modern world. The decriminalization of many of the old "taboos" – divorce, homosexuality – a strong campaign for women's rights, the reassumption of cultural freedom (censorship restrictions were abolished in 1978) and the fomentation of regional identities and self-expression are some examples of the changes that allow Spain to experience the joys and problems of freedom in the twentieth century.

Although no censorship laws would cause problems for the publication of *The Same Sea As Every Summer*, some of the material in the novel was still controversial in 1978. The explicitly erotic nature of the text and, particularly, the feminine perspective on sexual matters were new to Spanish fiction. The novel recognizes and validates woman's pleasure (clearly differentiating it from male pleasure), deals frankly with female sexuality, depicts homosexuality (particularly between women, another taboo) in a positive light, and reinforces these themes with the erotization of the text itself, through the use of female sexual imagery.[2]

The Same Sea As Every Summer is also an excellent example of the direction that the contemporary Spanish novel was to take, in its technique of depicting a national situation (Spanish value systems, the Spanish and Catalan cultural and social scene) within a wider framework of universal themes, and viewing both society and its morals with the critical, ironic distrust of the postmodernist. Thus the complexity of the text – its experimental form, fragmentary presentation, intertextuality, recondite style, allusive content, ambiguity, ironic and pessimistic overlay – reflects both the personal concerns of the writer and the generational concerns of contemporary European intellectuals.

The novel opens with the middle-aged narrator's return to the apartment of her childhood, an ostensible rejection of her unhappy life with an unfaithful husband. Her real purpose in returning, however (in a pattern common to many novels about middle-aged women), is to undertake a journey into the past to rediscover a happier, more authentic time in her life.[3] She redefines her motives, which evolve from her apparent desire to reject the present in an effort to reclaim her past, corroborated by insistent references to her search for old phantoms, for the child she used to be, and for objects and talismans that represent that happier period.

The narrator delves into her hurtful past, using a confessional technique to peel away layers of experience until she reaches the dreadful account of her first love's inexplicable suicide. This act of betrayal thus serves as a structuring motif that reappears in numerous variations as the story unfolds. Betrayal forms part of an archetypal paradigm in which love or trust will inevitably be repaid by desertion: her husband Julio's infidelities and desertions (the marital betrayal), the uncompromising expectations of her mother and daughter (betrayals of the narrator's desperate need for understanding and support), her father's betrayal of Sofía's love (and simultaneous betrayal of the social "pact" by publicly humiliating his wife), Jorge's suicide, and the narrator's betrayal of Clara. Falsification, social masks, and inauthenticity are explored as further examples of self-betrayal.

The narrator's return to her apartment and the past thus signals her desire to break with the pattern and regain her original innocence. However, her intentions are continually undermined by a narrative subtext that emphasizes the inalterable nature of the paradigm, with allusions to tales of betrayal in myth (Theseus and Ariadne) fairy tales ("The Little Mermaid"), literary classics (*Faust*), opera (*The Twilight of the Gods*), ballet (*Swan Lake*), cinema, and popular music. These references suggest that escape from – or even modification of – the pattern will be impossible.

The fortuitous appearance of Clara is another incentive for the narrator to recoup her lost innocence: she introduces the young woman to places associated with her own past life (the ice cream shop, the apartment, the opera house, the seaside cottage), employing symbolic references and spatial imagery to suggest that she and Clara will undertake a psychological and temporal journey into the self. These visits (often called rites or rituals) entail thresholds traversed and journeys of descent: down stairs, through dark hallways, into interior patios, and into the well, an ever-present symbol.

Descriptions of Clara show that she is the temporal double of the narrator and a mechanism to allow the older woman to recapture "lost time." Clara's physical traits, behavior, and social ineptness recall incidents from the narrator's adolescence. Thus the affair with Clara – a symbolic merging of the two selves – represents the negation of the present, the successful recuperation of lost time, and admission into the "green world" (which Annis Pratt identifies with nature) that is symbolically linked with the green sea of leaves below the apartment windows and the real sea where the epiphany takes place.

The women's affair constitutes a rite of passage into a world radically altered by their love, a world delivered from the dominance and egotism associated with the traditional division of lovers into self and other; their new, green-world love is completely unselfish and powerful enough to enfold – and possibly improve – all people.[4] Symbols of renewal and rebirth fill the descriptions: they swim in the sea; their lovemaking takes place in the children's bedroom; Clara weaves a symbolic cocoon from which the narrator will emerge transformed. Just as their love emphasizes difference and inversion, so the patterns they establish will reshape the world by replacing the customs and practices of patriarchal society – the only hope for breaking the inexorable paradigms.[5]

In this new world, binary or contradictory elements can

suddenly coexist;[6] characters become protean, sharing or interchanging traits. The narrator wonders which of them – she or Clara – is Beauty and which the Beast, and she sustains this changeableness by overlapping characteristics associated with other pairs (particularly Ariadne and Theseus); even the mother-daughter-lover triad appears in her description as another complex variation on this theme. As opposite elements are ultimately refashioned into androgynous unity, categories such as male/female, betrayer/betrayed are no longer valid. The Edenic perspective suggests that everything will be freshly created: even a new language is necessary to express this change, an intuitive language that the narrator carefully dissociates from reasoned discourse.

The timeless betrayal motif complements a plot that is developed within clearly identifiable modern coordinates: regional (Barcelona), social (well-to-do bourgeoisie), and temporal (the years following the Spanish Civil War). Descriptions of life at that time emphasize the stultifying atmosphere, the snobbishness, the empty lives, the materialism of her parents' generation as well as of her own generation – who, in a further variation on the paradigm – have betrayed the ideals that they had once promised to uphold. In contrast to the narrator's reclusiveness, the Catalans live publicly, placing great emphasis on appearances, attempting to outdo one another despite the apparent clanlike solidarity of the postwar years. The combination of splendor and tawdriness in the opera house symbolizes this way of life, as does the proprietary relationship of the Catalans to this "temple" and the cultural events which take place within its walls. Even at the seaside village, the idle bourgeois families relish the opportunity to relieve the summer boredom with gossip provided by Sofía and the narrator's father. The end-of-the-summer party at the casino – another public event – corroborates their love of ostentation (their frenzy to obtain the ugly wax roses as a sign of power) and malevolence (their delight in spying on the narrator's family). The narrator sets this behavior in a wider context: she continually describes her people as a race of dwarfs, as stunted children whose unlimited potential has never been allowed to develop. These characteristics are then textualized into the "once-upon-a-time" story about a king and queen (her parents) on their island. This "story" creates a myth (the Catalans' "splendor" and power) while simultaneously demythifying it (the Catalans' insularity, complacency, and self-importance).

The narrator's disillusionment stems in great part from her interaction with a social environment in which she is accepted only in subservient roles as daughter, wife, mother. Her account of the unwritten rules of behavior, codes to be assimilated, norms to be followed, role models offered and discarded, create a densely woven picture of twentieth-century postwar Spain. The narrator traces these attitudes throughout the fragmented narrative: her mother's disappointment that she is not like the others, despite family efforts to beautify and socialize her; the mother's apparent power, which gives way before the "real" authority (the father); the social pressures that force a wife to put up with her husband's philandering. The author undermines male authority by depicting the patriarchal figures in her life in terms of public spectacle: Julio's actions recall the vapid, studied gestures of television commercials; her father, despite his apparent detachment, is compared to a dramatist who prepares the script and assigns roles to the women. Frequent references to parts one must play, costumes, masks, and scripting emphasize the degree to which the system itself forces the narrator to sacrifice her uniqueness to the role that has been chosen for her, but without her consent. On the other hand, there is a wide-ranging exploration of the female world: the narrator's complex love-hate relationship with her mother, the thwarted bond with her daughter, the grandmother's role as victim of patriarchal manipulation, the dynamics of friendship among the women, the problems of an aging woman, the rejection of a male-oriented social system in favor of the naturalistic green world associated with the female principle. The introduction of Clara – whose New World origins are couched in terms of lush, green landscape – gives the narrator a pretext to attempt to try to regain her youth through female bonding, a quest she cannot sustain, but which Clara will perhaps be capable of continuing.[7]

The Same Sea As Every Summer probes the relationship between literature and life, with constant intertextual references (the betrayal theme, for example, and many others) and most obviously through the narrator's obsession in seeing her own life as literature. Her ideas have been formed by her readings, and recalling her childhood, she states that she learned to live the wrong way, choosing words, never realities. As if to confirm this, many of her recollections are actually literary constructs – true experiences seen through a superimposed literary model (the story of Jorge begins as a fairy tale; her visit to Marcos in London recalls Beauty and the Beast). The children's fairy tales from which she learned proper behavior are debunked as stories of norms and conformity, ending in unhappiness for the "rebel" who dares to venture beyond the expected: the various storybook personae assumed by the generic Prince Charming reveal that he is a fatuous opportunist who is truly unworthy of the total love which has been bestowed on him.

But the novel is also a novel about writing – writing (or rewriting) one's life. Much of the renewal quest relies on the theme of literature, which reveals life as a kind of script which the narrator is attempting to rewrite: her affair with Clara may be the chance for the Happy Ending, or for an entirely new text based on new relationships. The narrator begins her story by putting the young woman in familiar scenes – the places of her childhood – and then writes herself into the story, creating a complex literary relationship in which she is simultaneously author and character, yet ironically she is powerless on either level to modify the ending. The inalterable nature of the script is once again confirmed by the narrator's betrayal of Clara, and therefore of herself.

Game playing is still another metaphor for life and the dynamics of relationships on the individual and the social level.

The narrator draws parallels between the developing alliances and game strategies: rules followed or transgressed, moves on the chessboard, cards played, the necessity to continue the game to the end. On one end of the scale are the social games (Maite's use of Clara as an attempt to draw the narrator into the game; Maite's manipulation of her friends and lovers described as harmless social games); on the other are the "sacred" childhood games. The effort to change the rules of the social game, to change the nature of the game from social to sacred (that is, to break the code and modify the rules by means of the lesbian affair and return to childhood innocence) fails, just as the "indelible" literary text cannot be rewritten.[8]

According to the narrator, the affair with Clara offered her a chance to emerge from the parentheses of her banal, unhappy life and to renew her authentic existence (that of her childhood). Despite the rituals of renewal offered by the young girl, elements from diverse myths – classical, cultural, regional, social – even generational – intrude, overwhelm, and ultimately stifle the nascent green world enclosed in the patio of the bougainvilleas. Yet the ambiguity of the final words (which combine with the epigraph to reinforce the circularity implied in the title) do not entirely muffle the hopeful note associated with Clara's departure, which, if not triumphal, at least is not in defeat. Clara is left with choices which imply that the closed patterns of the Old World may not follow her to the New.

NOTES

1. For an overview of Tusquets's work placed within the context of Spanish women writers, see Janet Pérez, *Contemporary Women Writers of Spain* (Boston: Twayne Publishers, 1988), 159–62.

2. Linda Gould Levine offers some excellent examples of this in "Reading, Rereading, Misreading, and Rewriting the Male Canon: The Narrative Web of Esther Tusquets's Trilogy," *Anales de la Literatura Española Contemporánea* 12, nos.1–2 (1987): 203–17; Catherine Bellver treats this subject at length in "The Language of Eroti-

cism in the Novels of Esther Tusquets" *Anales de la Literatura Española Contemporánea* 9, nos.1–3 (1984): 13–27.

3. The feminist reconsideration of the conventions of the hero journey, the quest motif, and the novel of development in general is perceptively analyzed in Annis Pratt's *Archetypal Patterns in Women's Fiction* (Bloomington: Indiana University Press, 1981). Elizabeth Ordóñez looks at the quest motif in *The Same Sea As Every Summer* in "A Quest for Matrilineal Roots and Mythopoesis: Esther Tusquets' *El mismo mar de todos los veranos*," *Crítica Hispánica* 6 (1984): 37–46, as does Lucy Lee-Bonanno in "The Renewal of the Quest in Esther Tusquets' *El mismo mar de todos los veranos*," *Feminine Concerns in Contemporary Spanish Fiction by Women*, ed. Roberto C. Manteiga, Carolyn Galerstein, and Kathleen McNerney (Potomac, Md.: Scripta Humanistica, 1988), 134–51.

4. The rhetoric of love is discussed in Gonzalo Navaja's "Repetition and the Rhetoric of Love in Esther Tusquets' *El mismo mar de todos los veranos*," in *Nuevos y novísimos: Algunas perspectivas críticas sobre la narrativa española desde la década de los 60*, ed. Ricardo Landeira and Luis T. González-del-Valle (Boulder, Colo.: Society of Spanish and Spanish-American Studies, 1987): 113–29. See also Mary S. Vázquez, "Tusquets, Fitzgerald, and the Redemptive Power of Love," *Letras Femeninas* 14, nos.1–2 (Spring–Autumn 1988): 10–21.

5. Geraldine Cleary Nichols thoroughly and perceptively analyzes this theme and other important aspects of the novel in "The Prison-House (and Beyond): *El mismo mar de todos los veranos*," *Romanic Review* 75 (1984): 366–85.

6. Mary S. Vázquez discusses this opposition in "Image and Linear Progression toward Defeat in Esther Tusquets' *El mismo mar de todos los veranos*," in *La Chispa '83: Selected Proceedings*, ed. Gilbert Paolini (Baton Rouge: Lousiana State University Press, 1983): 307–13.

7. Several excellent articles study the female relationships in *The Same Sea As Every Summer*: Ordóñez, "A Quest for Matrilinear Roots," and Mirella Servodidio, "A Case of Pre-Oedipal and Narrative Fixation: *El mismo mar de todos los veranos*," *Anales de la Literatura Contemporánea* 12, nos.1–2 (1987): 157–74.

8. Mirella d'Ambrosio Servodidio, "Perverse Pairings and Cor-
rupted Codes: *El amor es un juego solitario*," *Anales de la Literatura
Española Contemporánea* 11, no. 3 (1986): 237–54 analyzes Tusquets's
second novel in the light of three codes (psychosexual, game, and
narrative); many of her remarks can be applied to *The Same Sea As
Every Summer*.

Volumes in the European Women Writers Series include

Woman to Woman, by Marguerite Duras and Xavière Gauthier
Translated by Katherine A. Jensen

Nothing Grows by Moonlight, by Torborg Nedreaas
Translated by Bibbi Lee

Music from a Blue Well, by Torborg Nedreaas
Translated by Bibbi Lee

Why Is There Salt in the Sea?, by Brigitte Schwaiger
Translated by Sieglinde Lug

On Our Own Behalf: Women's Tales from Catalonia
Edited by Kathleen McNerney

Mother Death, by Jeanne Hyvrard
Translated by Laurie Edson

Artemisia, by Anna Banti
Translated by Shirley d'Ardia Caracciolo

Maria Zef, by Paola Drigo
Translated by Blossom Steinberg Kirschenbaum

The Panther Woman: Five Tales from the Cassette Recorder,
by Sarah Kirsch
Translated by Marion Faber

The Tongue Snatchers, by Claudine Herrmann
Translated by Nancy Kline

Bitter Healing: German Women Writers from 1700 to 1830
An Anthology
Edited by Jeannine Blackwell and Susanne Zantop